A CONVERSATION WITH THE PRESIDENT

"Tell me how you feel about something," her mother said.

"About what?" Meg asked.

"Anything. Just tell me how you *really* feel about something."

"Okay," Meg folded her arms across her chest. "I don't like reporters, Secret Service agents, or starting school tomorrow."

"No argument there," her mother said.

"I wish we still lived in Massachusetts, I wish you were an English teacher, I wish . . ." She stopped.

"Do you really wish I were an English teacher?" her mother asked.

Meg shrugged.

"Just anything but President, right?" said her mother.

"It could be worse." Meg said.

"What do you mean?"

"You could be Pope."

THE
PRESIDENT'S
DAUGHTER

Ellen Emerson White

AN AVON  FLARE BOOK

AVON BOOKS
A divison of
The Hearst Corporation
105 Madison Avenue
New York, New York 10016

Copyright © 1984 by Ellen Emerson White
Published by arrangement with the author
ISBN: 0-380-88740-1

First Avon Flare Printing: October 1984

AVON FLARE TRADEMARK REG. U. S. PAT. OFF. AND IN OTHER COUNTRIES, MARCA REGISTRADA, HECHO EN U. S. A.

Printed in the U.S.A.

K-R 10 9 8 7 6 5

For my mother. Naturally.

CHAPTER ONE

Meg was ten minutes early. It was her mother's opinion that three minutes were more than sufficient, but Meg liked to play it safe. Less pressure that way.

She slouched into the tennis club, wearing old blue sweatpants, a baggy V-neck sweater, and a faded green Lacoste shirt. The woman at the front desk nodded, and Meg nodded back. It was Friday afternoon, so the place was pretty quiet, although commuters would be showing up any minute now for after-work drinks. Which meant that her mother would have to shake hands all over the place. Pretty embarrassing.

She sat down on a gold velour couch to wait, checking to make sure that no one was watching before swinging her legs onto the magazine table. *Tennis, World Tennis, Racquet Quarterly, Architectural Digest, Vanity Fair.* She had a tremendous urge to go up to the desk and ask for the latest issue of *People,* but repressed it. Sometimes people didn't have a sense of humor about things like that.

She checked the clock. Seven minutes of five. That meant that she had four minutes to go—unless her mother's plane was late, or she was tied up in Boston traffic. Some Fridays, that happened.

To occupy herself, Meg unwrapped the blue bandanna from her racket handle, not sure whether to tie it around her head as a sweatband or just hide it inside her racket cover. She could never decide if bandannas were cool or trendy—it was impossible to be both.

The front door of the club opened, and she heard a familiar voice: Glen, her mother's top aide.

"—at eight-thirty," he was saying. "And then, at nine—"

Her mother nodded, both dignified and beautiful in a blue silk dress and her London Fog raincoat. She saw Meg and

1

her face changed, the fatigue and political smile replaced by a grin. She crossed the hall with swift grace, and Meg stood up to receive an enthusiastic hug, smelling bold but understated perfume.

"I hope I'm not late," her mother said, glancing at her watch.

"No," Meg said. "I was just kind of early."

"Well, I'm sorry you had to wait." Her mother held her away. "Smile."

Meg smiled obediently.

"Oh, you look beautiful," her mother said. *"Much* older." She turned to Glen and her press secretary, Linda. "Doesn't Meg look beautiful without her braces?"

Linda and Glen nodded. They weren't what you'd call effusive types. More like what you'd call grumps.

"Well." Her mother checked her watch again. "We'd better get moving." She looked at Glen and Linda. "I'll anticipate seeing you shortly before eight."

Glen scanned his schedule sheet, his expression worried. "I think seven would be more—"

"I haven't seen my family since Monday," her mother said somewhat sharply. "Eight will be quite sufficient."

He sighed, but nodded.

"Thank you," her mother said. "I'll see you in a few hours." She switched her tennis bag to her left hand, putting her right arm around Meg. "Come on, let's not waste any court time."

"See you later," Meg said to Glen and Linda, then followed her mother down the hall to the women's locker-room. Watching her, Meg decided that her mother was the kind of person who made you wish that you had on pumps. Not that Meg could walk on pumps. Not that she really *wanted* to walk on pumps. Put-together, that's how her mother looked. As if she never had a grey hair. Except forty-four was kind of old for that.

"Mom?"

"What?"

"Do you color your hair?"

"No."

"Hmmm." Meg considered that. "Never?"

"Occasionally." Her mother turned to look at her. "Why?"

"Just curious."

Her mother lifted an eyebrow, but didn't pursue that.

Meg sat in the lounge part of the locker-room, slouched low enough to avoid the many mirrors. She wasn't heavily into mirrors.

Her mother came out in an *ellesse* pleated skirt/striped shirt outfit, walking over to the largest mirror to put up her hair, doing so with three deft bobby-pin jabs. She frowned at the mirror, retouched her makeup, then shook her head to loosen some of the hair in the bun. The Senator prepares to enter the public eye. She saw Meg watching and smiled.

"I only color it when it starts greying strangely," she said.

Meg put on her best solemn expression. "I guess only your hairdresser knows for sure."

"What, are you kidding? I do it late at night."

"Do you turn the lights out first?"

Her mother laughed. "Always." Leaving the locker-room, she glanced down at Meg's outfit. "What happened to all those clothes you got for your birthday?"

"I don't know," Meg said, a little self-conscious about the contrast between them. The Senator and slovenly daughter. "I feel like I'm not supposed to perspire in them."

Her mother nodded. "No point in ruining good clothes by wearing them."

Meg looked at her uncertainly, not sure if she were kidding, but they were already on the court, and it was too late to ask.

"Rally for a while?" her mother asked, on the other side of the net.

"Um, yeah, sure," Meg said, leaving her bandanna with her racket cover. Her mother was like, a phenomenal tennis player. Meg generally felt lucky to get a game off her, although she would play as hard as she could. Over the last

3

year or so, more and more games had gone to deuce, and sometimes Meg even won a set.

They kept the court for about an hour, her mother winning 6–3, 6–4. Meeting her at the net, hot and tired, Meg noticed that her mother was also flushed and trying to hide the fact that she was out of breath.

"Are you okay?" Meg asked, just to be sure.

"Fine." Her mother blotted her face with a towel. "Have you been playing a lot lately?"

"Pretty much."

Her mother nodded. "It shows."

"Hello, Senator," one of the women taking over the court said. "How's Washington?"

"Not bad," her mother said. "How's psychology?"

"Not bad."

"Have a good match." Her mother picked up her tennis bag, then draped her sweater around her shoulders.

"How do you remember all that stuff?" Meg held the door as they left the court area. "I mean, all the people you meet."

"Practice, I guess. I've never been one for mnemonics."

Meg nodded intelligently, rather than asking, "What are mnemonics?"

"I mean," her mother's voice was very casual, "I personally find that memory devices complicate things even more."

Meg blushed. She would have to work on her intelligent nod.

"Hey." Her mother paused by the club bar. "Feel like going in to get something to drink?"

Meg shrugged and followed her, trying to get her sweater to drape just as sportily around her shoulders. Or at least half as sportily.

The bar was crowded, and they sat at a table in the corner, a waiter hurrying over.

"What can I get you, Senator?" he asked, pen poised.

"Orange juice, thank you." She grinned. "It's not just for breakfast anymore."

"I believe," Meg said, "that I'll have a martini."

"That's what *you* think," her mother said. "How's orange juice sound?"

"Not as good as Tab."

Her mother nodded at the waiter, who nodded back and scurried off to get their drinks. When he returned, her mother took a sip of juice, glanced around at the other people in the bar, and leaned forward.

"How can you come and play tennis and be terribly healthy, then come in here and drink?" she asked.

Meg gulped some Tab. "Are you sure I can't have a martini?"

"What do you know about martinis?"

"Lots."

"Right." Her mother finished half the juice, still flushed from playing. She lowered her glass, looking at Meg thoughtfully. "You know, since it's just the two of us, I thought we could have a—"

"Senator Powers." One of the men from the bar was suddenly at their table. "I wanted to congratulate you on the work you did on the chemical dumping bill."

"Oh, well, thank you," her mother said. "How've things been going for you?"

"Not bad, not bad."

"Oh," her mother turned. "This is my daughter Meghan. Meg, this is Mr. Garvey."

"How do you do," Meg said.

"Hi," Mr. Garvey said briefly. "Senator, what I wanted to ask you was, the wife and kids and I are going down to D.C. for a week. What's the chances of us being able to get some gallery passes?"

"Call the Boston office," her mother answered, "and talk to Harriet. She'll arrange everything for you."

"Okay, thank you. Thank you very much," he said, and went back to the bar.

"Another day, another vote," Meg observed.

Her mother grimaced.

"How come you have to go out and give speeches tonight? I thought you were going to be home."

"Well." Her mother looked uncomfortable. "It's only two. I should be back by ten at the latest."

Meg nodded. It wasn't like this was the first time.

"Anyway," her mother said. "I thought since it's just—" She glanced around to make sure. "Since it *is* just the two of us, I thought we could have a talk."

Meg stiffened. "Am I in trouble?"

"No, of course not. I just want to talk to you."

Meg relaxed. "If it's about sex, I already know," she said, sitting back in her chair.

"Since we went over it about six years ago, I should hope it's sunk in by now. At any rate," her mother went on, "I've discussed this with your father—"

"What, sex?"

"Meg, come on, I'm being serious."

Recognizing the irritation in her mother's voice, Meg was quiet.

"I wanted to talk to you before I mention it to your brothers. Your father and I have given it a lot of thought. It's about the next election."

"You mean, you're not running?"

"I'm not running for Senate," her mother conceded.

"You mean, you'll like, live at home all the time?" Meg could almost feel her eyes lighting up or whatever it was that eyes did.

"Meg, I want to run for President."

Meg choked, losing half her mouthful of Tab on the table. She shoved her napkin onto the liquid, still coughing. "Are you kidding?" she gasped.

"No."

"Oh my God."

"A lot of party people have been approaching me. They think the country's ready for a serious woman candidate, and they think— Well, what do you think?"

Meg frowned. "Will you be in the primaries and everything?"

"At least New Hampshire," her mother nodded.

"Will you be able to be home at all?"

"Not much," her mother admitted. "I'd have to be all over the place campaigning."

"What'd Dad say?"

"I want *your* opinion, not his."

Meg studied her mother, healthy and alert, the thin neck and face dark against the white sweater.

"You look like a President," she decided.

"Now?"

"Yeah. You dress right. And you're tall enough."

"Well, thank you." Her mother laughed. "Think we can work 'five eight' into a slogan somewhere?"

Meg twirled her straw, thinking about all of this. "You're not—I mean—what happens if you win?"

"I guess that would mean I'd be President."

"My God." Meg shuddered, dropping the straw. "You think you'll win?"

"I'll be happy if I make a good showing in New Hampshire, forget anything else."

"My God." Meg shuddered again.

"Well, what do you think?"

"Can I have a martini?" Meg asked.

Getting home half an hour later, they found Meg's little brothers Steven and Neal on one side of the kitchen table, making a salad, while Meg's father sat on the other side, drinking Molson and frowning at the paper.

Steven was eleven, thin and pugnacious, with their mother's dark hair and eyes. Neal was six, still hanging on to somewhat blondish hair, much quieter than his brother.

"Hey!" Neal scrambled up. "It's Mom!"

"Hi." She caught him in a hug, dropping her tennis bag.

Steven shoved the lettuce away and moved in for his turn. Their mother hugged him, then Meg's father, which was a different kind of hug. Longer. They looked at each other, and Meg's father brought his hand up to her mother's cheek.

"You look tired," he said.

"Well"—she kissed him lightly—"I've been playing tennis."

"Mom, Mom, look!" Neal rushed out of the room, then

7

back in with a handful of school papers. "I got a hundred in spelling and everything!"

"Oh, well, let's see." She sat down and Neal climbed up on her lap, grass-stained and disheveled from soccer practice. "Wow, a ninety-five in math. Oh, that's great."

"Hi," Meg said to her father.

He smiled at her before looking back at her mother. "How was school?"

"Okay. How was work? Get lots of new clients today?"

"Hundreds." He leaned forward, touching his wife's hand. "I'm glad you're here."

"I'm glad too," she said, turning her hand over to hold his.

Meg looked at Steven, who pretended to gag.

"Bet Mom'll make you get a haircut tomorrow," she said, just to get him going.

He threw some carrot peelings at her as the phone rang, and they both jumped for it, Steven getting there first.

"Hello? . . . Oh, just a minute, please." He covered the receiver with his hand. "Mom, it's what's-his-name from Texas."

"Representative Palmer?" She took the phone as he nodded. "Brian, hi . . ."

"Party business," Steven said, trying to make his voice deep.

"Party?" Meg said. "Who's having a party?"

"Boy, do we have a dumb sister," Steven said to Neal, who laughed.

An hour and six phone calls later, they were sitting down to dinner, the phone hooked up to the answering machine, eating the stew that Trudy, their housekeeper, had made and the salad Meg had had to finish making. On weekends, Trudy usually went home to her apartment.

Their father frowned, which made him look like a stern tax attorney. His smile made him look like a jolly lumberjack. "Steven, we'd better see about getting that hair cut tomorrow."

Steven groaned and Meg laughed.

"You'll probably be even better at soccer if it isn't getting in your eyes all the time," their mother said reasonably.

"Me too?" Neal asked.

"You too." Their mother leaned over to cut his meat.

He watched her, his elbows on the table. "Were you important today?"

She made four quick horizontal cuts. "Not really."

"Did you talk in front of everyone?"

"I always do." She handed him his plate, indicating with her eyebrows for him to move his elbows.

"Boy." He reached in front of Steven for the bread basket, saw his father's expression, and sat back. "Would you please pass me the bread please?" he asked politely.

Steven took two pieces, then shoved the basket along.

"Boy," Neal said, taking two bigger pieces, "I bet all those Senators listen to you."

"Not always."

"Boy," he said. "You should be President."

She lifted her eyebrows at Meg, who shuddered.

"Meg, be a good munchkin and pass me the salt, will you?" she asked.

CHAPTER TWO

After the usual fight with Steven over the dishes—the fight they always had when Trudy wasn't around either to do them herself or officiate—Meg escaped upstairs with the excuse of homework. Actually, homework wouldn't have been all that terrible an idea, since the next night there was a dance at school, and she and her closest friend Beth Shulman were going to go along with a bunch of other girls and collectively stare at Rick Hamilton, which would undoubtedly be fruitless but entertaining. Then, Sunday night was out, because her parents were having a dinner party for an ambassador and his wife and some other political people. Party business, as Steven would say. Anyway, that would mean that they'd have to make appearances, be properly well-mannered and articulate children, and pass hors d'oeuvres. At least there would be maids and people around to serve dinner. She and Steven would definitely have made a mess with dinner.

"Looks like no homework this weekend," she said to her cat, Vanessa, who was washing in the upstairs hall.

Vanessa purred, rubbing against Meg's legs and following her into her bedroom. They had five animals, and technically, that meant that each member of the family should have one. But it hadn't worked out that way. Vanessa was hers and had been ever since the day Meg found her, a tiny grey kitten, wandering around outside the Chestnut Hill Mall and brought her home. Adlai and Sidney, the two Siamese, were her parents' cats and rarely deigned to leave their bedroom. Humphrey, the lumbering, arrogant tiger cat, didn't belong to anyone. He had shown up on their porch a couple of summers before and decided to move in, no matter what anyone else said about it. He took turns sleeping with everyone—"sleeping around," her father said.

Then, there was Kirby, their dog. They had gotten him at the pound right after Neal was born—so Neal could have a twin, Steven often said—and no one could agree on what breed of dog he was. He had grown up into a large shaggy brown and white dog with floppy ears and a shepherd head. The kind of dog whose loved ones were the only ones who thought he was beautiful. Kirby belonged to all of them.

Meg sat down on the bed, lifting Vanessa onto her lap. "You're mine, right?"

Vanessa stretched out her front paws, back arching, then settled down to sleep.

"I think"—Meg stood up—"that it's time for some Talking Heads." She was tempted to put on "Old Time Rock and Roll" and do her Tom Cruise imitation, but someone invariably walked in on her. Meg wasn't into public displays of dancing.

Her favorite song in life was Joan Jett's "I love Rock and Roll," but that was too rowdy for sitting down and being pensive. She settled for the Stray Cats because that way she could dance Vanessa around during the Stray Cat Strut. Dancing amused Vanessa.

She went back to her bed to be pensive. President. Good God. As far back as she could remember, her mother had been in the Congress. It was a given. When Meg was born, she'd been in the state assembly, and before that, the youngest Boston town council member ever, but all Meg could remember was Congress. First, the House of Representatives, then the Senate. Nothing like moving up the old ranks.

Her mother had had to take some time off when Steven was born, and they'd lived in Washington for almost two years when Neal was born, but basically it had always been like this—the family here in Chestnut Hill outside Boston and her mother living in an apartment in Georgetown, flying in on weekends and whenever else she could. They were all used to it, and as her mother put it, "tried to make the days they *were* together count." Those days always seemed to be hectic.

11

It was hard even to imagine what it would be like if her mother were a lawyer in her father's firm, or a teacher or something, and lived at home all the time. Not that Meg didn't wish it were that way. Whenever Congress recessed and her mother didn't have to be out among her constituents—possibly Meg's least favorite word in the English language—it was so nice. Kind of a luxury. Waking up and hearing those quick footsteps on the stairs made her feel complete inside, that everything was as it should be. The footsteps never stopped, almost as if they were rushing around to make up for the days they weren't there.

No one at school thought it was a big deal, thank God. They were used to it too. In fact, a lot of her friends were always saying they wished *their* mothers didn't have to be around all the time and yelling at them or whatever. Meg would have chosen the yelling any day.

She ruffled up Vanessa's fur, then smoothed it down again, just ruffling the fur on and around her head, creating an ugly, out of proportion beast. Quite the stray cat look.

It was funny—it had gotten so no one in the family even thought twice about it if her mother was interviewed on *Meet the Press* or *This Week with David Brinkley* or something. And it was an odd day if she wasn't mentioned in the paper. For a while, Meg had saved all of the articles, but it just got ridiculous. There were magazine write-ups too, like the one in the *New York Times Magazine*—a story about "The Leader of That Growing Minority: Congresswomen." With that one, she had even had her picture on the cover.

"A Minority of One," she said to Vanessa. "Female Presidents."

Enough of being pensive. She went over to the stereo to put on Bob Seger's "Stranger in Town" and do her Tom Cruise imitation after all. She took off her sweatpants and exchanged her tennis shirt for an old Oxford shirt of her father's. She set the record to the right song, turned the volume all the way up, and grabbed a hairbrush to use as a microphone. The music started, she slid across the floor in her Peds, and spun around to dance.

The door opened, and she stopped, in midgyration, to blush. "Don't you knock?"

"Well, I—" Her mother was trying, unsuccessfully, not to grin. "I—the stereo was so loud," she said lamely.

Meg turned the volume down, then put her sweatpants back on, her face very hot. "Did you want anything?" she asked stiffly.

"Well, I—" Her mother's eyes were bright, and she was shaking from keeping the laughter inside. "The stereo was so loud," she said again.

"Yeah, well"—Meg coughed—"what can I do for you?"

"How about 'Slaughter on Tenth Avenue?' " her mother suggested and broke up completely.

Meg scowled.

"I'm sorry," her mother said, controlling herself. "I didn't—I'm really sorry."

Meg didn't say anything, arms tightly folded.

"Come on, where's your sense of humor?"

"I don't have one," Meg said, trying to stay grouchy, but unable to keep back a small grin. Her Tom Cruise imitation was probably pretty funny looking. She studied her mother, soignée in a light grey wool dress. "How'd it go?"

"Not bad. A little tiring though."

Meg nodded, smoothing the fur on Vanessa's head. Her mother spent most weekends being exhausted.

"Well." Her mother moved toward the door. "I'm sorry I disturbed you."

"Mom?"

Her mother turned instantly.

"You, uh, going to bed or something?"

"No," her mother said. "I just thought—well." She came back in. "So. How are you feeling about things?"

"Which things?" Meg asked, to be difficult.

"Well, what we discussed this afternoon."

"Oh, *that,*" Meg said,

"Mmm, that," her mother said. *All The President's Men* was lying on the desk, and she picked it up, automatically smoothing the binding and putting in a piece of paper as a bookmark. "Were you reading this before, or did you start tonight?"

"Book report," Meg said, which was a lie. Actually, she kind of liked reading about politics—not that she would ever admit it. Reading, because you were going to get graded took the fun out of it. Besides, it was a lot easier to talk to all the political people who came over if she knew a little about it. "You going to call yours *All the President's People?*"

"God forbid," her mother shuddered.

"I'll, uh, probably have to watch saying things like that."

"Probably definitely," her mother agreed. She glanced over. "You're feeling a little better about the idea?"

"I don't know." Meg stroked Vanessa's fur down, making her face very serpentine. "I mean, it doesn't seem real."

"No, it doesn't," her mother said, and Meg watched her pace, wondering if she would do that someday, or be like her father who just tightened up and didn't move. "It really doesn't."

"What's it going to be like?"

"I don't know," her mother said, shrugging. "Undoubtedly full of depressing defeats."

"Sounds like fun."

Her mother stopped pacing. "I'm sorry. I'm not answering your question, am I?" She sat down at the end of the bed. "There'll be a lot of publicity, some probably very unfavorable. And your father will have to be away with me for some of the campaigning."

"What about us?" Meg asked, uneasy.

"I'm not going to *make* you campaign, if that's what you mean."

"So, I could, like, back another candidate?"

Her mother nodded, amused. "If you wanted to."

"Will it be mostly leafleting, or standing around having our pictures taken, or what?"

"Probably a little of both."

"Gross," Meg said. "I hate having my picture taken."

Her mother laughed. "I do like you, Meg," she said,

lifting her hand enough to move some hair away from Meg's face. "I feel like—you're growing up, and I'm missing it."

"You're not missing it," Meg said awkwardly.

Her mother nodded a very unconvinced nod, looking at her for a long minute. "You know," she said, "you are getting extremely attractive."

Meg blushed. "You're my mother. You have to say that."

"No, I don't." She kissed the top of Meg's head. "All I know is that there must be an awful lot of crushes over at that school."

"Yeah," Meg said. "And I have all of them."

"Be thankful. When I was your age, I was at an all-girls school, and I was absolutely terrified of boys."

Her mother? Afraid of men? Inconceivable. "Really?"

"Really," her mother said. "And I was tall. Height was the bane of my existence."

"Rough life."

"I know I thought so."

Neither spoke, listening to Vanessa purr.

"Was it hard?" Meg asked.

"Was what hard?"

"N-not having a mother around."

"Yeah, it was." Her mother laughed shortly. "Not that I have to tell *you.*"

"Mom."

"Well, it's not as if I'm around."

"It's different."

Her mother nodded, obviously not agreeing.

"It was a riding accident?" Meg both asked and said. This wasn't something they ever discussed.

Her mother nodded. "My mother wasn't a person who knew her limitations." She shook her head. "I don't know, it's hard to remember. I was so small."

Meg moved closer. "I always thought you were mean when you wouldn't let me take riding lessons," she said, looking at the thin, tight hand in her mother's lap.

"I suppose I was."

"I don't mean I think so anymore." She touched the hand for a fraction of a second and saw it relax. "Mom?"

"What?"

"Do you know your limitations?"

"No. No, I don't guess I do."

"I kind of figured." Meg tilted her head up to look at her, noticing the laugh lines around her mouth and eyes. Unexpected lines. Lines you would never see from a distance. "Are you going to win?"

"I very much doubt it."

"Then, how come you're running?"

"I don't know." The laugh lines deepened suddenly. "I guess I think I can win."

Her mother announced her candidacy in front of a huge crowd at the Prudential Center, the whole family standing behind her, the pictures hitting what seemed like every magazine in the country. Meg kept expecting to walk by a magazine rack and see her mother on the cover of *Popular Mechanics*.

The campaign became a routine like everything else. Her mother was home even less often, traveling around the country whenever she wasn't in Washington, calling at some point every night to talk to them all. Lots of weekends, Meg's father would fly out to be with her, while Trudy took care of Meg and her brothers. Sometimes, not very often, her mother would make it home for a day or two, and once, for just a few hours, so she could see Steven on his birthday.

When her mother *was* home, Meg got accustomed to the house being full of campaign people, a lot of whom Meg knew from her mother's Senate staff, even more of whom had been hired specially. Glen, who the press called the Boy Wonder, was her mother's campaign manager. Very jittery guy. Linda, her mother's press secretary, had only been on the Senate staff for about ten months, and Meg realized now that she must have been hired with the idea that her mother would be running for President some months later. So, it must have been in the works for a long time. Linda was obsessed with "images," and Meg didn't like her much. Smooth California blond combined with aloof Smith College poise. Meg suspected that Linda had been hired because she was able to be tough in ways that her mother wasn't—cutting off press conferences, dodging questions, withholding information until the appropriate moment. With the press, Meg's mother was apt to be either very candid or very funny. This made Glen and Linda nervous.

The rest of the top-level campaign people were an incongruous bunch. There were quite a few more men than women; this, Meg figured, because her mother didn't want to be thought of as the Female Candidate, but rather, judged ideologically. Her mother had never been obsessively active in the Women's Movement because, she said, she would far rather be associated with foreign policy and defense expertise and thus, in the long run, have a strong enough position to *do* something for women and minority groups. First, she had always told Meg, she had to get people to forget that she was a woman. It made sense. A lot of other female politicians were so sensitive to sexism that no one took them seriously on other issues. Her mother thought it was easier to work from *within* the patriarchy.

And, although nothing much would really happen until the Iowa Caucus, her mother was getting a lot of publicity, most of it favorable. Ultraconservative types were saying things about a woman's place being at home with her children, but her mother was so well-respected as a Senator that the negative publicity wasn't having much effect. She was the chairperson of the Senate Committee on Energy and Natural Resources, as well as a highly ranked member of the Foreign Relations and Judiciary committees. A pretty fair political package, as Linda would say.

Meg and her brothers had decided early on that their favorite campaign person was Preston Fielding. He was this very cool black guy who had been in charge of public relations in her mother's Washington office and was now a consultant on the national level. Titles aside, Meg had noticed that Preston just sort of did whatever needed doing. When other people had lost or forgotten demographic sheets or expenditure lists or whatever, Preston invariably had copies.

He would show up with a case of Heineken when everyone was getting uptight and grouchy; he seemed to know about six important people in every government agency—all of whom owed him favors; he was great at fund-raising. Important as all of that was, Meg liked him because he was so funny.

Every day, her life seemed to change a little more, all because of the campaign. Like the telephone company coming to connect four extra lines into the house. Or the Secret Service all over the place studying her house and the neighborhood, since they would have to start protecting her mother in January—an idea too scary to even *think* about yet. The post office was delivering so much mail that they came to the door with sacks instead of trying to use the mailbox. Meg would have to dig through the pile to find things like the L. L. Bean catalog. All of it seemed very unreal.

Maybe the hardest was when her father was out of town too. The house felt so empty. Steven would slouch around, pretending not to miss them, and Neal would have ten times as many bad dreams as usual. And Meg never knew what to do for either of them. Thank God for Trudy.

One Sunday night, when her parents were in Pennsylvania or someplace, Steven and Neal wandered off after dinner, Meg hanging around the kitchen to help Trudy with the dishes.

"I can take care of this," Trudy said, smiling at her over grandmotherly glasses. "You should do your homework."

"I don't have any," Meg lied, drying the spaghetti sauce pan.

"A sophomore in high school, and you don't have any homework?" Trudy clicked her tongue.

"Nope." Meg looked at the clock. "Wonder what Mom and Dad are doing."

"They're probably at a church supper," Trudy said, washing the salad bowl. "And your mother's getting ready to make a speech."

"Probably," Meg said, realizing the impulse to put the pan away harder than necessary.

"You know, Meg, if you need someone to—"

"I don't," Meg said. "I mean, thanks anyway, but I really don't." She closed the pan cupboard. Very quietly. "You think I ought to go see what Steven and Neal are doing?"

Trudy nodded. "We're almost finished here anyway."

Hearing the television, Meg went into the sitting room. Steven was sprawled on the couch, a New England Patriots notebook next to him.

"You do your homework?" she asked, for lack of anything better to say.

"Nope."

"Are you going to?"

"Nope."

She shrugged and sat down next to him.

"What is this?" She watched two cars crash, rolling down an embankment and exploding into fire.

"It's boring," he said.

"Where's Neal?"

"Dunno. He went upstairs."

"Is he okay?"

"Guess so."

"Well, maybe I'll go see what he's doing." She reached over to rumple his hair. "Why don't you watch something more cheerful?"

He shrugged.

"Be back in a while." She went upstairs and found Neal's bedroom door closed. The light was on, so she knocked. "Neal?"

"What?"

"Can I come in?"

He mumbled something and she opened the door to see him sitting up on the bed, looking very small and very sad.

"What's wrong?"

"Nothing."

"Are you sick?" When Neal was upset, he had a tendency to get sick to his stomach.

He shook his head.

"Well." She started to put her hands in her pockets and

19

realized that she had on sweatpants. "Can I keep you company?"

He shrugged, and she climbed onto the bed, sitting next to him.

"You've been pretty quiet tonight," she said. "You sure you aren't sick?"

"Yeah."

"Do you miss Mom and Dad?"

He nodded, moving closer, which was a signal for her to put her arm around him, which she did.

"He'll be home tomorrow."

He nodded.

"And maybe she'll come home this weekend."

"No, she won't." He burrowed closer. "She never does."

"Well, she can't help it, she has to campaign."

He shook his head harder, and she could tell by the shaking in his shoulders that he was crying.

"Come on, Neal, don't. Please, don't." She hated it when he cried—she never knew what to do. "Don't, okay?"

"How," he was trying to stop the tears, but not succeeding very well, "how can she be away if she loves us?"

You tell me. "She's away *because* she loves us," Meg said. Oh, good. Very good. She couldn't even convince *herself* with that argument.

He shook his head, also not convinced.

Okay, Meg, justify that. There will be sixty seconds for rebuttal. "Neal, running's important to her; she feels like she has to do it. If she didn't, she'd be unhappy, and she doesn't want to be unhappy around us because that would upset everyone. She's doing it now, so things will be better later." Not bad. She could almost fall for that one herself.

"But—" He hesitated, that having made an impression. "I miss her."

"I miss her too."

"I like it when she says good night." He snuggled next to her, smiling in one of the incredible mood swings of his age. "She smells so nice."

"She does," Meg agreed. She did. It wasn't even just perfume.

"And she holds me." He hugged himself, demonstrating. "And says that she loves me."

"Well, she does. You know she does."

He beamed up at her and she smiled back. Child psychology. She had found her career.

"Daddy smells nice too," he said.

"Yeah, he does."

"But different." Neal squared his shoulders in imitation.

"You're right." Observant little kid. Her mother smelled expensive. Unruffled. As if nothing she did required physical effort and she could be like *Bewitched* and just flit about at will. Her father was different. He smelled like flannel shirts, he smelled safe. Even in a dinner jacket, he smelled like flannel shirts. Comfortable.

"Meggie?"

"What?" She loved Neal's hair. Her mother generally cut it, wrapping him up in a little towel, using a pair of black-handled scissors. His upper lip always seemed to be smiling and, looking at him, she couldn't help hoping that he would never grow a mustache and cover it up. Except for milk mustaches. She loved his milk mustaches.

"I like the way you smell," he said, giggling.

"How do I smell?"

He turned his head to sniff her hand on his shoulder. "Ivory Liquid," he said, and giggled.

"I was helping Trudy with the dishes."

"Sometimes Noxzema."

"Sometimes." She traced his haircut with the Ivory Liquid hand.

"And," he took a long time deciding, "like outside."

"Yeah," she agreed. "I fall down a lot."

"No!" He pushed her in giggling impatience. "Like raking leaves. Like *doing* things." He tilted his head to peer up at her. "Steven smells like new sweatshirts."

"Like baseball gloves," she said.

"What about me?"

"Hmmm." She hugged him, pressing her face into his hair. "Like very old sneakers."

"I do not!"

"Marshmallows."

He laughed, shaking his head.

"Ski jackets."

"That's no good!" He tried to get away from her, giggling as she tightened her arm around his shoulders, keeping him from moving. She tickled him and he laughed uproariously, trying to push her hand away.

"Meggie!" He tried to squirm free, but she held on, not releasing him until a few seconds before he would start getting mad. "You're mean," he said, laughing weakly.

"I am not."

He tickled her and she managed, through the utmost self-control, not to react.

"You're not ticklish?" he asked doubtfully, pausing.

"Sorry, kiddo." She grinned at him. "Want to go watch TV with Steven?"

"Will you make popcorn?"

"Again?"

"And put in too much so we can watch the cover come off?"

She looked at him for a second, wondering vaguely why stupid little things always made people happy.

"Yeah," she said. "Sure."

CHAPTER THREE

A couple of weeks after Christmas, Meg went into Boston with Beth Shulman. After the divorce, Beth's father had given her a bunch of charge cards, and she loved to go into places like Sak's and Bergdorf's, look disreputable enough to irritate salespeople, then whip out her charge cards. Meg would often comment that this was extremely nouveau behavior. Beth would sigh deeply and say, in a very sad voice, Not everyone can be old money. Apparently not, Meg would say and they would laugh loudly enough for the salespeople to suggest that they think about going elsewhere. Actually, the concept of money kind of embarrassed Meg, and she would never say anything like that in front of anyone other than Beth. Oh, come on, Beth would say, *flaunt* it. No, thanks, Meg would say.

"Where's your mother get her clothes?" Beth asked as they looked through a display of sweaters in Filene's Basement. In Boston, if you were very cool, you *always* went to Filene's Basement.

"I don't know." Meg held up a very ugly maroon crewneck. "Lots of places. New York, mostly. Can you see anyone ever buying this thing?"

"And here I was," Beth said, "planning to buy it for you." She held it up and shook her head. "I don't know. I like you better in salmon."

Meg nodded. "Most people do."

"Just the other night, before he climbed out my window, Rick Hamilton said, 'God, Beth, why doesn't Meg wear salmon? She wouldn't look nearly as ugly if she wore salmon.' "

"Which night?"

"Wednesday? Thursday?" Beth shrugged. "Who keeps track?"

"Well," Meg said, "the thing of it is, he's been at *my* house every night this week."

"It's all right," Beth said gently. "You can have your fantasies."

Meg grinned. "Likewise."

"That's for sure." Beth dropped the sweater. "You want to go buy some records or something?"

Meg shrugged. "If you want."

"We could get some food."

"Yeah, I guess."

"Well, what do *you* want to do?"

Meg shrugged.

"Do you feel okay?"

"Yeah." Meg glanced around restlessly. "Let's get out of here, okay?"

"Whatever." Beth followed her out of the store, Meg walking very quickly. "Hey, slow down already."

"Sorry." Meg stopped on the sidewalk, putting her hands in her pockets to avoid the winter wind.

"What's your problem? You're being a real grouch lately."

"Yeah, I know." Meg sighed. "I don't know."

"Well, what is it?"

"I don't know." Meg hunched her shoulders. "Cold out here."

Beth zipped her jacket up, also hunching. "Very."

"Yeah." Meg looked up and down Washington Street, seeing grey slushy snow and hurrying commuters. "You mind going on a walk?"

"A walk," Beth said.

"Please? It's not far."

Beth grinned. "Not everyone has such a kind and generous friend."

"Guess I'm just lucky," Meg said, grinning back.

"Not that," Beth said, "I won't collect on the favor."

"What happened to generosity?"

"When it's this cold out?"

"We'll walk fast." Meg started down Washington Street

toward Government Center, veering down one side street, then another.

"It's getting dark for this sort of thing," Beth said.

Meg looked at the sky. "Yeah, kind of." She turned one more corner, stopping when she saw the storefront with the huge "Katharine Powers for President" banner across it, along with lots of red, white, and blue bunting and several large posters of her mother smiling.

"Hunh," Beth said, also staring. "I didn't know there was one down here."

"This is the main one."

"Yeah?"

"I've, uh," Meg let out her breath, "never been here before."

"There wasn't some kind of ceremony when it opened?"

"No. We just went to the Chestnut Hill one." Meg swallowed. "It's big."

Beth nodded.

"Really big." Meg stared at the posters, trying to relate the smiling candidate in pictures with the elderly, minorities, students, and other what Glen called "voting blocs" to the woman who did things like burn toast. The woman in the pictures—the *candidate* in the pictures—looked as if she were perfect. Friendly, kind, intelligent—but, it was scary. It was like when her mother's office sent out semiannual reports on what The Senator had accomplished lately. Looking at the pictures always gave Meg the creeps.

"Kind of weird," Beth said.

"Yeah." Meg looked away from the pictures. "I haven't seen her since the day after Christmas."

"Well," Beth said awkwardly, "I guess she's pretty busy."

"Yeah." Meg started walking. "Let's go."

"You aren't even going in?"

Meg stopped. "Why should I go in?"

"You dragged me all the way down here, and now you're not even going to check it out?"

"Well—no," Meg said uneasily.

25

"Come on." Beth started across the street. "Don't be a jerk."

"But I really don't want to."

"What about that favor you owe me?"

Meg sighed. "Just pretend we're regular people, okay?"

"I *am* a regular person," Beth said.

"You know what I mean."

"Yeah, I know what you mean." Beth flipped up her jacket collar. "Come on. We'll pretend we're spies from tne enemy camp."

"Swell," Meg said, following her.

Beth opened the door, and warm air rushed out at them. They stepped inside, and Meg was surprised to see the maze of activity going on. Normally at this stage of a campaign, things were apt to be pretty quiet. The room was crowded with people talking and laughing, phones were ringing, a radio was set to WBCN. There was a strong smell of coffee, both old and new, and doughnuts. The walls were covered with posters, and tables were stacked with buttons, bumper stickers, and leaflets. The people were different ages, but there were a lot of senior citizens and even more students. Some were stuffing envelopes; some were making lists of registered voters; some were on the phones, either taking or making calls, Meg couldn't tell.

They stood there for a few seconds, Meg feeling more and more uneasy; then a girl from one of the tables near the front came over, smiling, her hair tied back in a green bandanna.

"Hi," she said. "I'm Lily."

"I'm Beth," Beth said, shaking her hand.

"I'm—" Meg hesitated. "I mean, hi." She shook the hand the girl offered, not sure if she should have taken her glove off first. Her mother would have.

"Is this your first time here?"

Meg blushed and Beth nodded.

"Well," the girl said, smiling, "we have a lot of high school workers."

"No," Meg shook her head. "We're just kind of here because—well, we were just curious," she finished lamely.

"Then, let me show you around." Lily was very cheerful. "Do you know much about the candidate?"

"Uh, kind of," Meg said, not looking at Beth.

"Well, then." The girl began giving them some personal background on the candidate, as well as issue positions, as Meg blushed, wishing she'd never had the stupid idea of coming down here.

She focused on a photograph of her mother talking with energy officials—they all had on hard hats and everything. Her mother looked concerned, interested, informed. Ridiculous in the hat. So this was what was coming out of all those late-night conferences around the kitchen table. Probably no one would ever know that slogans like "The Way to Honest, Open Government" made her mother laugh, that she thought they were empty clichés. "Image, Kate, image," Glen would say. "Trite, Glen, trite," her mother would say.

As she listened to the girl explain the candidate's interest in education and women's issues, she couldn't help wondering if workers had a speech ready for every kind of person who might come in. If they were older men with thick calloused hands, would they get a speech about unions and Social Security?

"Have you met her?" Meg asked, interrupting.

"Well, not personally," the girl admitted. "But I've heard her speak. She's wonderful. You can just tell how honest she is."

"How?"

"Well, it's her attitude mostly, although anything I've ever read substantiates it. Have you ever heard her speak?"

"Yeah," Meg said.

"Me too," Beth said. "Once, when I was little."

Meg elbowed her.

"Well then, you know what I mean," the girl said. "She doesn't hesitate when she answers questions, she doesn't have stacks of notes up there with her, she's not afraid to say what she thinks. I don't know—I guess it's sort of hard to pin down. But I know I could never support anyone I didn't trust."

27

"Is it true that she broke ranks with the party and voted with the President on the missile bill?" Beth asked.

Meg shot her a look, which Beth returned innocently.

"My God, no," the girl said. "The Senator's positions are strongly—"

Meg looked around some more. Everyone in the room seemed enthusiastic and confident. Excited. It was pretty impressive to have so many people working before the primaries even started.

"Would you like a couple of buttons?" the girl asked.

Beth nodded, taking two, Meg blushing and shaking her head.

"We have a bunch at home," she muttered, shifting her weight.

"Is your family working on the campaign?"

"Sort of." Meg heard Beth choke back a laugh. "Is this place always so crowded?"

The girl nodded. "Every time I've been in here. Like tonight's Tufts Night, and a lot of these kids are from there. Most of the colleges around here have Nights every couple of weeks. It's crazy in here on Harvard and Radcliffe Night, because that's where she went. Plus, a lot of senior citizens' groups and unions have Nights too. And church groups. She pulls in a lot of the church groups."

"I thought her position on abortion was upsetting people," Meg said.

"I guess the Old Guard types," the girl conceded. "But we still get an awful lot of people in here. Oh, Bruce," she moved to intercept a man in a dark blue suit who was coming out of the office in the back. "Come over here and talk to some people." The girl dragged him over, and Meg flushed, recognizing Bruce Gibson, who she'd met quite a few times in her kitchen.

"Meg, hi," he said. "What are you doing down here?"

She turned even redder. "I don't know. We were just kind of walking around and—"

"Well, great." He seemed very happy to see her. "You haven't been down here before, have you?" He turned to the

28

girl. "Lily, this is Meghan, the Senator's daughter, and—?"

"My friend Beth," Meg said.

Bruce smiled. "And her friend Beth."

"Really?" The girl's eyes got very big. "Wow. Why didn't you say anything?"

"I don't know. I guess I felt—"

"Well, come on. We should introduce you to everyone."

"No, I—" Meg hung back. "I'd really rather not. It's getting late and we—well, we just wanted to—"

Bruce rescued her. "It *is* getting dark. Do you two need a ride home?"

"Oh, no," Meg shook her head very hard. "We'll take the T. Only, is it okay if I use your phone? I ought to let my father know I'm running late."

"Sure. C'mon back here."

They followed him through the maze of tables, boxes, and workers to the cluttered office in the back, half-empty Styrofoam cups of coffee everywhere.

"How're things going?" Meg asked.

"Great," he said. "Our big worry was your mother's early fund-raising power, but the donations are pouring in. Unions, women's groups, all kinds of people. Once she starts winning, we'll be up for the big money."

"You're that sure she's going to win?" Beth asked.

"Absolutely."

Her mother sure could inspire dedication. Unreal. Meg picked up the phone, dialing. "Oh, hi, Dad?" she said when he answered. "I'm still in Boston. I got sort of held up."

"Did you think to look outside?" His voice was irritated. "I thought I said I wanted you home early."

"Yeah, I guess you did."

"Well, where are you? I'll have to come pick you up."

"Dad, we can just—"

"Where are you?"

"Mom's headquarters. We can just get on the—"

"Really?" His voice was more pleased now. "What are you doing there?"

"Just looking around?"

"What do you think?"

"It's really busy, there's like all kinds of people here."

"Well, maybe later on you can start doing some work down there."

"Yeah," Meg agreed. "Look, we're just going to go out and get on at Government Center, okay?"

"I'll pick you up at the station."

"Okay. Be there in about twenty minutes."

She hung up, Beth called her mother, then they went back out to the crowded room with Bruce, Meg noticing that everyone was looking at her. Lily must have spread the word. Meg nodded at them, taking a button to pin on her jacket.

"So," Beth said as they walked to Government Center.

"My mother voted with the President?" Meg asked.

"I was making conversation."

"Right," Meg said.

They took the D Line train back toward Newton, Beth getting off at Reservoir where her mother would be waiting, Meg getting off a stop later at Chestnut Hill. Her father was in the parking lot and started up the engine when he saw her.

She got into the front seat. "Hi."

"Where's Beth?"

"She got off at Reservoir."

"Did she have a ride?"

"Her mother."

He nodded, turned on the headlights. "Next time, I want you home when you're supposed to be."

"Yes, sir."

"And enough with the 'sirs,' " he said, reaching over to give her a scarf a tweak.

"Anything you say, sir."

He laughed, putting the car into reverse and driving out of the lot. "What did you think of the headquarters?"

"It was okay." Meg slouched against the seat. "I hate those pictures though. She doesn't look—I don't know—real, in them." She glanced at him. "Are they all staged?"

"I don't think they're staged so much as there's a photographer following her everywhere she goes.'' He braked for a stop sign. ''It's advertising, that's all. You have to win the election before you can do anything.''

''So you do anything to win?''

''No, of course not. It's just—'' He started to turn the corner, then frowned, pulling over. ''Sorry. I can't talk and drive.''

''Kind of like walking and chewing gum?''

''Kind of,'' he agreed. ''You really shouldn't worry, Meg. Have you *ever* seen your mother do something unethical?''

''Well—no.''

''Neither have I,'' he said. ''And I don't expect her to change now.''

''I don't know,'' Meg said. ''I guess.''

''Meg, all I can tell you is this: Your mother is absolutely, totally, almost sickeningly honest. She doesn't do anything she doesn't believe in. She humors them—''

''Them?''

''Glen, the staff, you know. She humors them,'' he went on. ''But once she gets out there, she does what she wants. And she says what she wants. She doesn't do things because they 'look good.' ''

''So how come what she does looks so good?''

''Because it's what people want to see.'' He let out a hard breath. ''I don't know what to say, Meg. I can't believe that I'm sitting here telling you something you should already know.''

''I guess.'' Meg jiggled her knee up and down, thinking. ''Is she going to win?''

''I don't know.''

''Do you *think* she's going to win?''

''I don't know. But I think everyone's going to know she was in the election.''

''Hmmm.'' Meg thought about that. ''Do you want her to win?''

Her father didn't answer right away. ''I don't know,'' he said finally. ''I want her to be happy.''

''Wouldn't being President make her happy?''

31

"I'm not sure," he said, both gloved hands resting on the steering wheel. "It's almost as if—she wants a woman to be President, she wants that desperately, and at this point, she knows she's the only one around who can pull it off."

"What about ambition and power and stuff like that?"

"I don't know, Meg." He shook his head. "I don't think your mother's obsessed with either—it's more of a challenge kind of thing with her." He shook his head again. "She's a very complex woman. A very wonderful woman," he added more quietly.

Meg let a few respectful seconds pass, knowing that he was missing her. There had been times when her parents hadn't seemed quite so much in love—maybe not even in love at all. It hadn't been like that for a long time, but that didn't stop Meg from worrying, especially with her mother being gone twice as much as usual.

She looked at her father, thinking about what a nice man he was. Probably the nicest man she knew. She remembered suddenly being the star of the Thanksgiving play when she was in third grade. The part had required pigtails and a little blue dress, both of which she had. The play was in the afternoon, and her father had come, one of the few men in the audience, a man sitting up front with Steven, who was in nursery school. After the play, he came backstage to get her, his smile very proud. He gave her some flowers—she couldn't remember what they were, daisies, maybe?—then picked her up in a big hug, and the three of them went all the way into the city to have hot fudge sundaes at the original Bailey's. Then, that night, Trudy stayed with Steven, and she and her father went to see *The Sound of Music*. He had always been able to make them feel special.

Seeing him sitting next to her, his face healthy and windburned, as if he never sat behind a desk or read *The Wall Street Journal*, Meg obeyed an overpowering urge to hug him.

"What was that for?" he asked as she pulled free before he could hug back, sitting on her side of the car, embarrassed.

"I don't know." She blushed, staring out t'   igh the

windshield. She almost never gave in to urges to hug people. "I like you."

"Well, I like you too," he said.

"Steven's probably burned the house down by now."

"Probably." He started the engine, then looked over at her, shaking his head. "You're very much like her."

Meg blushed. "I am not."

"When your grandfather was alive, he used to sit there for hours, watching you. He said it was frightening."

"Well, I guess I *look* like her," Meg said. "But I mean like, she's—and I'm—"

Her father just grinned, glancing over his shoulder to check for cars, then pulling out into the street.

CHAPTER FOUR

Right after dinner that night, the phone rang.

"I've got it!" Meg yelled from the kitchen. "Hello?"

"Hi," her mother said. "How are you?"

"Okay." Meg sat down at the table. "Where are you?"

"Detroit."

"I thought you were in Iowa."

"I was." Her mother yawned, and Meg had a momentary disturbing flash of her sitting alone and exhausted in a hotel room somewhere. "I flew up because we ran into some luck today."

"What happened?"

"The autoworkers pledged their support, isn't that great? The union, I mean."

"Wow," Meg said. "That's really good, isn't it?"

"It's *tremendous,*" her mother said. "I really wasn't expecting it. Certainly not this early." Her mother yawned again. "What did you do today?"

"Nothing much. Beth and I went in and kicked around Filene's Basement."

"Did you pick up anything? Aren't they still having after-Christmas sales?"

"Yeah. We were mostly just looking around though. Meg mouthed the word "Mom" as Steven came in.

"Well, you really need a new ski jacket. That thing you're wearing around now is disgraceful."

"I like it," Meg said.

"Then get the same kind."

"Yeah, but—" Meg pushed her brother's hand away from the phone. "Steven, wait a minute, will you?"

"Come on, let me talk," he said impatiently.

"I said, wait a minute." Meg pushed him harder. "When are you coming home again, Mom?"

"I think maybe next weekend," her mother said. "So do me a favor and get the jacket, and maybe we can all go up to Stowe for a couple of days."

"Wow, really?" Meg lowered the phone. "Mom says she's coming home, and we can maybe go skiing next weekend."

"Well, let me talk to her."

"Okay already." Meg lifted the phone back up. "Steven's being a jerk, Mom, so I'd better let him talk to you. That's really good about the autoworkers."

"Thanks. Take care of yourself, okay? It sounds as if your cold is pretty much gone."

"Yeah. Where are you going tomorrow?"

"South."

"Just in general?"

"It feels that way. Actually, Atlanta; then I have to head up to Washington by Monday." Her mother laughed. "It sounds as if you'd better put your brother on."

"Yeah, really." Meg shoved him again. "I'll talk to you tomorrow.

"Okay. I love you."

"Yeah, me too," Meg said quickly. "I, uh, went to your headquarters in Boston today; they were pretty neat. Um, here's Steven."

"God, about time." Steven grabbed the phone from her. "Hi, Mom, where are you?"

Meg got up, moving to the door.

"Dad? Neal?" she called. "Mom's on the phone!"

"Oh, good." Her father came in from the sitting room. "I thought it might be."

"Wow, let me talk!" Neal rushed in, trying to get the phone away from Steven. "Come on, it's my turn!"

"God, wait a minute, will you?" Steven pushed him.

Hearing the familiar note of irritation in his voice, Meg laughed. "Neal, don't bug him. He just got on."

Neal scowled, slouching into a chair to wait.

"She still in Des Moines?" her father asked,

"Detroit."

"What's she doing there?"

"The autoworkers said they're going to support her."

"Really?" His expression was both surprised and impressed. "My God, she's cleaning up on the unions." He tapped Steven's shoulder, indicating for him to hurry up.

When her father was on the phone, she and Steven and Neal waited at the table.

"Guess what Mommy said?" Neal leaned forward on small crooked elbows. "She bought me a cowboy hat in Texas! A real one!"

"How queer," Steven snorted, his mouth full of Oreos he'd found on top of the refrigerator.

"Yeah, well, she got you one too." His face fell. "That's supposed to be a surprise."

"Yeah?" Steven looked eager. "What color are they?"

"If you really think it's queer, we can have Dad tell her to take yours back." Meg helped herself to some Oreos, giving one to Kirby, who wagged his tail and retreated under the table to eat it.

"Meg, shut up, okay?" Steven said, blushing.

"Dad's being mushy on the phone," Neal said, stuffing an Oreo into his mouth.

"I love you, Katie," their father was saying. "Be careful, okay? . . . I have to worry, I can't help it . . . Right . . . Okay, I will . . . I love you too." He listened for another few seconds, then hung up to see Meg grinning, Steven pretending to throw up, and Neal giggling. "Little brats." He picked up what was left of the package of cookies. "Come on, who wants to go watch the Celtics game?"

"Gross," Meg said. "I hate hockey."

"Cute," her father said.

She spent the next couple of days looking forward to going skiing, but began to lose enthusiasm as she realized what it was going to be like. The first warning came on Monday night when her father remarked to the three of them that "there would be some politics going on that weekend, and they all had to be prepared for that." What she had seen as a relaxing family weekend was going to be more of a three-day campaign session. Glen was coming, Linda—who

Meg had decided to call the Ice Queen—was coming, campaign coordinators were coming—and Meg didn't feel like going.

She didn't communicate that to her brothers, both of whom were so excited that the weekend was all they talked about. She was anything *but* eager.

Wednesday night, hearing her father wandering around downstairs—he wandered a lot when her mother wasn't home, especially after they were all in bed—she got up and went downstairs, finding him coming out of the den.

"What are you doing up?" he asked, automatically checking his watch.

"I don't know. I'm not tired."

"Terrific." His expression was wry. "It's going to be fun waking you up tomorrow."

"What are you doing?"

"Not a lot." He reached forward, touching her forehead with the back of his hand. "Do you feel okay? You're not coming down with anything, are you?"

Oh, good idea. If she were sick, she wouldn't have to go. "I don't know," she said. "I just can't sleep."

"Well. Would you like me to make you some warm Tab?"

"Would that help?" she asked uncertainly.

He laughed. "No." He sat down on the stairs, indicating for her to sit next to him. "What's wrong? Are you still upset about this weekend?"

"I don't know. I thought it was going to be just us."

"She's running for President," he said. "There's no way it's going to be 'just us' for a long time."

Meg slouched down, not wanting to hear that.

"Oh, come on." He put his arm around her. "It's not going to be that bad."

"Will people be taking our pictures all over the place and asking questions and everything?"

"Probably."

"Sounds like fun," she said grumpily. "What am I supposed to say to reporters?"

"We've gone over that, Meg. Just be polite and friendly.

And don't worry about it. Your mother's staff will keep them out of the way—that's what they're there for."

Meg kicked at the bottom stair with her right foot.

"World champion fretful child," her father said.

"Don't make fun of me."

"I'm sorry. Look," he kissed the top of her head, "don't worry. It's going to be fine. Your mother's staff will handle everything—I promise. All you have to do is stand there and smile."

"Look daft, you mean?"

"I'll buy that," he said, grinning, then hugged her closer. "It's really going to be fine."

"Do you promise?"

He nodded.

"Can I quote you on that?"

"Sure," he said.

They got to the Inn at the Mountain right before dinner on Friday night. The place was full of reporters and cameras, and her mother's staff was very excited. Her mother had a press conference, and then there was a quick photo session—naturally. They ate at the Inn, in the Fireside Tavern, a dinner that wasn't exactly restful, but they *were* together, as her father kept pointing out.

By the time they finished, it was too late to do anything else. Her parents had gotten two suites—one for Meg and Steven and Neal; the other for themselves, also to be used for campaign planning. Steven and Neal went right to bed, so they'd be wide awake for skiing in the morning. Meg wasn't tired, so she hung out in the main room of her parents' suite, watching the same kind of strategy session she usually saw around the kitchen table. And, as usual, her father was making jokes that only her mother seemed to think were funny. Everyone else was too busy being serious. Too bad Preston hadn't been able to come. He and her father really seemed to have a good time together. It was Meg's theory that Glen and Linda never had a good time.

After about an hour, she gave up, deciding that the session was going to go on all night.

"Going to bed?" her father asked, as her mother glanced through a thick sheaf of reports.

"Yeah." She yawned. "I'm pretty tired. Are you guys going to do this all night?"

"We're going to call all of the other candidates, see when they're going to bed, and stay up fifteen minutes longer," her father said, and her mother laughed, touching his shoulder with a caressing hand.

"Well," Meg said. "Good night."

Her mother smiled. "Eight o'clock breakfast sound good?"

"Yeah." Meg shrugged. "Sure. Good night," she said to the room in general, getting a couple of nods, a couple of good nights, and a couple of grunts in response.

"Make sure you lock your door," her father said, "okay?"

"But I'm expecting someone," Meg said, amused to see three sharp glances from campaign people.

Everyone seemed very busy and distracted, so she left, feeling a little lonely. Since it wasn't going to be a family weekend, she should have asked if Beth or someone could come. But on a family weekend, it didn't seem right—not that it would have mattered much. She stood outside the door, listening to Jim—who had worked on every Democratic Presidential campaign for the last thirty years—talk about New Hampshire and the primary. Well, her leaving sure hadn't upset things much.

She went down to the other suite and unlocked the door. It was very quiet. Too quiet. She changed into her nightgown, thinking about Vanessa. Missing her.

She was just finishing brushing her teeth when there was a small tap on the door. Her mother. For a confident person, her mother always knocked very shyly. Meg finished rinsing and put the little plastic cup down on the sink.

"Is that you, Arthur?" she called.

She heard her mother laugh and went out to open the door.

"Did you come to tuck me in?" she asked.

"I came to make sure you were all right." Her mother looked worried. "Are you?"

"Yeah. Sure."

"Good." Her mother glanced at her watch.

"What," Meg said, "you have to get right back there?"

"No. I just wanted to make sure that you were going to get enough sleep."

Meg flushed. She had probably been a little too quick to be hostile there. "So, uh, you going to read me a story?"

"Sure," her mother said. *"The Cat in the Hat* sound okay?"

"Yeah." Meg went into her room, getting into bed and pulling up the covers in four-year-old anticipation.

"I used to love reading to you." Her mother automatically turned down the spread. "You always got so excited."

"Yeah." Meg kept her arms around updrawn knees, remembering those nights: the theatrical way her mother read, how she'd always been able to tease her into reading two or three instead of just one. She pulled her knees in closer, almost wishing she were Neal's age again and could still be cuddled. Parental cuddling was nice. She missed parental cuddling.

"Meg?"

She released her knees, sitting up straight. "I was just thinking. "I'm sorry about this weekend." Her mother sat at the bottom of the bed. "I wish it could be just us, too."

Meg shrugged affirmatively, bringing her knees back up.

"It's not bothering you too much, is it?"

"Not really," Meg said. "Some of your campaign people are kind of grumpy though."

"Some of them certainly are."

"They don't even laugh at Dad's jokes."

"And he's really terribly funny." Her mother laughed, and Meg wondered which one of his remarks she was remembering.

"How come you hired such grumps?"

"They're not *all* grumps."

"How come Preston's the only one who isn't a grump?"

"Because I need a team of highly organized, serious people." Her mother's face relaxed out of her political expression. "You're right. I like Preston too."

"Glen's kind of a pain."

"He's a perfectionist, that's all. You just have to get used to him."

"Linda too?"

"Oh, she's all right."

"Ice Queen," Meg said disparagingly.

"Is that what you call her?" Her mother tried to look serious, but Meg could see the amusement in her eyes. "That's terrible, Meg."

"She's like a robot. I swear I've never heard her say a sentence that didn't have the word 'image' in it."

"I might remind you that she's in a profession in which women have to work twice as hard."

"So are you."

"Right," her mother nodded. "And for all we know, there's a country full of people who think I'm an Ice Queen." Half of her mouth moved into a smile. "And worse."

"No, they don't."

"The other day," her mother settled herself more comfortably, "I gave a speech at a Rotary Club luncheon and afterward, at the reception, a man told me that I was a harlot."

"What did you do?"

"Well, you know me," her mother said. "Always quick on the uptake. So, I said, 'What?' He repeated himself, I said, 'Oh,' and he walked away."

"At least you told him off," Meg said.

"I guess I'm used to it."

Meg scowled. "Do lots of people say crummy things to you?"

"There're a few in every crowd," her mother said, shrugging. "Anyway, that's why Linda's the way she is. If you spend that much time with your defenses up, it gets to be a habit."

"But you're not like that."

"To a degree I am. You have to be."

41

"Yeah, but—"

"Oh, come on," her mother said. "Let's talk about something *other* than politics."

"Are you going to win?"

"I thought we weren't going to talk about politics."

"I just wondered. I mean," Meg gestured toward the door, "all these reporters up here and everything. Isn't it pretty good to have so many following you around?"

"Well, at this point, they're following everyone."

"That many?"

"Probably not," her mother admitted. "I don't think it means much though. At least not until after the caucus."

"The Iowa Caucus," Meg said, her mother nodding. "How're you going to do, you think?"

"It's hard to say." Her mother smoothed the blanket with one hand. "The polls have me up near twenty percent now. If I do well in the debate they're having, that'll help. I don't know."

"Who're you worried about the most—Kruger?"

"Well." Her mother folded her arms, considering that. "He's doing well. So is Hawley. And you can never tell about Mertz. Every four years, he throws a scare into people."

"What about Mr. Sampson?"

"Oh," her mother brushed that aside, "no one takes him very seriously. But who knows? Maybe Clay Grundy will come from nowhere and take a lot of votes. He's been spending most of his time in New Hampshire, and he just might be a threat there. I don't know."

"What about the election?"

"You mean, the real one?"

Meg nodded. "Are we going to win? The party, I mean."

"One would certainly think so," her mother said. "I mean, with Crandall officially out of it. I think the incumbency factor was the only advantage they had."

"But you're not prejudiced or anything," Meg said.

Her mother smiled. "Not even vaguely." She stood up. "You should probably get some sleep."

"You should probably go rescue Dad from the grumps."

"Yes." She bent to tuck in the blankets, then hugged her, long enough for Meg to feel awkward. "Good night."

"Night."

Her mother moved to check the window lock. "I'll go look in on your brothers," she said. "Then, I want you to come and put on the chain lock, okay?"

"But then Arthur won't be able to get in."

"I'm sure he'll think of something," her mother said.

CHAPTER FIVE

Heading for the lift line for a third time the next morning, Meg felt someone glide up next to her, and turned to see Linda, stiff but well-groomed in her light green ski suit, smiling that sterile smile.

"Would you like to share a chair up?" she asked.

"Sure," Meg said. Being trapped on a ski lift had to be the ultimate example of a captive audience.

"I thought we should get to know each other better."

Oh, boy. Her mother had undoubtedly put Linda up to this. Meg smiled and nodded.

"H-how is it?" Linda gestured up the mountain.

"A little icy."

Linda looked nervous. Scared, actually.

"It's not that bad," Meg said quickly. "Just stay away from the fall line."

Linda nodded. "Your, uh, your mother tells me that you're very good," she said conversationally.

"I don't know." Meg leaned forward against her poles for a few seconds, stretching. "Steven's probably going to be the best out of the three of us."

"What about Neal?"

"Well," Meg straightened up, moving forward in line, "he's been doing it since he was three, so he's pretty good, but Dad doesn't like him skiing alone, so we take turns keeping him company." She smiled. Keeping Neal company was sometimes one of her favorite parts of skiing. He never stopped laughing. She loved to watch him square his little shoulders, push off down a slope, and giggle all the way down. She glanced at Linda. "Have you been skiing long?"

"Not particularly. I guess I prefer tennis."

Or, probably, *Jane Fonda*'s *Workout* tape. Linda had

that kind of body. Actually, Meg—who considered herself to be in fairly good shape—had tried the workout once with Beth and Sarah Weinberger, neither of whom did more than an occasional flight of stairs, and had found it so difficult that she had to fake a sudden, extreme headache.

They didn't say much of anything else until they were in the chair and on the way up the mountain.

"Eric told me he saw you talking to someone from the *Times* this morning," Linda said, shifting her poles to her right hand.

Maybe her mother hadn't initiated this after all. "Oh, the *Times,*" Meg said. She hadn't been sure where the man worked. "I knew he was from one of the papers."

"What did he ask you?"

Meg thought back. "I don't know. It was no big deal."

"Well, can you try to remember?"

"He wanted to know how the skiing was here, and I said that it was really good." Meg moved the zipper on her new CB jacket—her mother had insisted—up and down, thinking. "Then, he asked if I liked coming up here, and I said yes, and he said it must be nice to be spending time with my mother, and I said yes, and he said it must be hard to have her away so much, and I said that we missed her and everything, but that she was always there if we needed her." She glanced over. "Is that okay?"

"That's fine." Linda's smile was significantly less sterile. "I should have realized that you'd be pretty well politicized."

"But it's true. I wouldn't have said it if it wasn't true."

Linda just nodded, seeming very pleased by her performance.

"She always comes if we really need her."

Linda nodded.

"Like on Steven's birthday. She flew home and everything."

"No one is saying that she didn't." Linda's voice was calm. "You just have to remember that your mother isn't running for school committee; she's running for President. We have to be very careful."

"We?" Meg asked.

"In the future, I'd rather that you didn't talk to any reporters unless I'm there or someone from my staff is sitting in."

"Yeah, but—"

"I'd like that to be the policy."

"But—" Meg released a slow, frozen breath, ordering herself not to get irritated. "What if someone comes up and asks me a question? Do I say, I'm sorry, I can't answer that unless someone's with me?"

"We need to be careful, that's all. People have an image—"

Meg grinned, in spite of herself.

"—very important that you and your brothers come across as happy, well-adjusted—"

"Fake it, you mean?"

"That's not what I said."

Meg grinned, then recognized two familiar shapes twisting down a slope below them: one small and darting in bright red, the other tall and graceful in royal blue.

"There's Mom and Neal," she pointed.

Linda looked down, wincing as the figure in blue took a jump over an uneven patch of snow and stayed airborne for several feet before landing easily, smoothly.

"Your mother is sometimes incautious," she said.

"A few years ago, she broke her leg," Meg said, remembering how the incident had been both frightening and amusing—frightening since she and Steven had been skiing with her when it happened, but amusing because of all the pictures *Newsweek* and everyone printed of The Senator crutching her way around Capitol Hill.

"It's over if she breaks her leg," Linda said grimly. "A candidate, particularly a woman, is supposed to be invulnerable."

"Invincible," Meg contributed.

Linda was not amused.

They dismounted as the lift got to the top, Linda's descent unsteady.

"Which trail would you say is the least demanding?" Linda asked, sounding more nervous than she looked.

"Toll Road," Meg said, pointing to the right. "And take the crossover."

Linda nodded her thanks. "Please try to be careful with reporters," she said. "Everyone will be glad to help you."

Meg nodded, and they separated, Meg gliding down to Hayride. There was one particularly icy turn, and she'd almost fallen on her first run down, so she wanted to try it again and see if she could get it right. She took her mirror sunglasses out of her jacket pocket and slipped them on. To be a very cool skier, one *always* had to wear mirror sunglasses. Hers were blue.

She paused at the top of the trail, studying the terrain to see how she could attack it differently this time. She took a deep breath and jammed her poles into the snow, shoving off.

She made a few quick parallel turns, enjoying the speed, enjoying the challenge of the ice. Whipping along, carving neat, short turns, she considered slowing before the difficult turn, but decided not to, enjoying the rushing wind too much. She cut the turn a little late, and her right ski skidded on an icy patch, sending her down in a hard tangle of skis and legs. She lay on her back for a minute, staring at the clouded sky, annoyed at her own stupidity in trying to take it too fast. Nothing like being incautious.

There was a spray of snow as someone stopped next to her and, focusing on dark curly hair and a tanned face, Meg decided that she believed in God.

"You okay?" the boy asked, his voice flippantly concerned.

"Yeah, thank you. Just hit some ice." Embarrassed, Meg got her right ski on, using her poles to push herself up.

"Let me give you a hand." He moved a thick glove underneath her elbow.

"Thank you." She knocked the snow off her jacket. The trouble with wearing jeans when you skied was that the snow soaked in, and when you got to the bottom, everyone knew that you had fallen.

"My name's Dave." He brushed some snow off her back, and she blushed, the touch somehow intrusive. "What's yours?"

"Meg."

He studied her for a second, eyes going down. "How old are you?"

"Almost sixteen." She sighed, realizing that unexpected romance would have been too much to hope for.

"Would have guessed older." His eyes moved again.

"How old are you?" She turned to avoid the scrutiny, reddening more.

"Be nineteen in a couple of months. I go to Dartmouth." His voice was superior.

"Good school," she said.

"Yeah." He bent to adjust a buckle, balancing on one pole, and she wondered if she should seize the moment and make a quick escape. He straightened. "You hear we've got a celebrity up here this weekend?"

"Oh?" Meg tried not to groan aloud.

"Yeah," he nodded. "Presidential candidate. You ever heard of Senator Powers?"

"She's the woman, right?"

"Yeah." This nod was patronizing, and he spoke in the authoritative voice of a college freshman taking Politics 001. "Of course, she'll never win."

"Why not?"

"We need a *man* in the position."

What a jerk. "We do?"

"Absolutely," he said, not even noticing that she'd stiffened. "Certainly Powers is probably qualified, and she gives a good speech, but she wouldn't have the authority, especially in dealing with world leaders. If she's lucky, Kruger or someone'll ask her to be his running mate—that'd be a better place for her."

"Why?" Come on, Dave, let's see how much further you can put your foot in your mouth.

"No responsibility," he said.

If he puts it in any further, he'll choke.

"I mean," Dave shifted his weight onto the other pole,

"She'd probably be good at functions—she's poised, and God, no one can say she isn't good-looking. But, you have to have a man at the top."

Heimlich maneuver time.

"But," he smiled at her. "I'm sorry to go on like that, I couldn't expect you to be interested."

"Why not?" Meg asked in the voice of a champion Ice Queen.

"Well, you're—" He paused, searching for the word. "I mean—"

"Look," she cut him off. "Before you say anything else, maybe you should know something."

"What's that?" The smile was patronizing again.

"Senator Powers is my mother."

"Y-your mother?"

"My mother," she nodded, pushing off and down the slope again. "Thanks for helping me up."

That night, she and her family had dinner at the Trapp Family Lodge, all having gotten through the day without broken legs. Right after their salads were served, her father frowned suddenly, glancing at her mother, who followed his gaze to the bar and laughed.

"Meg, there's a boy over there who can't take his eyes off you," she said. "Steven, be a nice kid and pass me the salt, will you?"

Meg looked over and recognized Dave with two other boys.

She returned to her salad. "He's looking at you, Mom."

"No, he isn't." Her mother checked again. "It's very definitely you."

"Believe me, it isn't." Meg kept eating.

"Yeah, who'd look at Meg?" Steven said, grinning.

"A lot of people would," their mother said. "Your sister is very attractive."

Both Meg and Steven snorted, then Meg frowned at her brother.

"You're not supposed to agree," she said.

"Hey, except for your face, you're fine," he said.

"If you hadn't been born without a brain, you'd probably be okay too." Meg managed to grab a piece of garlic bread right out from underneath his hand.

"How about a truce?" their father suggested. "At least until after dinner."

"Oh, but we love each other." Steven moved his chair over next to hers, putting his arm around her. "Don't we, Meggie?"

"Oh, yeah." Meg kept eating.

Her father frowned at the bar. "I don't like it. He's too old to be staring at you."

"He's only eighteen," Meg said. She glanced up to see the whole family looking at her. "Oh, guess I shouldn't know that." She shrugged, picking up her knife to cut a piece of lettuce, deciding to start some trouble. "He's a pretty good kisser for an old guy." Without even lifting her eyes, she could feel their heads turning toward the bar.

"What's his name?" her mother asked casually.

"Why would I know his name?" Meg asked. "Hey, can I have a martini?"

CHAPTER SIX

They skied all day Sunday, had dinner at yet another reporter-crowded restaurant, then drove home, not getting in until pretty late. Very tired the next morning, Meg fumbled her way through school, thankful that there wasn't a Student Council meeting or anything that would mean she'd have to stay after. She didn't actually fall asleep until her last period class, which was history, and always pretty boring. Her teacher, Mr. Bucknell, was a real pain, always talking about her mother and trying to get Meg to drop campaign secrets. Not that she knew any. She wasn't even sure if there *were* any.

"Meghan?"

"What?" She jerked away, hearing the irritation in her teacher's voice. He was scowling nearsightedly, gripping his tie with one hand, which made her uncomfortably suspicious that he might have called on her more than once. The grins on the people sitting near her made her suspect that even more. "I mean, yes, sir?"

"I *do hope,*" he stretched the two words out, "that you don't mind my interrupting your little nap."

Well actually, sir, now that you mention it . . . "I'm awake," she said.

A couple of people laughed.

"Well, I am," she said to everyone sitting in her section of the room.

"She thinks, therefore she is," Rick Hamilton said, and more people laughed.

Meg blushed, but returned the cocky grin he gave her, deciding that he was probably the sexiest—

"Meghan," Mr. Bucknell said impatiently.

"Uh, yes, sir?" She focused toward the front of the room.

"We were discussing the Iowa Caucus, and I thought you might be able to give us some insights on the subject."

"Um, well." Meg searched for something to say. "It's a week from tomorrow."

"Does your mother have any specific campaign strategy?"

The man never quit. She looked at Beth, who scribbled a note that said "Tell him about the bribes." Lots of help. This was the only class she had with Rick Hamilton all day, and Mr. Bucknell seemed to go out of his way to embarrass her. If only he would—you know, Rick was really incredibly good-looking. Arrogant grin, wavy hair, really sexy eyebrows. She had a thing for guys with acrobatic eyebrows. Usually the only way she could ever keep awake in this class was by trying to stare at him without getting caught. Beth and Sarah Weinberger almost always got caught. Meg figured she had about a .500 average. Not that he'd be interested in her anyway; he always went for the tall, blond—

"Meghan?" Mr. Bucknell sounded very testy, practically choking himself with his tie.

"I'm sorry," Meg said. "I just really don't know anything."

"Oh, come on, she must have mentioned something. You spent the entire weekend with her."

Nothing like having a private family life. Was every day going to be like this? She looked at Rick, who obviously thought all of this was—damn it. He caught her that time. Flushing, she looked at her desk. Now he would know that she liked him. God, what a day.

"What about the debate?" Mr. Bucknell asked. "Has she got any special strategies for the debate?"

"I don't think so."

"Well," he kept trying. "What about positions? Like gun control. What's she going to say about gun control?"

Wasn't he ever going to give up? "I'm kind of not supposed to comment on that," she said quietly.

"What?" He took a step backward, looking so theatrically stunned that most of the class laughed.

"That's telling him, Meg!" someone shouted.

"Well, class." Mr. Bucknell's eyes made a slow sweep of the room. "What would this school be like if *all* our students went around saying 'No comment?' "

The same people laughed again.

"The *next* thing you know, Meghan will be taking the Fifth."

A few people laughed, but more people gave her sympathetic looks, switching back to her side.

"Maybe you'd feel better having an attorney with you in class?" he suggested, and Meg made herself meet his gaze, not looking away until he did.

Then, she stared down at her books. Why couldn't her mother be a psychologist? Or a writer? Or a professional tennis player? Only then, her gym teachers would be after her—she could hear it now: "Well, Wimbledon's coming up. Meg, do you think you can give us some insights?" Would she have to be Catholic to join a convent?

The bell rang and she gathered up her books, wanting to get out of there as fast as possible.

"Don't forget," Mr. Bucknell said. "I want the answers to the chapter seventeen questions handed in tomorrow. And, Meghan, would you mind staying after for a minute?"

Yes. Meg paused halfway to the door.

"Tell him yes," Beth said, right behind her.

"Meghan." Mr. Bucknell didn't sound as if he were in the mood for any smart answers.

Meg sighed and sat back down. When everyone was going, Mr. Bucknell leaned against the table at the front of the room, folding his arms.

"I don't think I asked you anything *too* terrible," he said.

"I'm not supposed to go around talking about things."

"We just want to share the experience. I think we're very fortunate to have a candidate's daughter in here, and I've been trying to get some good discussions going. We can all learn a lot from this."

"But I'm not supposed to talk about things."

"No one is asking you to give away campaign secrets," he said mildly.

Yeah. Sure.

"I was thinking that you might be able to get her to come in one day and speak to the class."

Meg shrugged, wondering when her mother would find time to do something like that if she didn't even have time to come home.

"Meg, I really don't mean to give you a hard time."

Then, how come you keep doing it? Meg didn't say anything.

"If you're having a hard time with the idea of your mother being a candidate, you should share *that*," he said.

"I'm not."

"It would be perfectly natural."

"But I'm not." She checked the clock. "I kind of have to get going."

He sighed, unfolding his arms. "Maybe in the future, we can both try to be a little more cooperative," he said.

Meg nodded, standing up to leave.

"Meg?"

She turned.

"I was very impressed with your paper on the Reconstruction. You seem to have a real grasp of the material."

Flattery would get him nowhere. "Thank you," she said.

Beth and Sarah were waiting for her in the hall.

"So?" Beth asked.

Meg glanced over her shoulder to make sure she had closed the door on her way out.

"He wants me to try and be a little more cooperative," she said. "I told him he'd have to speak to my attorney about that."

"Wow." Sarah's eyes widened behind her glasses. "What'd he say?"

Meg and Beth grinned.

"Well, I don't know." Sarah shrugged defensively. "Meg might do that."

"I bet you said, 'Yes, sir, anything you say, sir,' " Beth guessed.

"I told him I'd get back to him," Meg said.

"Tell me, Miss Powers." Beth made her hand into a microphone. "What is your mother's position on gun control?"

"Well." Meg leaned back against a locker, assuming a pseudothoughtful, pseudointellectual stance; standing like any one of a number of her mother's aides. "The Senator is a little torn on this issue. She carries several guns in her purse, but she doesn't like the idea of just any old person being able to get one. Also, she's sponsored several bills on teacher executions and—"

"Wow," Sarah said. "Does she *really* carry a gun?"

Her father got home later than usual that night, having had to appear at a couple of fund-raisers in lieu of her mother. On Thursday, he was flying out to Iowa to be with her for the last ten days before the caucus. Even though only about 10 percent of the people in Iowa voted in it, it was a big deal because it was the first vote of any kind—other than straw polls—in the election. Iowa was pretty conservative, but Meg figured that her mother had a pretty fair chance since she had an outstanding record on agricultural issues. There was also the college vote. She'd probably get most of that.

"Daddy!" Neal saw him first, as Meg, her brothers, and Trudy sat watching television after dinner. "We missed you!"

"Well, I missed you too." Their father bent to hug him.

"I've got your dinner warm in the oven if you're hungry, Russell," Trudy said.

"Thank you, that sounds great." He straightened up, rubbing a tired hand across the back of his neck, then loosened his tie. "But don't worry, I can get it myself."

"Don't be silly. It won't take but a minute." She bustled out to the kitchen.

"How'd it go?" Meg asked, opening her biology book to make it look as if she'd been doing homework.

"Not bad. Crowded." He yawned, taking off his jacket, making Neal laugh by putting it on Kirby. "Your mother call?"

"Yeah." Steven opened his math book, seeing Meg open her chemistry book. "She said hi."

"Don't be a jerk." Meg reached across the couch to hit him. "She said for you to call her back around eleven, Dad."

"Guess what?" Neal climbed onto his father's lap. "She said she had a meeting with the President today and everything! *He* called her up to talk to her!"

"*He* wants her support on that foreign-aid bill," Meg said.

Her father glanced over. "Been reading the papers lately," he observed.

Meg shrugged. At school, she worked just hard enough to get good grades—candidates' children were kind of supposed to, but newspapers and magazines and things like *McNeil/Lehrer* were different. She liked knowing what was going on. Sometimes, when Mr. Bucknell managed to get the class into a political discussion, she would have to chew her pen or drum on her desk to keep from joining in. If she said anything, people would probably think she was showing off or had asked her mother for the answer. Like, in Student Council, instead of running for an office, she was just a representative, and she and Beth would sit in the back being attitude problems. They never volunteered for anything, although when they were assigned to committees, they did whatever needed to be done quickly and responsibly. Being an attitude problem was one thing; being ill-bred was quite another.

After watching television for a while, she went upstairs to do some homework. Mostly, she got A minuses. Getting A's made people expect too much. Meg wasn't one to overachieve.

She did some French and geometry, then moved over to her bed to read, Vanessa joining her. Lately, she'd gotten pretty hooked on mysteries, especially this series about a Boston detective named Spenser. Most of his cases were in and around Boston, and it was fun to read the books and know where everything was.

Hearing her father laughing and talking down in the front

hall, she glanced at the clock and saw that it was just past eleven. He hadn't wasted any time calling her mother. Listening to him laugh, she smiled, the sound making her feel very warm and safe. Her parents hadn't always gotten along so well.

The bad time—that is, the bad time she could really remember—had been before Neal was born. It had been when she was six and seven, so parts of the whole thing were kind of blurry, but she remembered the tension. She definitely remembered the tension.

It had started around the time her mother had been elected to the Senate, moving up from the House of Representatives. Her workload and constituency had gotten bigger, and suddenly, she was home even less often than before. Then, when she *was* home, her father did a lot of work at his office while she and Steven spent the weekends with her mother. And they didn't eat dinner together. She remembered for sure that they all didn't eat dinner together.

In those days, she never understood what was going on if she got up early on a Saturday morning to watch television and found her father asleep on the couch. It just seemed strange. She remembered how unhappy her parents had been, and she remembered the extra hard hugs she got from them separately. She remembered the low angry voices in the kitchen, then the back door slamming and her father not coming back until almost too late to say good night to them. Once, coming into the dining room, she found her mother crying and had been terrified because parents weren't supposed to do that. Then, during the week when her mother wasn't there, her father would be quiet and sad, not laughing the way he usually did, getting furious if she and Steven did something like spill milk, then getting sad again and grabbing them in the very hard hugs. It had been scary because Meg could never understand what was going on, and no one ever talked about it. At any rate, not to her.

Sometimes she heard things though, some of which she had a feeling she would probably never forget. Her mother sounding very bitter once and saying to her father, "See you at Christmas," as she left for Washington. That had been scary because it was July. "We've done separation," her father had said another time, his voice very sarcastic. "Maybe we could have a trial 'togetherness.' " That time, her mother had slammed the back door. Steven was too young to know what was going on, but Meg had heard the word "separation" and knew people in her class whose parents had gotten divorced. Most of them talked about how their fathers didn't live at their houses anymore, and Meg had worried that that might happen to them, and then she and Steven would be all alone.

One day, her father *did* leave, Trudy taking care of them. He came back after what seemed like years, but was probably only three or four days. He took her and Steven out to this really neat hamburger restaurant, gave them a lot of hugs, and said they were all moving to Washington. They went to a little house in Virginia, and about half the kids in their new elementary school had a parent, usually a father, who worked in the House of Representatives or in the Senate with her mother.

It was kind of funny—funny-strange as opposed to funny-amusing—because right after they moved down, her mother was sick a lot and would go to bed early. She was also getting fat. Her parents explained about this new little brother or sister that neither she nor Steven was too excited about getting, and sometimes Meg put her hand on her mother's stomach to feel it kick. It kicked hard. Now, her father was always helping her mother around and bringing her special things—things they never bought, like potato chips.

When the baby came, she and Steven decided that it was very ugly. They got to like it, especially when it smiled, and they got used to calling it Neal. As he got older, he wasn't as red and ugly anymore, and she and Steven decided that he was very beautiful. Her parents had always thought he was beautiful.

After about two years, they moved back to Massachusetts and her father went back to the firm full-time. In Washington, he had worked at home and over the phone mostly, being a consultant, flying back to Boston only when it was really necessary. Looking back, Meg realized that he had spent a lot of his time during those two years working on investments and talking to their broker. Her father was the self-made type, as opposed to her mother who, as an only child, had been given a lot and inherited even more. Meg's father was the kind of person who invested in computers before they were hot, then pulled out before the market was glutted. About the only thing Meg knew about finance was that one didn't spend one's principal.

Back in Massachusetts, her parents still fought sometimes, but they were happy more times and even did things like kiss each other, which Meg and Steven found hysterically funny. Her father laughed more, and her mother's face lost the dark circles under her eyes that even makeup had never helped much. Meg still got all hung up if they argued about *anything*, but when they fought now, it was about predictable things like her mother working too hard and her father turning the heat down.

Too tired to read, Meg dropped the mystery next to her bed and reached up to turn the light off. It was good to hear her father laughing downstairs—that meant that things were okay. A Presidential campaign couldn't be all that great for a marriage. Especially when the *last* time her mother had tried for a more responsible political position—except she wouldn't worry about that right now. Not with her father sitting down there laughing. That was probably the one bad thing about her parents getting along—they ran up an incredible phone bill.

CHAPTER SEVEN

Friday night, one of the seniors on the tennis team, Monica Jacobs, had a party. Definitely the social event of the season. Meg couldn't help being glad that her father had gone to Iowa—he would have asked a lot of questions about whether or not parents were going to be there, if there was going to be alcohol, all that kind of stuff. Trudy's questions were never very demanding, although she did want to know who was driving and told Meg to stay out of cars with young men. Meg said she would do her best.

She got a ride with Ann Mason, who was a junior and had her license. Beth came too, along with three juniors they knew from Student Council and newspaper. Meg was never sure what she thought about these parties. She couldn't decide if her parents let her go because they didn't know what the parties were like or because they trusted her. Both were possible. One thing, she always made sure she rode with someone like Ann Mason, who she knew wasn't going to get drunk or anything if she had to drive. Meg always figured that, if you were going to die, there were much better ways to go.

"I have to get the car back by one," Ann said, parking in front of Monica's house. "So don't anyone go off with anyone. Or," she corrected herself, "if you do, be back by twelve-thirty."

"Watch yourself," Beth said out of the side of her mouth.

"Yeah," Meg said. "You should talk." Meg, always afraid of publicity, had never gone off with anyone, except at a dance once. Beth was more inclined toward an occasional fling.

They had arrived fashionably late, and the party was already pretty crowded and very noisy, the stereo blasting "Money" by Pink Floyd. Meg unzipped her ski jacket, looking around the darkened entrance hall and living room, hot and crowded, loud with somewhat drunken male laughter. The wrestling team was apparently out in full force.

"Let's get rid of our coats," Beth said, and Meg followed her. The coatroom was almost always the parents' bedroom, unless there were siblings. In this case, it was the little sister's room. Smurfs and Matt Dillon.

Before dropping her jacket on the bed, Beth took out a pack of cigarettes. She always held a cigarette at parties. Newports.

"Wow," Meg said, watching her light one. "You are so cool."

"I know." Beth released a slow stream of smoke. "It's a lot for you to live up to."

"It's a lot for me to live *down*."

"Ha," Beth said, glancing in the white plastic mirror to adjust her hat. It was a grey felt with a small red feather. Very stylish. Meg would never have the chutzpah to wear a hat.

They went out to the kitchen, each taking a Miller from the refrigerator. Usually, Meg had one beer—she had never actually gotten drunk. Partly because her father trusted her not to, and partly because she wasn't sure how it would affect her. Lots of times at these things, people got sick—especially sophomore girls—and Meg couldn't stand the thought of that kind of public humiliation. Besides, paranoid or not, she always worried about the possibility of publicity. If she were going around getting drunk at parties, people would undoubtedly hear about it. People like parents, who were also voters, who were also constituents—from the way people like Linda acted, maybe worrying wasn't as paranoid as she thought.

"Oooh," said Fred Bierny, a senior and captain of the wrestling team, as he came in to get more beer and saw the ones they were holding. "Big bad sophomores." He nudged Meg. "What would Mom say?"

"That she should have had Heineken," Beth said.

Yeah, well," Fred took out two beers, draining half of

61

one in a long gulp, "think I'll go get a camera and send the picture to the *Globe*."

"Hell," another guy from the wrestling team said. "Just call Channel Four and get them out here."

"Give her a break," the boy behind them, Greg Knable, said, moving through to the refrigerator.

Meg blushed, sipping her beer. Greg Knable always intimidated her. Not only was he tall and handsome in a dark curly-haired sort of way, but he was the president of the Student Council, star of the basketball, cross-country, and baseball teams, and on about six thousand other extracurricular activities. He also got good grades. The really intimidating part though was that his father, a wealthy, successful businessman in every clichéd sense of the phrase, was vehemently, publicly, *constantly* against everything her mother did and said. He was always trying to make her look dishonest or ineffectual or power-mad or whatever he could think of to get people to vote for a more conservative senator. It was even stupider because if she was with either parent, and they ran into Mr. Knable at the tennis club or someplace, everyone would be sickeningly polite. Her mother said it was civilized. Meg thought it was hypocritical.

At any rate, she was never quite sure how to act around Greg. His friends usually made cracks, but he seemed pretty embarrassed about the whole thing. There were other kids in the school whose parents didn't go along with everything her mother did, but Mr. Knable was one of the only really active ones. Usually, if she was around Greg, neither of them brought up politics, but since the only place she regularly saw him was at Student Council meetings, the topic was hard to avoid.

"So." Greg opened a can of beer. "How's it going?"

She looked around, saw that Beth was giving someone a cigarette, Fred was trying to pick up this girl from her French class, and that Greg was definitely talking to her.

"Not bad," she said. "How's it going with you?"

"Not bad."

"I hear you got into Amherst early decision. That's really good."

"Yeah," he said. "I was pretty happy. My father went there and everything, so he's really"—he stopped—"pleased," he finished.

"He must be."

"Yeah." Greg blinked and concentrated on his beer.

"Looking forward to being able to take courses at Smith and Mount Holyoke?"

"Yeah." He grinned. "I can't wait."

Meg grinned back. "I can imagine." Greg was pretty well known as a womanizer.

"Hey, everybody, look!" Fred said. "A peace treaty! Historical moment here!" He put a heavy arm around Meg's shoulders. "Think your parents'll ground you for talking to him?"

"Fred, don't be a jerk, okay?" Greg muttered.

"Anything you say, Romeo." Fred winked at him and opened his other beer.

Meg kept her eyes on her hands, too embarrassed to look up and see Greg's expression.

"I, uh, I told someone in the living room that I'd kind of be right back," she said.

"Yeah," he said.

"That's really good about Amherst."

"Thanks."

She looked up, saw that he was also red, and hurried out to the living room.

"Hey." Beth caught up to her. "Were they being jerks to you?"

"No. Just stupid Fred."

"Don't even listen to him."

"Yeah, I know." Meg gestured across the room toward some people from their class. "Sophomores."

"Let's go," Beth said, heading over.

The party got better as the night went along—more crowded, more noisy, and more interesting. She was in the middle of an argument—well, more like a friendly but intense discussion—with Isaac Pechman, who didn't like the

63

Talking Heads, when she caught sight of his watch and noticed that it was past eleven-fifteen.

There was a network news special on about the Iowa Caucus after the local news and she wanted to watch at least the first few minutes. Her mother had done really well in the debate, which had been on Wednesday, and the polls had been going up ever since. Not only did she want to see what the network news team thought about the whole thing, but there would probably be some film footage on the various candidates and she kind of wanted to see that too.

So, when Isaac decided he wanted another beer, Meg went to find Monica, who was pretty drunk and having a marvelous time at her party. After being told that there was a television upstairs that Monica was perfectly happy to have her "check" for a minute, Meg went up to find it, deciding that she'd just watch for a couple of minutes, just to see if her parents were going to come on, then go back downstairs.

"Where you going?" Some guy who must have crashed the party tried to grab her as she went by. "Keep me company, babe."

"Excuse me," she said, continuing past and hoping he wasn't drunk enough to follow her. Once upstairs, she found the room with the television—the parents' bedroom—and tuned it in.

The door opened as the commentators of the news special were introducing each other and outlining the format and content of the show.

"Sorry," a boy said. "I thought this was the bathroom."

"I think it's down to the right." Then Meg blushed, realizing that it was Greg.

"Hey, what are you doing?" He came all the way in. "You a television addict or something?"

"Despite Senator Powers' unexpected victory in Wednesday's debate," the commentator was saying, "Iowa is expected to go with the more conservative Hawley in Tuesday's caucus. Polls have indicated that Hawley is holding his lead with approximately twenty-eight percent of the vote, Powers moving up to twenty-three and a half percent, Kruger close behind at nineteen percent."

"Oh," Greg said.

"Yeah."

"She's jumped a couple of points."

"Yeah."

"You, uh," his hands went into his pockets, "want me to leave?"

"I'm just watching for like, a couple of minutes," she explained. "See, I thought I'd just check and see if—"

"Of course you're watching," he shrugged, sitting down on the bed a couple of feet away from her. "Hell, I know I would."

They watched as a film clip showing Senator Hawley earlier in the day came on.

"Do you have any opinion as to the outcome of Monday's caucus?" a reporter was asking.

"No comment." Mr. Hawley, tall, slightly balding and very tough, kept walking.

"Do you think Mrs. Powers' victory in the debate will have an effect on—"

"No comment."

"Well," another reporter tried, "what about—"

Senator Hawley was ushered away by Secret Service agents, his campaign manager and press secretary blocking reporters away. Secret Service protection had started for Presidential candidates a few days before—not having seen her mother, Meg had almost forgotten. Kind of scary to remember.

"I'm sorry," the press secretary said. "Mr. Hawley has no comment at this time."

"Kind of a rude guy," Greg said, drinking some beer.

Meg nodded. "That's what my mother says."

A clip of her mother earlier that day flashed on, and Meg sat up straighter, seeing her parents, Glen, Linda, what looked like agents, and a bunch of other people walking along, everyone looking quite cheerful in comparison with the Hawley contingent.

"Senator Powers, how do you feel about the caucus?" a reporter asked.

"Excited," her mother said, eyebrows jumping up.

Everyone laughed.

"I'm being serious," she said, her expression self-amused, but in no way embarrassed. "I really love to watch democracy, I love the way it works." She grinned. "Isn't this a great country?"

Most of the group laughed.

"Do you think you're going to win on Monday?" someone asked.

"I wouldn't presume to predict," her mother said. "What do *you* think?"

People laughed again, and the clip ended, going back to the commentator, who was smiling.

"Well," he said, "two very different candidates."

Meg glanced at Greg to see his reaction.

"She's too funny," he said. "Is she always that funny?"

"Not always. They just *show* it when she is."

"Yeah." He slowly crumpled the beer can, then tossed it into the trash can by the bureau. "I don't know. She should be more serious."

"She is. It's not her fault when they don't show it. What, you want her to be like Hawley or someone?"

"I don't know." He put his hands in his pockets, not having anything to do with them now that the beer can was gone. "I guess my parents kind of like Griffin."

"He'll probably get the Republican nomination."

"That's what my parents figure." He shifted his position. "I'll be eighteen by then."

"I'm not even going to ask," Meg said.

"Don't," he agreed. "Hell, I don't even know."

"—Powers certainly scores high on agricultural issues," the commentator was saying. "With Representative Kruger being the next—"

"You know." Meg changed the channel, stopping at a station that had a basketball game in progress. "I kind of like to watch basketball too."

He grinned, and they watched for a few minutes, companionably silent, Meg having no idea who was playing except that it was two college teams. Villanova and somebody.

"We should probably get going downstairs," she said as the game switched to a commercial.

"Come here," he said.

"What?"

He leaned over and kissed her, his arm going around her waist, and Meg automatically kissed back, but recovered herself almost as quickly and pulled away, feeling the flush move into her cheeks.

"Why'd you do that?" she asked.

"What do you mean, why?" He kept his arm around her waist.

"Because you like me, because I'm a girl, or because you feel sorry for me?"

He laughed. "All three," he said.

"What?" She moved away from his arm. "Where do you get off feeling sorry for me? There's no reason to feel sorry for me!"

"Okay then," he said. "Because I like you."

"Oh, come on. You mean, because I'm a girl."

"I like girls," he agreed. "What's so bad about me liking girls?"

"Nothing." She swallowed, knowing that she wanted to kiss him, that he still wanted to kiss her, and that they probably weren't going to again.

"Oh, sorry," a boy said from the doorway. "Thought this was the bathroom." He pushed away from the door frame, continuing down the hall.

"I guess we should get going downstairs," Greg said after a minute.

"Yeah." Meg reached forward and turned off the television.

They got up and walked awkwardly downstairs, a couple of feet apart, not talking.

"You're going to love Smith and Mount Holyoke," she said finally.

He smiled, touched her hand for a second, and they separated to rejoin the party.

CHAPTER EIGHT

On the night of the caucus, the house was filled with people from the campaign, as well as a few reporters. Originally Meg and her brothers had been scheduled to go to Iowa, but her parents—mainly her mother—decided that it really wasn't worth their missing school. Meg thought that was too simplistic and figured that either her mother thought she was going to win and that it would be more important for them to miss school at certain points further on in the campaign, or—and this was what Meg suspected—because she thought she was going to lose, and she didn't want all of them to be there for that.

Whatever the reason was, they stayed home. Preston had brought over an extra television, so there were three set up in the sitting room, and all the networks were on at once. People brought in a lot of pizza and things to drink, and it was more like a party than anything else, although campaign workers had to take turns manning the phones, which never seemed to stop ringing.

After helping Trudy make sure that everyone had everything he needed, Meg sat on the rug in front of the televisions with Steven, who was gobbling pizza, Neal, who was looking around with huge eyes, and Beth, who was spending the night. Kirby lay in front of them, eating the pizza crusts Steven gave him, which Steven always called "pizza bones." Strange kid. The cats were all closed up in her parents' bedroom so that no one would let them outside.

There was a flash of light and all four of them jumped.

"Good," the *Globe* photographer said. "Can you all maybe turn a little so I can see everyone's faces?"

"Are we going to be famous?" Neal asked.

"Come on, Meg," Meg said to Beth. "Aren't you going to smile for him?

"I don't want to," Beth said. "I'm a Republican."

"Yeah, but she's your *mother.*"

Beth sniffed. "She's a bleeding heart, that's what she is."

"Girls," Steven said sternly, imitating their father.

"We're boys," Meg said.

"No way," he said. "You're too ugly to be boys."

"Yeah, well, you're too ugly to—"

"What do you all think of this?" Her mother's best friend, Andrea Petersen, bent down next to them, and they all sat up politely. Some of her parents' other friends had come over as well—this was probably a lot more fun than Iowa.

"I think it's neat," Steven said, reaching for more pizza.

"I think it's loud," Neal said, still looking around.

"What's with you, Meg? Don't you think?" Mrs. Petersen asked.

"Only twice a day," Meg said, grinning back. "And I used them up already." She liked Mrs. Petersen. She and her mother had been friends since Radcliffe, or as Mrs. Petersen put it, "back in the days when Kate was a simple English major." "Simple is right," her mother would say and they would both laugh uproariously. Mrs. Petersen was one of the few people around whom her mother relaxed. "Oh, Mrs. Petersen, you know my friend Beth, right?" she asked.

They both nodded.

"Do you want some pizza, Mrs. Petersen?" Steven asked, reaching onto the coffee table to get a clean plate.

"No, thanks." She touched her waist. "Not all of us have your mother's metabolism." She straightened up. "My God, I never thought I'd be over here watching her run for President." Her smile widened. "I'm invited to the Inauguration, right?"

"Yeah," Meg said. "You can stand in for me."

"You wouldn't go to the Inauguration?" Beth asked.

"No way," Meg said. "Wear some frumpy gown on national television and have a bunch of Senators dance with me because they felt sorry for me standing all alone? You've got to be kidding.''

Mrs. Petersen laughed. "What if the gown weren't frumpy?"

"Stand there all alone in some skimpy gown on national television?" Meg asked.

Mrs. Petersen laughed again, heard someone calling "Hey, Andy!" from across the room and went over there after gesturing, "Excuse me."

"You really wouldn't go?" Beth asked.

Meg shrugged. "At this point, it isn't really an issue."

"Yeah, but still."

"Hey, kids, where're the smiles?" Preston sat down next to them. "Candidates' kids gotta smile."

They all smiled.

"Oh, good, very good," he said, leaning back to get a beer, terribly stylish in dark brown flannel slacks, ankle-high leather boots and a V-neck tan lamb's wool sweater with no shirt underneath. "Some scene we got here," he remarked, tilting his brown felt hat over one eye. He looked at them with the uncovered eye. "You know why your mother's going to win?"

"Because everyone loves her," Neal said happily.

"Not just that, kid." Preston took the hat off and put it on Steven, who tried to adjust it to the same tilt. "Because the lady's got style. People like style."

"Do I have style?" Neal wanted to know.

Preston grinned. "Sure, kid. You got the makings of one fine-looking dude."

"Steven too?"

"Ab-solutely," Preston stretched the word out. "And Meggo here," he slung an arm around her shoulders. "Meggo's got it too." He nodded at the grey sweatpants tucked into her hiking boots. "Very nice, kid. All you need is here." He pulled at the neck of her Icelandic sweater. "A nice scarf here, and you'll have 'em at your feet."

"Who?" Neal asked.

"The world, kid." He looked at Beth. "Good, the friend has style too. Only you might want this up." He reached over to adjust her collar, then studied the result. "Good. Very good."

"Does Daddy have style?" Neal asked.

"Russell?" He shook his head. "I don't know, kid. I think Russell-baby needs some help."

"You call him Russell-baby?" Steven asked from underneath the hat.

"Sure," Preston said, shrugging. "What else? You can call him that too, kid. Tell him I said it was okay."

"What's wrong with the way Dad dresses?" Meg asked, amused.

"Well, Meggo, it's like this—bourgeois. Upper bourgeois, maybe, but bourgeois. Moccasins, Oxford underwear, still wearing the old B-school jackets—" Preston shook his head sadly. "No style whatsoever."

"He went to L school," Meg said.

"Same difference, kid."

"Can you help him get style?" Neal asked, sounding as if he weren't sure if he should be worried or giggling.

"Sure," Preston said. "Give me a few weeks of intensive—"

"We interrupt this program for a special news bulletin," one of the televisions said, flashing to a commentator sitting behind a desk in the network's New York studio.

"Shhh," half the room hissed, and Meg felt a sudden tension rippling up her back.

"With most of the returns in from today's Iowa caucus," the announcer read from a sheet of paper lying flat in front of him, "Senator Katharine Powers is the projected winner in an unprecedented—"

The room exploded into thirty separate cheers.

"—holding strong with almost thirty-five percent of the vote, her nearest competitor, Senator Thomas Hawley, well behind with only—"

Meg stared at the pandemonium in the room, at people jumping and shouting and hugging each other, at Steven and Neal and Beth who looked as stunned as she felt.

"—tuned for further details, and we'll have a complete report at eleven—"

"We interrupt this program for a special report," another television said.

"This makes her the front runner!" someone yelled.

"We're gonna do it!" someone else shouted. "We're gonna go all the way!"

Neal pulled on Meg's arm. "Does this mean Mommy's President?"

"It means she might be," Meg said, looking at the piece of pizza Steven had dropped facedown on the rug. The pizza looked like she felt.

"I thought she wasn't supposed to win," Beth said quietly.

"She wasn't," Meg said, feeling almost dazed. "All the polls said—" She shook her head. Projected—holding strong—unprecedented—

"Isn't it great?" someone shouted at them. "Aren't you proud of your mother?"

They all nodded, Meg gulping some Tab to calm her stomach.

"Now, we'll move to the Des Moines Sheraton where Mark Wilson is on the scene," a commentator said. "Mark?"

"Thank you, Lila," a man holding a microphone in a noisy, crowded hotel lobby said as the camera switched away from the New York studio. "This is Mark Wilson, and I'm standing in the—"

"Shhh!" several people said, the celebration stopping so everyone could gather around that television.

"Sources have said that the Senator will be coming down to—yes, there she is. We'll be moving in to—"

Meg watched as the camera focused on her mother, surrounded by people and flashbulbs, dignified in a deep blue dress. Her father was standing next to her with a very large, very proud grin. He said something to her, she smiled, and Meg saw their hands touch before her mother turned to face the cameras. She waved briefly with her left arm and most of the hotel lobby, as well as the sitting room, broke into applause.

"Senator, how do you feel?" a reporter shouted.

72

"Very happy." Her mother's smile changed into a grin. "Very excited, very—very inarticulate."

The people in the lobby laughed in obvious camaraderie.

"Did you expect to win, Senator?" another reporter asked, managing to get his voice heard over the others.

"I make it a practice never to *expect* anything," her mother said.

"Where do you go from here, Senator?"

Her mother's grin got a little bigger. "New Hampshire."

After the caucus, her mother was on the covers of both *Time* and *Newsweek,* which really freaked Meg out. Everywhere she went, she either saw a picture of her mother, or heard people talking about this woman who was the first serious threat to the Presidency. It was kind of like a bandwagon, like all the people who must have run right out to get stock in Xerox when people got the first inkling that this way of copying might be a big deal.

Because New Hampshire was an easy drive, they spent weekends with her mother, and Meg found herself doing some campaigning—mostly just handing out leaflets and buttons. Steven was all set to run around shaking hands, but when asked to concentrate on leafleting, worked with exhausting enthusiasm. At first, Neal helped them leaflet, but he was kind of afraid of the crowds and would spend most of his time with their parents, holding onto whichever one— usually their father—had a free hand, probably winning hundreds of votes with his smile, which was now missing two front teeth and even cuter. Steven kept telling people it was a hockey accident.

One Sunday afternoon at a shopping mall in Manchester, she and Steven ran into Senator Hawley's children, three swaggering and obnoxious boys wearing ties. They surrounded Steven, knocked his box of buttons out of his arms, and told him he'd better get the hell out of there if he knew what was good for him. Meg hurried over to help, and the two older boys—both of whom were bigger than she was, although probably only one of them was her age—made comments that were both chauvinistic and obscene. This infuriated Steven, who was ready to take on all three of them, and Meg was starting to get a little scared, when one of the boys yanked her leaflets away from her, scattering them on the ground. For some reason, this struck Meg as being extremely funny, and as she stood there laughing, the three Hawleys apparently realized what jerks they were making of themselves and left, an angry Hawley campaign worker meeting them on the way and taking them to another part of the mall. People who had witnessed the scene helped Meg gather up her leaflets and Steven get his buttons back into his cardboard box, quite a few remarking that they were very well brought-up and that that said good things for their mother. Meg said thank you and everyone went off with a button and a leaflet apiece. The scene obviously won a few votes.

The incident got back to her parents and after that, Meg noticed that there was always an adult worker lurking nearby. Linda pulled them aside, said they were very well politicized, and had handled a difficult situation quite maturely. Meg still thought the whole thing was funny, and after he stopped being mad, Steven agreed with her.

They would ride in a limousine driven by Secret Service agents, more agents riding in a car behind them. Because the limousine was crowded, Meg always got stuck on a jump seat, which made her carsick. The Secret Service didn't want them to open the windows either. Her mother would be slumped against the seat, gulping coffee and wearily reading the report her advance team had prepared on the next town, scribbling last-minute changes in whatever speech she would be giving while Glen practically had a heart attack.

"Kate, every time you start ad-libbing, I age three years," he'd groan.

"But I always ad-lib," her mother would point out.

"I know. Believe me, I know."

"I've been giving these same speeches for days, I get bored." Her mother would frown and scratch out another paragraph.

They'd pull into the next town and her mother would get out of the car, suddenly cheerful and refreshed, projecting the air of relaxed, friendly confidence that people seemed to find so appealing. Usually the speeches went well—crowds were big, audiences receptive—but not always. Sometimes the advance team had over- or under-anticipated the number of people who could come, and once no one came at all because the staff had publicized the wrong time. Standing in the empty auditorium, Meg could tell that her mother was furious, but almost as quickly, she was amused and sent someone out to get hamburgers, which they ate sitting on the stage.

"You gonna fire someone, Mom?" Steven asked, his mouth full of cheeseburger.

"That depends on whose mistake it was," her mother said, arching an eyebrow at Glen.

"These things happen, Kate," he said.

She nodded. "They happen *once*." Then, she grinned. Enough said?"

Seeing Glen nod, Meg glanced over at her mother. Kind of weird to see her being an administrator.

"Well, Glen finished his hamburger. "Why don't we get out of here and head over to Sunapee?"

Meg sighed and looked down at her barely touched hamburger. She was kind of enjoying hanging out on the stage.

"Is that really necessary?" her father was asking.

"No," her mother said, to Meg's surprise. "Glen, I'm going to take this as a sign that I need a break."

"But—" He started.

"Can we really stay here?" Meg asked. "I mean, for a while?"

"Don't make me feel so benevolent," her mother said. "Of course we can. I think we all need it." She yawned. "I know I do."

So they sat on the stage, and ate hamburgers, and didn't discuss politics once. It was Meg's favorite afternoon of the campaign so far. Of course, right after that, they got into the car and went to Sunapee, and her mother made two speeches, but still. For a while there, it had been almost as if her mother weren't running for President. Almost.

CHAPTER NINE

The day before the primary, the headline above the lead editorial in the Manchester *Union-Leader*—New Hampshire's biggest newspaper—was "KATHARINE POWERS: VERY OPEN AND VERY PRESIDENTIAL." It was a big deal because everyone in the state read that paper and it often influenced primary results. Indeed, her mother won, with almost 40 percent of the vote, the media analysts saying that it would have been higher if she were anti-gun control. Then, she won the Florida primary with a somewhat lower percentage; the Massachusetts primary with a much higher one. Local Senator makes good.

Primaries became the routine, with her mother doing very well in the Northeast, less well in the Bible Belt, where Hawley talked a lot about Tradition and Family Unity, the concept of Motherhood implicit in this. Funny no one ever asked where *his* family was. And when they were there in pictures—the three boys standing behind their parents, all of them smiling—Meg couldn't help wishing that everyone knew how rotten those kids were. Hawley was too, taking a very hard line on defense, trying to make her mother's more diplomatic inclinations seem weak and potentially dangerous to American security. Her mother didn't sling mud back, both because she didn't operate that way and because every time Hawley opened his mouth on that subject, she got more votes from people who supported the nuclear freeze movement. And there were a lot of them.

But even though Meg was very impressed by the way her mother was doing, and also kind of proud, she got tired of only seeing her on the news or in photographs, and only talking to her when she was alone in some hotel room or phone booth. Somehow, no matter how angry or resentful Meg was feeling at that particular moment, she couldn't bring herself to say anything mean because she kept picturing her mother being lonely and sad, halfway across the country. Sometimes *all* the way across. So, on days when she knew she might say something rotten, she—not too often because her father would get suspicious—managed to be in the shower or on a walk with Kirby around the time her mother was supposed to call. In a way, Meg thought of it as doing her part to help The Candidate.

When her mother *did* come home, she was exhausted. She would try to get up to have breakfast with them and do normal parent things, but was always so tired that everyone was afraid to ask her. Like Meg wouldn't even *suggest* a game of tennis.

Wandering around late at night, she would come into the kitchen or sitting room, find a table covered with papers and graphs, stacks of folders, cold mugs of coffee—and her mother, sitting up, but asleep, her head propped on one hand. Sometimes, after Meg woke her up, her mother would go up to bed, but more often, she would go to the kitchen to get more coffee and keep working. She got mad fast too, probably too tired to control her temper, and it would erupt unexpectedly, as if she had been holding it in for days, erupt into sudden fights which, as far as Meg could tell, were mostly with her. She knew she should be understanding, remember how much pressure her mother was under, how tired she was, but most of the time her temper would come crashing out to meet her mother's, and the fight would end only when one of them left the room.

One night around one-fifteen, finding her mother hunched over reams of paper in the sitting room, Meg woke her up.

"What?" Her mother jerked awake, looking around in confusion. "What's wrong?"

"Nothing," Meg jumped a little at the quick reaction. "I just thought you should maybe go up to bed."

"I have work to do." Her mother fumbled for her cup of coffee, tasted it, and shuddered.

"You should go up to bed. It's really late."

"I think I can manage that decision by myself." Her

77

mother wearily pushed up her sleeve to check her watch, then frowned. "What are *you* doing up?"

Meg shrugged. "I always stay up."

"Terrific, you always stay up." Her mother scowled, lifting up a folder about fossil fuel or MX missiles or whatever else it was that she was studying. "You wouldn't if I were around."

"Yeah, well," Meg tried to keep her temper from coming up and out, but didn't succeed. "You're not around, are you?"

Her mother's folder slammed down and Meg couldn't help flinching.

"Let's not start that again, okay?" Her voice was controlled—of course—but Meg could hear the anger in it.

"Yeah, really," she agreed. "Wasted energy on my part."

Her mother's jaw tightened, and Meg could see the flush starting into her cheeks.

"Well." Meg folded her arms. "Guess I ought to leave—I'd hate to waste any of your valuable time. Maybe we can make an appointment to see each other next month." She paused, knowing that she should just shut up and leave the room. "If you have time, that is."

"I said, cut it out!" Her mother's voice was less controlled.

"No," Meg shook her head, still trying to tell herself to shut up and leave the room, still not doing it. "You said not to start again. I didn't hear anything about cutting it out—"

"Meg, get out of here!" Her mother jumped up so fast that she knocked over her coffee. "Just leave me alone. Just—" She saw the liquid spreading over her papers. "There! Are you happy?" She picked up the mug and dumped out the rest. "Does that make you happy?"

"Mom," Meg backed toward the door, wishing that she'd just shut up and left, that she hadn't—"I didn't mean to—"

"Oh, yeah, you did! You know damn well you—"

"Katie," Meg's father said from the door, and her

78

mother stopped, visibly trembling, taking a long, slow breath to try and control herself.

Meg glanced at her father and found such an expression of fury that she took an involuntary step backward, her heart beating a little harder against her rib cage.

"Get up to your room," he said.

"Oh, good," she said, nodding. "As usual, you're going to listen to my side of it too."

His eyes got colder, and she backed up another step, knowing that it was unreasonable to be scared, but scared anyway.

"Get up to your room," he said. *"Now."*

She bolted past him and halfway up the stairs, then stopped to lean against the railing, trying to get her breathing and heart to slow down as hot, clumsy tears started down her cheeks.

"Okay," she heard her father saying gently in the sitting room. "It's okay. Come on, it's okay."

She let go of the railing, running the rest of the way upstairs and into her room, crying harder. Vanessa, startled by her entrance, jumped off the bed, scurrying out of the room. She got into bed, bringing the blankets and her knees as high as they would go, shaking so hard that the tears wouldn't come out right, feeling angry and guilty and very, very alone.

The next morning, still feeling angry and guilty, she stood in her closet, figuring out what to wear to school. She smelled perfume before she heard anything and knew that her mother had come into the room.

"I'm leaving now," her mother said.

Meg nodded, not turning around.

"Come on, Meg, I'm not going to be back for a couple of weeks. I don't want to leave with us still angry at each other."

"Does that mean you're staying?" Meg grabbed a shirt and a pair of pants, carrying them over to the bed.

"You know I can't."

Meg didn't answer, going over to her dresser to get socks and underwear.

"Meg, I'm sorry. I lost my temper."

Meg shrugged, pushing up her nightgown sleeves and going back to the bed.

"Is that what you're wearing to school?"

Meg frowned, realizing that she'd picked out plaid madras pants and a striped Oxford shirt. "Yes," she said.

"Very attractive." Her mother came over and put a hand on Meg's shoulder, ruffling it up through her hair. "You're not going to break down and smile?"

"It's not funny," Meg said, even as a little grin escaped.

Her mother also grinned, sitting next to her on the bed, and Meg looked at her, noticing the perfection of the green silk dress, smelling the light, penetrating perfume.

"You look pretty damn beautiful," she said grumpily.

"I'm not sure if that's a compliment,"

"I'm not sure either."

"I admire your honesty." Her mother put her arm around her. "It *irritates* me, but I admire it." She brushed a light kiss across Meg's hair. "Let's not be angry, okay?"

Meg shrugged.

"Okay?"

"You're going to miss your plane."

Her mother nodded, automatically glancing at her watch.

"You'd better get going." Meg got up, taking the striped shirt back to her closet.

"It's not always going to be like this," her mother said.

Meg hung up the shirt, selecting another, a pale yellow one.

"It really isn't."

Meg frowned at the pale yellow shirt and exchanged it for a pale blue one.

"You are the most obstinate person I've ever met."

Meg turned and looked at her. "I'm not sure if that's a compliment," she said.

"I'm not sure either," her mother agreed.

Meg turned back to the closet, choosing a white shirt instead.

"Kate?" Meg's father called up the stairs. "It's almost seven!"

"I'm on my way," her mother called back. She looked at Meg. "I'll see you soon?"

"Whatever." She carried the white shirt over to her bed, hearing her mother's small sigh. She listened to her walk out to the hall, then couldn't stand it anymore and went after her, catching her on the stairs. "Mom?"

Her mother stopped.

"Be, uh," Meg blushed, not meeting her eyes, "careful, okay?"

"You too." Her mother smiled. "Wear the blue shirt."

Meg looked at the white one, then nodded, and her mother went down the stairs.

When school ended, the plan was that they would all go on the road with her mother, her father taking a leave of absence from the firm. They would campaign with her, and when she had to go to Washington to be a Senator—which she did less and less these days—they would campaign without her. Not only was Meg dreading that part of it, but since she and her mother still weren't getting along too well, which meant that she also wasn't getting along with her father, she didn't look forward to all of them spending a lot of time together. But Steven was the one who really got upset about the idea, furious that he'd have to quit Little League, and frankly refusing. He always surprised Meg when he got upset—Neal was different because he was little, but Steven was so independent and secretive about things that when he blew up, people paid attention.

It was decided, finally, that Meg and Steven would stay in Massachusetts with Trudy until the Democratic Convention, which was the first week in August. Then, depending on what happened at the Convention, they would all spend August—which was when Congress recessed—campaigning, or if her mother didn't get the nomination, they would spend the month in the "home district" where, presumably, her mother would campaign out of force of habit. Meg didn't want to think that far ahead.

It was kind of lonely around the house, but restful—she and Trudy never fought, and Steven seemed to be able to find things to do with himself. Since there hadn't been any trouble, like the police calling and saying he was smashing streetlights or something otherwise delinquent, Meg didn't worry about him. He had gone through a period of streetlight smashing when he was about nine and a half. Kind of an expensive hobby.

Since she wasn't going to be around for the whole summer, she couldn't really get a job, so she spent most of her time playing tennis and going to movies with Beth and Sarah. A few guys from school called and asked her out, but since she knew they were asking because she was related to a certain Presidential candidate, she always politely refused. It was Beth's opinion that at least a *couple* of the guys might have been more interested in Meg than her mother, but Meg didn't even consider the possibility.

It was late July, almost August, almost the Convention, and Meg woke up at eight, glancing at the clock, then falling back onto her pillow. There was no reason to get up this early—not if she didn't have to. Vanessa, Adlai, and Sidney were all on her bed, and she patted each of them, getting two sleepy purrs and one long, somewhat toothless yawn from Sidney.

Hearing a noise from downstairs, she stiffened. Someone was in the kitchen, obviously trying hard to be quiet. At first, she was scared, thinking it might be a burglar; then she relaxed. How many burglars sat down to have bowls of cereal?

It wasn't Trudy, because she could hear her sleeping—Trudy had sinus problems, so she kind of wheezed—so, it had to be Steven. Only, what was he doing up so early? It could be some sports thing—he was always putting himself on exercise programs and jogging plans. Definitely his mother's child. He'd been so quiet lately—maybe he and his friends were up to something.

Yawning, she climbed out of bed, and the cats followed her as she went downstairs to check. Steven was hunched at the kitchen table in his baseball uniform, eating a bowl of Cheerios.

"Since when do you have games this early?" she asked.

"God, Meg." He straightened up, startled. "You always gotta sneak up on people?"

"We would have been worried if we'd gotten up, and you weren't here."

"I wrote a note." He gestured with his spoon.

"I thought Little League was over."

"It is," he said shortly.

"How come they let you keep the uniform?"

"They didn't."

"Oh." She sat down. "So, is this like an exhibition game?" It had to be something like that because she and Beth and Trudy had gone to his last game.

"All-Stars." He kept eating.

"You made All-Stars?"

"Yup."

"When?"

"Dunno. Couple weeks ago."

That figured. Steven would probably sign with the Red Sox, and no one in her family would have heard about it. "How come you didn't tell me?"

"Didn't tell anyone." He got up to get more orange juice.

"Why not?"

"Dunno." He sat down.

"But you should have, we all—"

"Yeah, sure." He hunched over the cereal. "Just leave me alone."

He was a lot like her mother, the way he kept everything inside. Only he was a lot more hostile about it. She got up to get herself some cereal.

"Are you playing?" she asked.

"Yup."

"What position?"

"Pitcher."

"That's really good."

He shrugged.

She noticed how neatly he'd put on his uniform and wondered how long it took him. Looking at the little black cleated shoes, scuffed but well-shined, made her feel suddenly sorry for him, realizing how awful he must have felt to have done this great thing and not have anyone know about it.

"Steven." She put her bowl down, forgetting about the cereal. "How come you didn't tell anyone?"

"You didn't ask."

"How would I know?"

"I've been to practice every stupid day! You never even asked where I was going! No one did!"

"Well," she flushed, knowing he was right. "I figured you were going to play baseball with your friends."

"Yeah." He scowled. "I bet you don't even care I had my picture in the paper."

"When?"

"Couple days ago."

"Well." She felt even guiltier. "Did you save it?"

"Dunno, I forget."

"Well, go get it, I want to see it."

"Because you feel bad." His voice was as hurt as it was angry. "That's all. I didn't show you 'cause all you care about is going out with your friends and playing stupid tennis. You could care less about me."

"Steven, that's not—"

"Oh, yeah? How come I heard you on the phone that time Trudy went out saying you couldn't go anywhere 'cause you had to stay home with Stupid Steven?" He mimicked her voice, and Meg flinched at the accuracy of the inflections.

"Well, I—" She twisted in her chair, uncomfortable. "I didn't mean—"

He just scowled, putting his bowl down for Kirby.

"What time's your game?" she asked after an uneasy minute.

"Ten, what do you care?"

"Where is it?"

"The field."

"Who're you playing?"

"Dunno, Medford." He stood up. "I don't care if no one comes."

"Do you care if someone *does* come?"

"You have a stupid tennis lesson." He put on his cap, very carefully adjusting it in front of the mirror. Preston's influence.

"Yeah, but"—she coughed—"I'm really not," she coughed harder, "feeling so well. I kind of thought I'd cancel."

"Yeah, sure."

"I mean, all that running around. And I'm really," she coughed extremely hard. "Very sick."

"Yeah, sure."

"The doctor says," she rested her forehead in her hand, "that I only have a month to live if I don't rest today. He thinks I should go to a baseball game or something."

"Yeah, well—" He had to grin as she had a long fit of coughing, falling off her chair. "You'd really skip it? To come to the game?"

"Of course."

"You don't have to or anything, it's not so big. I mean, I don't care if no one—"

"I wouldn't miss it." She got up from the floor. "Do you mind waiting until I get dressed so I can come watch you warm up?"

He looked so happy that she felt even guiltier for having paid so little attention to him recently.

"Yeah," he said. "I can wait."

CHAPTER TEN

After that, feeling like a complete and absolute skunk, Meg made an extra effort to pay attention to Steven and include him in things she did. He started looking happier and she felt like even more of a jerk for not realizing that just because he didn't advertise, he needed attention and maybe even needed *her*.

Her parents and Neal came home a few days before the Convention so everyone would have time to pack and so her mother, who Meg noticed was much too thin, could have a brief rest. Steven's good mood was contagious, and everyone got along very well—the house probably hadn't been this relaxed since the campaign started. It was ironic because the most important part of the campaign was still to come—one way or the other—but it was nice.

One weird thing was having the Secret Service around again. They had this like, command post set up on the porch. Her mother spent part of each day lying in the sun, and it was kind of amusing to think of the Secret Service having to be there. Her father didn't think it was so damn funny.

"Dad?" Meg came out of her room on the afternoon before they were going to leave, in the middle of trying to pack. "What kind of stuff am I supposed to bring?"

"Well, I don't know." He paused in the hall, grinned at the battered old Radcliffe sweatshirt and tennis shorts she was wearing. "Not that kind of stuff."

"You sure?"

"Very." He leaned forward to ruffle up her hair, keeping his hand there. The night before, he'd come into her room while she was reading *The Brethren*—she didn't know a whole lot about the Supreme Court—and sat on her bed for a while, which made it pretty hard to read. "How's it going?"

he'd asked finally, and she'd said, "Fine." "I missed you," he said, and she said that she'd missed him too. "Well, I love you," he said. "I wanted to be sure you knew that." She'd blushed and focused on the book cover until he gave her a hug, kissed the top of her head, said it was late, and she should get to sleep. She didn't argue.

"Ask your mother what to pack." He took his hand away. "She knows those things."

"Preston said tube tops and plastic miniskirts."

He laughed. "Preston was kidding."

They heard the back door slam as her mother came into the house.

"What's she whistling?" Meg asked.

Her father listened for a second. "Rhapsody in Blue."

"How come she doesn't whistle things like the McDonald's song like everyone else?"

He grinned.

Her mother came up the stairs, still whistling, wearing white shorts and a pale yellow unbuttoned Oxford shirt over her bathing suit. Meg looked at her, deciding that she must have recessive genes. Three days in the sun, and the woman was Rhapsody in Bronze. Forget running for President; she should have been doing Bain de Soleil commercials.

"Hi," her mother said, reaching out to move the hair her father had just ruffled back out of her face, keeping her hand there.

When her parents felt guilty, they always touched her head. Meg frowned briefly, wondering why that was.

"You look pretty good for being so old," she said aloud.

"Thanks a lot." The hand left, and her mother studied herself with a critical eye. "Do you think I got too much color? I don't want the delegates thinking that all I do is lie around the beach all day."

"*I* think you look great," Meg's father said, and her mother smiled a tiny smile.

Yeah, really. Who was her mother kidding? She knew how good she looked. She just wanted someone to say it. Meg pushed her sleeves up, glancing from one parent to the other. They wanted to be romantic. If Meg left right now, they would start being romantic.

"I think I'll go get some watermelon," she said. "Mom, later will you show me what kind of stuff to bring?"

"What you have on'll be fine," her mother said, Meg not sure if she were distracted, or being funny.

"Well." She shifted her weight self-consciously. "Guess I'll see you guys later." By the time she got to the bottom of the stairs, she heard them laugh softly, already being romantic. She blushed and headed for the kitchen.

She ended up packing dresses, with skirts for being casual. Oh yeah, real casual. Too bad she didn't have any plastic ones. The Convention was in Manhattan—her mother's hometown—and they flew down the next day, and a Secret Service limousine drove them in from La Guardia. In fact, it was really a motorcade. Her mother was getting so important it was scary. When they got into the city, they drove down Fifth Avenue toward the Plaza, where they'd be staying. Judging from the crowds on the street, New York was pretty proud of this native New Yorker who was running for President. Meg stared at all the people, wondering for a swift uneasy second if her mother was actually going to win. The concept of her winning—actually *winning*—was something Meg hadn't really thought about. She rubbed her hand across her forehead, the idea very scary.

"Wow." Steven shifted to the other jump seat and peered out through the tinted windows. "Are they all here for you, Mom?"

"I went to a very large high school," her mother said.

Meg smiled weakly. Actually, her mother had attended an exclusive private school on the Upper East Side, but it was the right moment to make a joke.

The motorcade pulled up in front of the Plaza, stately and impressive, next to Central Park, the epitome of classy hotels. As Preston said, the woman had style.

Her mother was probably supposed to be the first one out, but Meg felt so claustrophobic that she jumped out as agents opened the car door. As the crowd cheered, seeing someone with shoulder-length dark hair, she stopped, horrified.

"Not me," she said quickly.

"They know it's not you," Steven snorted, out of the car after her.

"Come on, kids," an agent said. "Hustle it inside."

Her mother was on the sidewalk now.

"I've been singing 'New York, New York' all the way over in the car," she said.

People cheered louder, some shouting, "Come on, Kate!"

"One thing for sure," her mother was always able to make her voice heard without seeming to be shouting, "it's great to be home!"

More cheers.

Meg watched her move along the edge of the road. What a politician. At least Meg had never seen her kiss babies. She'd probably die laughing if she saw her mother kissing babies. Once, in New Hampshire, she had shaken hands with Meg and Steven, then looked horrified and given them hugs. If the crowd didn't know who she and Steven were, they probably thought her mother was kind of weird.

"A real pro," Preston said, next to her.

Meg nodded.

"Come on," he said, his hand on Neal's shoulder, gesturing for Steven to come over too. "Let's get you guys inside and see about finding some Cokes"—he grinned at Meg—"and Tabs."

"What about Mommy and Daddy?" Neal asked.

"They'll meet us upstairs." He ushered them into the main lobby. "Now, let's—"

"Won't they worry?" Steven asked uneasily.

"What, you don't trust me, kid? I just talked to Russell-baby." He guided them over in the direction of the elevators.

"Is it going to be like this all week?" Meg asked.

He looked around the crowded lobby, cameras going off, people staring, agents lurking nearby. "Kid, this is minor league."

* * *

The first couple of days of the Democratic Convention
passed in a blur of shouting crowds and bright flashbulbs.
The families of all of the politicians—including Mrs. Hawley's sons, who seemed to be on their best behavior—had
special reserved seats, and quite a few television cameras
congregating nearby. The first two nights, Meg and Steven
spent most of their time out on the floor, fascinated by the
pandemonium, grumbling when someone got up to make a
speech for Senator Hawley or whomever, cheering wildly
whenever anyone got up for their mother. There were noisy,
foot-stamping demonstrations for candidates—complete
with chanting and sign waving—that sometimes went on for
as long as half an hour. They were so exciting that Meg
wished she didn't know that they were all staged. Maybe
''artfully encouraged'' was a better phrase. Demonstrations
were sort of a convention tradition.

The third night though, the night of the balloting, the family stayed in a room off the convention floor, where it was
easier to keep track. Her mother, Mr. Hawley, Mr. Kruger,
and several others had been officially nominated, but everyone knew that the contest was between two people.

The room was cluttered, and full of confusing activity,
like the *Hill Street Blues* station house. Aides were hurrying
in and out, yelling things at each other, taking and making
phone calls. Her mother stood in one corner drinking coffee
out of a Styrofoam cup and nodding a lot as people talked at
her. Her father was pacing around, Neal trailing after him.
Preston, who was spending his time on the floor charming
uncommitted delegates, came in every hour or so and gulped
soda so he wouldn't lose his voice. It was easy to tell who the
campaign floor workers were, because they were all hoarse.

Meg and Steven hung out near the televisions, watching
everything that was going on, both on the sets and in the
room.

''It should like, start soon,'' Steven said, yanking at his
tie.

Meg nodded, glancing down at her score sheet. Listed
next to each state and territory were the number of commit-

ted delegates her mother had, the number of uncommitted who had been persuaded to cast their votes for her, and an empty space to write down the number of votes each state actually cast. She also had a calculator so she could keep track of the total number of votes as she went along. A candidate needed 1,967 votes to be the nominee. Her mother had well over a thousand guaranteed votes from the primaries; Mr. Hawley had somewhat under a thousand. No one else was even close. And her mother was *very* close. Meg shut her eyes, wishing very much that she could put her mind on autopilot.

"Think we can get some food?" Steven asked.

She opened her eyes. "Are you *hungry?*"

"Well, yeah. I mean, kind of."

"So, see if there are any of those doughnuts left."

He returned with three. "Sort of stale," he said, taking a bite. "Want one?"

She shook her head. This was much too nerve-wracking to think of food. The chairman was, unsuccessfully, trying to call the floor to order, and she wished the stupid thing would just start already.

"We have to do it on the first ballot," she heard Glen say for about the tenth time that night. "Hawley could pick up a lot on the second, and the third would be—" He shrugged, indicating a free-for-all.

"How close are we?" her mother asked, her voice tense.

"So close," Glen put his thumb and index finger almost together. "So damn close, Kate. This close, Kate." He moved them barely apart.

Her mother smiled weakly, hands fluttering up to straighten the collar of her light beige shirt, her sunburn very dark in comparison.

"Two more uncommitteds from California!" A man on a telephone that connected to the convention floor shouted. "That's a positive!"

Meg scribbled that on her score sheet, hearing other pens writing around her.

"I can't stand this," her mother said, refilling her coffee cup.

"The great state of Alaska," a voice droned on the television.

Meg glanced up, startled. How had she missed the beginning? People gathered around the televisions to watch.

"How many so far?" her mother asked, and Meg could see the hand holding her Styrofoam cup shaking.

"Forty-one," several people said.

Meg frowned at her score sheet. Forty-one? It should only be forty so far.

"Picked up one in Alabama," someone said.

Meg nodded and wrote that down, vaguely aware that her own hand was shaking.

The balloting went on and on, each state's announcement followed by tremendous applause and cheering, including an abortive Hawley demonstration that the chairman managed to quell. Most of the delegates seemed to be standing around talking, jumping and waving signs every so often, waiting for their state's turn to speak. The television commentators kept switching to reporters "on the floor" who tried to make themselves heard over all the noise, talking about the mounting tension and excitement among the delegates.

"What do you know about tension?" Meg's father shouted at that television. "I'll give you tension!"

"Dad's losing it," Steven muttered.

Meg had to laugh. "He's not losing it." She looked at her father, who was pacing back and forth over the same five feet of the floor, tie askew, sleeves rolled up, and—she had to look twice to believe it—smoking a cigarette. She had never seen him smoke before. In fact, when she and Beth were in the seventh grade, he caught them smoking in the backyard, gave them a long lecture about the stupidity and health dangers of the habit, and grounded Meg for a week. "I think you're right," she said to Steven.

"Come on, Idaho!" someone yelled.

Meg wrote down the number Idaho gave. Just over five hundred now. And her mother had picked up eighteen extra votes along the way.

"Two definites in Wisconsin," Preston said, coming in.

"And a maybe. The maybe is seventy, eighty percent." His voice was noticeably hoarser, and he took the Coke someone offered, gulping half of it.

Meg added the two votes to her score sheet, next to Wisconsin. Then she added them to her space of uncommitted votes. Adding them to her mother's guaranteed votes showed how close they were. They were very, very close. Because of the guaranteed votes, the nominee was usually obvious long before the last state had cast its votes. So even though they were only in the five hundreds, Meg knew that her mother only needed twenty-four more uncommitted votes. Twenty-four, and they were only on—"Hey! That's another!" someone yelled, as Indiana finished casting its votes.

Twenty-three. And they were only on Indiana. She closed her eyes. This was starting to get really scary. Maybe she should go hide in the ladies room for a while, or—"Hey, kid."

She straightened, seeing Preston next to her chair.

"I have to talk to you seriously, kid," he said, his voice low.

She swallowed nervously. That sounded bad.

"See, kid"—he put his hand on her shoulder—"I don't want you to look in that back corner for a few minutes."

Automatically, she glanced over.

"Hey!" he said. "Thought I told you not to look."

Quickly, she looked away.

"The thing is," he said, "that it's very hot out there, and I'm going to go over in that corner and change my shirt. I don't want you to lose control or anything."

She stared at him, then realized that he was being funny. "That's a joke?"

He grinned. "Yeah, kid. It's a joke. Relax, okay?"

"Yeah, but—"

"Let's see a little laugh at my joke, okay?"

She managed a feeble smile.

"What, I'm not a funny guy?"

She smiled in spite of the fact that her mother had just gotten two extra votes from Iowa.

"Much better," he said, then turned to Steven aiming several quick mock punches at him before continuing to the back of the room.

Meg looked at the televisions. Every state had to make a big production out of its announcement, each delegate struggling to get on camera. This was going to take forever.

"Wyoming, here I come!" Preston said, getting smiles from most of the people who heard. He left the room, buttoning his cuffs.

Meg looked around, seeing her father leaning up against a table, fist-curled hands tight in his pockets. Neal was leaning next to him, in imitation that was either unconscious or not. Neither of them had cigarettes. Steven was twisted up in his chair, his tie and jacket off, his shirt untucked. Her mother was standing with a cup of coffee—how many was it now?—very stiff, her face absolutely expressionless as she picked up four extra votes in Louisiana.

This was not fun.

"Oh, come on, Fran," her father said when the Massachusetts delegation finally came on, and a woman with a microphone shouted the votes to the convention chairman. "Give her all of them!"

"You know her, Daddy?" Neal asked.

"Sure. Look there's Mr. Foster," he pointed. "On her right. And remember Mr. Taylor? He's behind the girl with the hat."

When Michigan announced its votes, Meg stiffened. Automatically, she wrote the numbers down, then punched them into her calculator. She added the rest of the guaranteed votes to that number, and the result was 1,967. Good God. That meant that her mother was—was going to be— she let the calculator slide out of her hand, hearing it drop on the floor from somewhere far inside her head.

Glen, very quite, was saying something to her mother who nodded, and there was a brief noticeable silence as she detached herself from the group around the television and went to the back of the room with her coffee. There was something impenetrable about the set of her shoulders as she stood there, staring at the wall, and no one went after her.

That meant that it was true. Her mother was—that meant—she glanced at her father who was hanging onto the table, staring at the televisions, looking as stunned as she felt. Someone yanked on the sleeve of her dress, and she turned to see Steven with his tie and jacket back on, his expression very worried.

"What?" she asked, her voice unexpectedly squeaky.

He shook his head, dragging her off to the side.

"Steven, what is it?"

He glanced at their mother who still hadn't moved. "Did she lose?" he whispered. "Everything's different."

"She won."

"What?" His eyes got huge.

"She got more of the uncommitteds in Michigan than they thought she would, and it gives her enough to win."

"But—what about Mr. Hawley?"

"She *won,* Steven."

"Yeah, but—" He looked around, still whispering. "Why's everyone so quiet?"

"It's not official." Meg listened to Missouri shout its votes, her mother getting almost all of the uncommitted instead of the two, maybe three, that had been predicted.

"Bandwagon," someone said quietly, other people nodding.

"You look like you're gonna cry," Steven said.

"I do not!" She almost forgot to keep her voice low.

"I feel like I am," he said.

"Yeah, me too." Meg glanced at the television and saw that her mother had over a thousand announced votes, over a thousand votes, and they were only on New Jersey. Her mother was still stiff in the back of the room and what, ten minutes ago, had been eager shouting around the televisions had turned into quiet, nervous voices.

"There's something happening out here," a hoarse reporter was telling the viewing audience, struggling to stay in front of his Minicam as chanting, excited delegates jostled for position. "You can feel it happening! We're getting close to a nomination here!"

"Glen?" her mother said, not turning around.

He scurried to the back of the room, and they talked for a minute, everyone else watching. He nodded and returned to the televisions. Without ever seeing how it happened, Meg noticed that people were starting to leave the room until the family, Glen, and a couple of his assistants were the only ones left.

"Well." Glen grinned at New Mexico presenting its votes. "I think the three of us'll head out onto the floor, see what's doing. I'll be back later, Kate, and we can talk."

She nodded. "Thanks, Glen."

The door closing after them seemed very loud.

"Well." Her mother smiled shakily and came back up to the front of the room, where she poured herself a fresh cup of coffee. Meg's father reached over with his hand, and she took it, holding on very tightly. "Meg, tell me about your tennis lessons. How've they been going?"

Meg stared at her. *"Now?"*

"Why not now? What's wrong with now?"

The woman was cracking up. The pressure had finally gotten to her, and she'd cracked. First her father, now her mother. Glancing back at the television, she saw New York shout out a tremendous chunk of votes, her mother's total creeping higher.

"Steven, tell me about your game against Medford again," her mother said.

"We lost," he said.

"Tell me about your home run."

"I hit it over the fence."

"You can just feel the tension down here!" a somewhat disheveled reporter was shouting on one of the sets. "Victory is close, and you can feel the anticipation, feel the—"

"Neal, tell me what you like best about New York," her mother said.

"The horse," he breathed.

"When you rode in the carriage?"

"I loved the horse," he said.

"Well, come over here and tell me about it." She glanced at Meg's father, who smiled, lifting his hand to cup her cheek, then focused on the television closest to him

Meg watched her mother sit down across the room, holding Neal on her lap while he told her about the horse, while North Carolina gave its votes.

"And *then*," Neal was out of breath from the joy of the memory. "Then, the man gave me an apple, and I put my arm up," he demonstrated—"and the horse—the horse put down his head, and—"

She was listening. Her mother was about to get the Democratic nomination for President, and she was sitting there listening to Neal tell her about Central Park—she wasn't even putting it on. If Meg had told her about tennis, about how she had learned a new second serve, a sort of derivation of the American Twist—she would have listened to that too.

Meg looked at her father, who was staring straight ahead, several inches above the televisions. She moved next to him, and he smiled, putting his arm around her. Steven moved in on the other side, and the three of them stood silent, not watching television.

Suddenly, Puerto Rico had presented its votes, and her mother had 1,965 only two more needed for the nomination.

"Kate," her father said.

Her mother straightened with a look of utter terror, and he nodded.

"Let's go watch for a minute, Neal," she said.

A bulky man in a too-tight pale green leisure suit was holding the microphone as the cameras moved in on the Rhode Island delegation.

"The distinguished state of Rhode Island"—he shook a strand of dark greasy hair off his forehead—"yes, Rhode Island and Providence Plantations, the smallest but greatest state in the Union, would like to—"

A woman in pink polyester pants got in front of him, waving wildly.

"Hello, Cranston!" she shrieked.

"Would like to," the spokesperson went on. "Is proud to—"

"Say it!" Meg's father shouted.

"—twelve votes for the next President of the United States, Senator Katharine Vaughn Powers—"

He never got the rest out as the entire convention went wild, signs waving, confetti flying, balloons dropping down from the ceiling, as everyone screamed at once, screamed and cheered.

In the room, no one made a sound for a long second, then Meg burst into tears—which she hadn't planned on doing—and everyone was hugging everyone else.

"The first time ever!" the hoarse reporter was yelling. "The first time in the history of the United States! The first time—"

Everyone was hugging and laughing and crying, and Meg thought of Rocky suddenly, feeling victory surging up her back and neck, into her head and arms, laughing and shouting even as she shivered harder, seeing the faces of women on the convention floor, faces sharing the same electric happiness, faces feeling the same quivering excitement, faces crying because a *woman* had won, because a woman was going to run for President, just because.

CHAPTER ELEVEN

Meg had thought that the primary campaign had been about as intense as a campaign could get. She was wrong. As Preston had said before, minor league. There were many more magazine cover stories, and her mother was never *not* on the front page of the newspaper. Every newspaper. The phones rang constantly—even the unlisted line. She had given up her Senate seat and chosen Mr. Kruger as her running mate. The Republican candidate was Congressman John James Griffin—Jay-Jay to his friends. He was from New Mexico, a wealthy and flamboyant man, buoyed by the retiring President Crandall's enthusiastic endorsement and support. Mr. Griffin was big and bulky, and Meg thought he looked like the word "obsequious" personified. Her mother called him "the last and greatest of the big-time Babbitts." Naturally, Meg had laughed intelligently at that, but later had to ask her father what it meant.

"*Babbitt* was a book by Sinclair Lewis," he explained. "He was what you'd call a good old boy."

"Oh," Meg said, with an intelligent nod.

"Bible belt, goes to the Athletic Club to drink his lunch, conforms to everything anyone says—you know. Your mother thinks he's a sexist, unscrupulous puppet."

Meg laughed. Reporters would have loved hearing that. "Is he?"

Her father laughed too. "Let's just say that his principles aren't as high as your mother's."

Meg hesitated. "How high is that?" she asked finally.

He sighed. "Very high, Meg. How many times are we going to have this conversation?"

"I don't know." She blushed. "Probably pretty many."

"Well, why don't you discuss it with *her?*"

"I can't do that," Meg said, horrified. For one thing, it

would hurt her mother's feelings; for another, would she really tell Meg the truth? If she weren't honest, that is. How could someone be the Democratic nominee for President without, somewhere along the way, having done a few—

"Meg, look," her father said. "Do you think of *me* as an honest person?"

"Well, yeah. Sure."

"Would I respect someone who wasn't?"

"Well—"

"Would I, Meg?" he asked, looking right at her.

"No," she said.

"All right then."

She nodded.

"I'm much more demanding than you are," he said. "Remember that."

She nodded.

The first day of school was terrible. For one thing, she got Mr. Bucknell for U.S. history. But worse than that, even people she had known since kindergarten didn't seem to know how to treat her. When she walked into a room, conversations stopped, and people acted as if she had developed an incredibly contagious disease over the summer. Beth was the only person who treated her like a normal human being—even Sarah seemed awed.

"You know," Beth said as people moved to let them through the hall, "this is kind of like hanging out with Moses."

"Yeah, I know," Meg said. "I'm having a terrible time taking a shower lately."

"Yes," Beth said, sounding slightly ill. "I noticed."

Meg laughed. "Thank God *someone's* still acting normal."

"It's a lonely life," Beth said. "Sacrificing myself like this."

"Thanks."

"Don't mention it." Beth stopped before going into Mr. Bucknell's room. "Do me a favor, will you?"

"But you just said don't mention it. Now I owe you a favor?"

"Yeah." Beth indicated the room with her eyes. "Don't let him harass you—you don't have to put up with that."

Meg sighed. "Yeah, well, what am I supposed to do about it?"

"Tell him off."

"Oh, yeah," Meg said. "Absolutely."

The bell rang, and they both looked at the door. Mr. Bucknell came over to close it and saw them standing there.

"Meghan," he said, frowning, "regardless of your family situation, you're not entitled to special privileges."

"Yeah, Meg," Beth said. "Get in there already."

Now he frowned at her too. "The same holds true for you, Elizabeth."

"My parents are divorced," Beth said to Meg. "It's been very hard for me."

Meg nodded. "Decay of the family structure."

"Girls, I'll be quite happy to put you on tonight's detention list."

They grinned at each other and went into the room.

The three Presidential debates were among the most important events of the campaign. They were being sponsored by the League of Women Voters and would be televised. Live. The first one was held in Philadelphia, the last week of September. Meg, her father, and brothers flew out of Logan Airport the day of the debate, meeting her mother at her hotel.

That night, during the last hour or so before it was time to go to the studio, they were all in her parents' suite, which was crowded with campaign people, the Secret Service out in the hall guarding the doors. Meg sat on the couch, wearing a skirt that even *felt* expensive. Neal and Steven were on either side; both in ties and jackets, Steven looking like quite the ruffian with the black eye he'd gotten a few days before. Since her mother had become The Candidate, he'd been getting in more fights than usual. Linda had quietly suggested that he use some Cover Stick on his eye, but he had said that no *way* would he wear makeup.

Everyone else in the room was pacing around being tense, except for maybe Preston, who was leaning up against a windowsill, resplendent in a dove-grey three-piece suit, silk tie and handkerchief, and a wide-brimmed hat tipped over his right eye. He kept saying that "everyone should just, like, relax, because the woman is going to be great," but they all seemed too uptight to agree.

If Meg thought about it, she could really have a crush on him. She watched him pour her father a drink, then one for himself. Then, he offered the decanter to the three of them—Neal giggling, Steven nodding, Meg blushing. Preston kind of brought new dimensions to the word sexy. It was funny though—out of all the people in the campaign, who would have guessed that her father would hit it off with the very suave, very cool Preston? Preston still made fun of his "B-school" jackets, and her father called him "The World According to *GQ.*" They had a regular squash game together, and her father would wear grey sweatpants, a shapeless Lacoste and a hooded sweatshirt while Preston would show up in a silky nylon warm-up suit with very white shorts and carefully coordinated Adidas or *ellesse* shirt. Now, standing by the window making jokes, they both wore grey suits, but the resemblance ended there.

"You sure you kids got enough to eat?" her father asked.

They all nodded, just back from eating in the hotel restaurant with Preston and a couple of agents.

"Stuffed their little faces," Preston said. "Except for old Meggo. The kid wants to be as sickly as Madame-Prez-to-be over there."

Her mother gave him a saluting wave from across the room, going through her voice warm-ups as the campaign hairdresser and makeup artist worked on her.

"Are you hungry, Meg?" her father asked.

"I'm fine," she assured him, blushing. She always had trouble stuffing her face in front of people. Steven and Neal never seemed to have that problem. Meggo. Be nice if everyone called her Meggo. It sounded—sporty. Very sporty.

"Good blood, bad blood, good blood, bad blood," her mother was saying over and over again, having finished her scales and now working on articulation. From her expression, Meg could tell that she wasn't too delighted about having Claude, the hairdresser, work on her.

"Why's she doing that?" Neal whispered.

"So her voice'll be warmed up, and she won't fall all over her words during the debate," Meg explained.

"Red leather, yellow leather, red leather, yellow leather," their mother was saying now, winking at Neal as he giggled.

"Okay, Kate, now like we said." Glen scanned his briefing notes. "Relaxed, but not too relaxed. Pleasant, but not too funny. Friendly, but presidential. If things are going well, you should maybe even sit down while he's talking. Or take notes. You look great when you take notes."

Her mother nodded. "Peter Piper picked a peck of pickled peppers."

"Be serious, but smile. Confident, but not arrogant." He lowered his folder. "Any questions?"

"How many pickled peppers did Peter Piper pick?"

"Very funny." He returned to his folder. "Just don't let him rattle you—the man is famous for it. His people are going to want to make you look emotional or bitchy."

"Peter Piper picked altogether too many pickled peppers," her mother said.

"Don't blow up if he starts getting sexist—if any of them do. That panel might be a little patronizing. Squelch them, but be calm about it."

"Friendly even?" Meg's father suggested.

"Peter Piper perpetuated pickled pepper pandemonium," her mother said, and her parents smiled at each other from across the room.

"Be serious," Glen said. He looked at her hands. "Think we ought to put some nail polish on her, Claude?"

"When I've been soaking in Palmolive all day?" her mother cried. "I'm not a 'her,' okay, Glen?"

"I know, I'm sorry." He bent down, checking her profiles, then studying her from the front. "You're too thin, that's what you are."

"The monitor put about ten extra pounds on her," Claude said. Her mother had done a couple of practice debates on videotape, Glen and Linda shooting questions at her.

"She still looked emaciated." Glen straightened up. "Try to look as tall as you can, Kate. Griffin's a big guy."

"Linebacker," Meg's father said disparagingly.

"If Russell-baby thinks that, you *know* the man's big," Preston said to Meg and her brothers.

"Sisters assisting selling seashells at the seashore," her mother said.

"Any way you can fill her cheeks out a little?" Glen asked Claude, gesturing to his own face. "The video picked up some shadows."

"Sisters *resisting* selling silly seashells at the seashore," her mother said, glancing at her watch. "We don't have time anyway. I told you I wanted this half hour completely clear."

"But—"

"You may brief me to your heart's content in the car." She frowned at the mirror and picked up a brush to redo her hair.

"But Linda has them downstairs, waiting for a statement—"

"On my way down," her mother said. "Now, please. I need this."

Glen grumbled but left the room, gesturing for everyone to follow him. Preston, the last one out, paused at the door: "Moses supposes his toeses are roses," he said.

"Moses supposes erroneously," her mother said.

Preston laughed and joined the others in the hall, and for a minute, the room was quiet.

"Well," her mother said.

"Simple Ceasar sipped his snifter, seized his knees and sneezed," Meg's father remarked from the window.

Her mother laughed, checked the mirror one more time, and put down the brush. "Do I look all right?"

"Pretty," Neal said.

"Beautiful," his father said.

"Not too thin?" She came and sat on the couch, leaning forward and turning on the television in time to hear the opening credits of *Family Feud*. "My goodness, we can do better than that." She turned it off.

Meg's father came over to stand behind her, squeezing her shoulders.

"I'm fine," she said.

"Relax."

"I am," she said. "Meg, let me see if I can do something with your hair. It's a little funny on the left side."

Meg went over to the mirror. "Funny-amusing or funny-strange?"

"Either way." Her mother picked up the hairbrush, and Meg could see her hands shaking.

"You're going to be great, Mom," she said.

"I—I don't think so." Her mother shook her head. "I just don't—" She stopped brushing and looked at her hands. "I think you'd better do it. I'm only going to make things worse." She paced across the room, pausing in front of Steven. "How's your eye?"

"Black," he said.

"My macho kid." She gave him a gentle tap on the cheek, then went back to pacing.

When the knock came on the door, they all jumped.

"It's time, Kate," Glen said from the hall.

"Well." Her mother swallowed, looking at Meg's father. He nodded, and she smiled weakly.

"Kate?" Glen had his we're-off-schedule voice.

"Well." She took one final look in the mirror, then strode to the door, stopping only long enough to give each of them a quick tense hug. "Are we ready? God, I'm really worried about *S*'s." She opened the door. "Simple Ceasar sipped his snifter, seized his knees and sneezed. Simple Ceasar sipped his—"

They had seats in the first row with Mr. Griffin's family: his wife—Bouffant City—a daughter and a son, all of them husky people with healthy New Mexico tans and strong determined voices.

"We look like twerps next to them," Steven whispered.

"Except Dad," Meg agreed. "They look like—politicians. You think they took lessons?"

He nodded. "Probly. We look like little kids who watch *The A-Team.*"

"We are."

"Yeah." He leaned in front of her. "Dad, what happens if we forget and clap?"

"Reform school," their father said.

"Well, what if Mom says something funny?"

Their father grinned. "Laugh as hard as you can."

Meg looked at him, noticing the tightly clenched right fist. Not as relaxed as he seemed.

Stagehands were bustling about, testing microphones, filling the glasses of water on each of the two podiums, double- and triple-checking everything. The four reporters who would be asking the questions filed over to the table with the moderator and sat down. The small audience abruptly stopped talking.

"Is it starting?" Neal asked, his voice loud in the silence.

Their father nodded, putting his finger to his lips. As the two candidates walked onto the stage, Neal barely restrained a small squeak of excitement, which almost set Steven off, and Meg had to give them both a quick warning elbow.

Her mother *did* look small up there but not nervous. Mr. Griffin was more obviously jittery, fiddling around with his microphone, straightening his tie. Her mother looked calm and alert, excited and cheerful. Meg wondered how much effort that was taking.

The noisy hush faded to silence as it got closer to airtime. Mr. Griffin was acting very jolly, as if his aides had told him to come out and be Santa Claus. Her mother looked a lot better, being pleasant and relaxed. She had won—or lost, depending on how you looked at it—the coin toss and would be going first in the debate. She stepped out to shake Representative Griffin's hand and he accepted with a too-solicitous air.

"You look very nice." His voice brought the image of a man meeting a hideously ugly blind date and trying to be polite about it.

Meg imagined her mother saying, "Thank you, you sexist, unscrupulous puppet," and almost laughed.

"Thank you," her mother said, sounding very amused. "*I* washed my hair."

Mr. Griffin's hand went to his carefully groomed head, which looked as if it could survive the most driving rainstorm. This time, Meg did laugh and was thankful that a lot of other people did too. She glanced over at the Griffin family and saw three very tight smiles.

Then they were on the air. Her mother and Mr. Griffin were being introduced, and Meg could feel her father and brothers sitting as tensely as she was. A member of the panel was asking his first question, and her mother was answering in a clear, friendly voice. Simple Ceasar sipped his snifter, seized his knees and sneezed. Mr. Griffin was leaning on a casual elbow, hands folded, as if neither concerned by nor interested in her answer.

"Thank you for *really* answering that," the reporter said, sounding surprised by the lack of campaign rhetoric in her answer. "I'd like to follow up with . . ."

The moderator called "Time" just as her mother was finishing, and it was Mr. Griffin's turn to answer the two questions.

"I must say," his voice was jovial, "with such an attractive opponent, one almost wishes that there didn't have to be time limits."

The Griffin supporters in the audience all grinned; her mother's supporters sat up straight. Worried, Meg looked at her father, whose fists had clenched, at her mother, who was polite and unruffled. Lots of times, debates could be lost for really stupid reasons, like the time Jimmy Carter had quoted his daughter Amy in reference to nuclear arms. Glen had said that Mr. Griffin was going to come out swinging, playing up every possible suggestion that a woman would be inadequate for the job. "If you can keep your head when all about you are losing theirs,'' her mother had said, and Glen nodded.

Mr. Griffin ran overtime on the follow-up too, and Meg wondered if his campaign managers were backstage committing suicide. Her mother leaned forward for the rebuttal, then paused.

''I'm sorry, Representative.'' She moved back, very gracious, her expression so friendly that even her worst enemies wouldn't be able to describe her as being bitchy. ''Did you get a chance to finish?''

Now her mother's supporters grinned, and her mother started in on the rebuttal, speaking logically and succinctly, finishing with time to spare.

Good, Katie, good! Meg could hear her father's unspoken praise as he strained forward in his seat, eyes on the stage.

Her mother was sitting now, one leg gracefully crossed over the other, listening with obvious interest as Mr. Griffin fielded the next question. When it was her turn, she answered the question directly, providing a casual underlining of the more general answers he was giving. The panel seemed pleased—not something Meg could point out exactly but more like a feeling in the air. She turned enough in her seat to locate Preston, two rows behind them, and he nodded, giving her a thumbs-up signal.

Further on in the debate, her mother absently slipped off her blazer, hanging it over the back of her chair, and Meg pictured Glen fainting backstage. A candidate wasn't supposed to be *too* relaxed. But her mother always said that blazers were masculine and spent more time taking them off than putting them on. Her action didn't go past Mr. Griffin who, in finishing up his remarks on his question, glanced over and commented that ''if he'd known this was going to be casual, he would have worn a sports shirt.'' Her mother just smiled, getting up to answer the question.

''I'm sorry,'' she said with just the right note of endearing self-deprecation, gesturing slightly behind her. ''A habit of mine.''

All four reporters on the panel smiled, and the simple elegance of her silk dress was suddenly more presidential than the blazer had ever been. The dignity came across even more as she answered the question as if she had never been flustered in her life. As she sat down, quite a few people in the audience clapped, television crew members frowning at them. Her mother's expression was, as it had been throughout, pleasantly relaxed, and now Meg wondered how much effort it was taking for her not to grin. Meg probably would have grinned.

Mr. Griffin didn't make any more unnecessary remarks, trying to create his own air of presidential dignity, an effort that came too late. At the end, her mother initiated a closing handshake with graceful confidence. Game, set and match to Senator Powers.

Meg wasn't sure if the cameras would be flashing across the families, and it probably wouldn't look that great to be cocky or overconfident, but she grinned anyway, so proud that she was kind of embarrassed. The lights came up, everyone off the air, and Meg saw her father and brothers grinning too. Her mother, leaving her podium to go shake hands with the panel, looked over, giving them a very small wink.

Late that night, after a noisy and crowded celebration in her parents' suite, Meg watched cable news in the suite she was sharing with Steven and Neal, to see how the press had reacted. People had watched the news in her parents' suite, but joining them would have made her feel like a jerk. Everyone would have been looking for her reaction, or her parents might have noticed or something. Far better to watch privately.

"The turning point was the blazer incident," a political analyst was saying, "Not only did Mrs. Powers show a remarkable sense of poise, but in the simple act of taking off her blazer, demonstrated a presidential elegance, the special quality a woman could bring to the office. Mr. Griffin was outclassed from that moment on. I think we were privy to something very special this evening."

The station had done polls both before and after the debate, and her mother had jumped eight points. She and Mr. Griffin were almost even. Almost even.

Meg turned off the television and went over to the window, looking out over Philadelphia. The city where Rocky ran up the steps. She turned, looking at the wall in the direction of her parents' suite. Almost even. Good God.

CHAPTER TWELVE

Her mother did well in the second and third debates, and the pollsters decided that the election was too close to call. At school, everyone was wearing either a Powers button or a Griffin one. People with buttons for her mother would wink at her in the halls; people with Griffin buttons would smirk. Luckily, there were a lot more Powers buttons. Teachers, who weren't supposed to show political bias, didn't wear buttons, but Meg could tell from their attitudes—and sometimes her grades—whom they were supporting.

Mr. Bucknell came up with a swell idea. On the Monday before the election, the school could have a mock election and—the idea got even more swell—Meg and David Mason, the Student Council president, could play the parts of the candidates and give speeches at a schoolwide assembly.

So, protestations overruled, Meg found herself sitting on the stage on Monday afternoon, quite certain that she was going to throw up. Her kingdom for a fire drill.

Her mother, amused by the whole thing, had insisted that Meg borrow her blazer—the one from the first debate—and as she sat on the stage, Meg regretted giving in. People were really going to think she was a jerk. David Mason was wearing a three-piece suit and had slicked down his hair to look like Griffin. Meg wondered if she looked like her mother. She was wearing the same kind of dress and the exact same blazer, but that probably wasn't enough.

A faint expensive perfume lingered in the wool, and for a second, Meg felt as if her mother were right there with her. She sat up straighter, deciding that even if all else failed, she would maintain presidential elegance.

"And now," Mr. Bucknell was saying at the podium.

Oh, God.

"Even though I know they need no introduction," he

said, "I'd like to present Representative John James Griffin on my left and Senator Katharine Powers on my right. Mr. Griffin will make the first statement."

Hokum. She had allowed herself to be forced into hokum.

There was great applause, along with some catcalls—terrific—and Meg thought she saw flashcubes go off. Like wow, they were making it look as if reporters had come. She would never live this down.

David read his statement, gesticulating and shouting that he was going to build up defense, lower taxes, balance the budget, blah, blah, blah. Same old thing. Consciously imitating her mother, she sat very straight, her right leg crossed over her left. Be relaxed but not too relaxed. Pleasant but not too funny. Friendly but presidential. Elegant, even. Simple Ceasar sipped his snifter, seized his knees and sneezed.

The lights were still there, giving her a headache, and she looked out at the audience, realizing with a deep sickening thud in her stomach that there *were* reporters. Reporters and what looked like television cameras and—someone had called the press. Mr. Bucknell must have called the press. She glanced over at her history teacher, who smiled at her. Oh, God. He had actually called the press.

Panicking, she closed her eyes. In keeping with her mother's style, she hadn't written her speech down, and she didn't know what to say, and David was almost finished, and—she was going to throw up. It was as simple as that. She was going to throw up, and it would get on television.

She would have to kill herself. Except, if she killed herself, there would be all kinds of publicity and her mother would lose the election, and it would be all her— David had finished his statement and everyone was clapping wildly.

"Senator Powers?" Mr. Bucknell asked from the podium.

She took a deep breath, trying to pull her expression under control. Be presidential. Be very presidential. She stood, crossing—elegantly? gracefully?—to the front of the stage, blushing as there were quite a few whistles but making herself keep going. There were cheers and shouts of encouragement too, mostly from the junior section, which Meg, indeed, found encouraging.

"Thank you," she said to Mr. Bucknell. She managed to smile at the audience, noticing with an inner terror that the television cameras were running. Did her mother feel this scared when she got up to speak? Legs shaking, muscles tight, hands perspiring? "Well." She let out her breath. "I guess I should start off by saying—" She paused, taking off her blazer, then smiled. "I'm sorry, they make me uptight."

Everyone laughed, and Meg grinned, putting it over the back of the chair.

"At any rate," she said. At any rate *what?* "I must say that I've enjoyed the campaign—I've gotten to meet so many marvelous people. My opponent, of course" she nodded elegantly at David, "people all over the country, half of Iowa, *all* of New Hampshire—" She smiled when that got a laugh, deciding that maybe this wasn't so bad after all. Kind of fun even. "And I can only say that I've enjoyed it. It's"—she paused—"it's a very special country. I mean, it really is, we should all be proud. There's no other place like it, it's—well, maybe it's why I ran for President. This country is so great, and I really wanted to be able to do something to—to make it better. I have ideas, you have ideas, we all have ideas. What we need is *action.* Cooperative action. We need to forget party differences, racial differences, sexual differences. In spite of everything, we all have something in common. We're all Americans, every one of us. We need to use it, we need to be proud of it. I know we can do it, I think everyone knows that. I want us *to* do it. We can. And we will." She stopped, out of things to say, and for lack of anything to do, smiled elegantly. "Thank you very much."

To her surprise, people clapped and cheered, and she stood there uncertainly, not sure if she should sit down, or acknowledge it, or—sit down. As she sat down, Mr. Bucknell gestured for her to stand up, and she heard the school band—*quel* hokum—playing "Yankee Doodle Dandy."

They weren't supposed to sing, were they? No, they were supposed to march out. Not *quite* as bad as singing.

Everyone else went out first, the band marching along in the rear. As soon as the auditorium had cleared somewhat, and before Meg could get out, the reporters and camera people came hurrying down to the stage. Meg recognized Alice, a woman from Linda's staff, with them.

"Meg, they would like to ask you a few questions," she said.

"Yeah, but—" Meg shifted her weight, very self-conscious. "I mean, I sort of have to go to chemistry."

Alice gave her a this-is-*very*-important look.

Meg smiled weakly. "Then again," she said.

Alice nodded.

That afternoon, she jittered around until six o'clock, waiting for the news to come on.

"What's gotten into you, Meg?" Trudy asked, stirring the spaghetti.

Meg shrugged, looking at the clock. Quarter of six. "I thought Dad was going to be home by now."

"All he said was before six-thirty."

"Six-*thirty?*" Meg asked. The news would be over by then.

"If you're that hungry, why don't you have an apple or something?"

Meg shook her head, too jittery to be hungry. When she got home from school, Trudy had asked how the speech went and she had said, "Okay." She was too embarrassed to admit that she was probably going to be on the news, but she did kind of want them all to see it. Even though she would probably look like a jerk. Alice had been there because someone at Channel Four had called campaign headquarters in Boston to ask if it was true that The Candidate's Daughter was giving a campaign speech. The reporters had asked a lot of questions—like had her mother helped her write the speech and that sort of thing with Meg trying to be dignified and mature, rather than kicking the floor and blushing a lot. Mostly, she had kicked the floor and blushed.

She wasn't sure if the reporters had influenced the voting, but Senator Powers had won the school election almost unanimously.

"Meg," Trudy said.

She looked up.

"Would you like to grate this cheese?" Trudy indicated a wedge of Parmesan on the counter.

Meg checked the clock. Five of six. "Um, if you want." She glanced at the television on top of the dryer. "Can I turn on the news?"

"Sure." Trudy was closer, and put the set on. Channel Seven. Yeah, Channel Seven had been there.

Meg sat at the kitchen table to grate the cheese, watching as the anchorman talked about the election—polls, predictions, interviews, film footage of her mother.

"And today," the commentator said, "out in Chestnut Hill—"

Meg stopped grating the cheese, blushing furiously as she saw and heard herself on television.

"Meg." Trudy stared at the television. "You're on the news."

Meg went back to grating cheese. "Hunh," she said, being as blasé as possible. "How about that."

On election day, her mother was in a terrible mood. Meg was in a pretty lousy mood herself, but it was nothing compared to her mother's. Her parents had gone early that morning to vote on national television, but except for that, her mother had stayed in the house. Glen wanted the family to go watch election returns at the Ritz, so they would be near campaign headquarters and her mother could make whatever announcement had to be made, but her mother wanted to stay at the house, so the family could watch privately. Glen gave in: just a few campaign people staying to man the phones, along with some reporters; as well as the Secret Service, of course. Even Trudy left.

Right after her parents got home from voting, her mother sent someone out to get her "a trashy novel"—*any* trashy novel—then took it into her bedroom, closing the door.

Meg didn't really see her until late afternoon when some of the early returns were coming in. Meg and her father were already in the sitting room, watching.

"I suppose I'm losing," her mother said grimly, standing at the door.

Meg's father smiled. "It's barely started. You're running about even."

"Well." She glanced around, frowning. "Where are the boys?"

"Outside playing soccer," Meg said.

Her mother frowned at her father. "Isn't it rather dark for them to be out?"

He glanced at the window. "It's barely dusk."

Her mother frowned and left the room and reappeared shortly with Steven and Neal, who looked as if the soccer had deteriorated into a leaf fight.

"Boys, why don't you go up and take showers," their father suggested, "and then, we'll see about some dinner."

They looked at each other and went upstairs, for once not making any smart remarks. Meg watched them go, kind of wishing she could think of a plausible reason to leave as well.

"Um, anyone want anything?" she asked. "I'm going to the kitchen."

Her parents shook their heads and she escaped to the kitchen herself where she sat at the table, drinking orange juice and eating graham crackers.

When she heard her brothers come downstairs, she trailed them back to the sitting room, where her mother was more uptight than Meg had ever seen her, moving from one chair to another.

"I feel like making dinner," she said, standing up. "Anyone want dinner?"

"Katie," Meg's father started, "we were going to send out—"

"I feel like it," she said, cutting him off. "How about omelets? We all like omelets."

"I hate omelets," Steven muttered.

"You love omelets," their father said, cuffing him.

"Better not have any vegetable crap in them." Steven said and their father cuffed him again.

They went out to the kitchen, Meg returning to her orange juice and graham crackers, consciously ignoring the sounds of campaign people answering the phones ringing in the living room.

"Oh, God." Her mother took the egg carton out of the refrigerator. "We only have two stupid eggs. How can I make omelets with only two stupid eggs?"

"I could go out and get some more stupid eggs," Meg said.

"Yeah," Steven snickered. "The smart ones don't get caught."

Their father cuffed them both, then gave Meg five dollars.

"Go find Glen and tell him to send someone out for some intelligent eggs," he said.

"If he can catch them!" Steven shouted after her.

Someone dutifully ran out and got eggs, and her mother threw together vegetable omelets. The frenetic burst of cooking only made her more jittery, and she didn't eat hers, pacing around the room instead. Meg, wasn't hungry either, but she played with her omelet, pretending to eat. Steven scraped his vegetables onto her plate and she stuffed them into her omelet so no one would notice.

"Maybe," her mother gulped some coffee, "maybe I'll go brush my teeth. Yes, I think I'll—"

Glen appeared in the doorway. "We've got some returns coming in. Channel Four."

Her mother rushed out of the kitchen, mug in hand, and they all followed her, leaving the omelets.

"Mom's like, flipped out," Steven said to Meg.

Meg nodded. "That's for sure."

The numbers on the television gave Mr. Griffin an early lead.

"Well, that's it." Her mother sipped coffee, very grim. "I knew I didn't have a chance. Who wants to be stupid President, anyway?"

"Katie, you knew you weren't going to do well in South Carolina," Meg's father pointed out.

"Terrific," her mother said. "They hate me in South Carolina."

"Katie—"

"Don't call me that! You make me sound like a poodle!" She blinked, as though surprised by the outburst, and put down her mug. "I'm going up to brush my teeth."

"How long is this going to take, do you think?" Meg asked when she was gone.

Their father looked very tired. "Probably all night."

Voting results trickled in. Every hour or so, journalists would come running in to ask questions, take pictures, then go back to the living room. It was kind of funny, because when the reporters were in the room, Meg would watch her family being pleasant; then, when they were alone, everyone would be grouchy again. She sat in a rocking chair on one side of the room, drinking a can of warm Tab, wishing she could go upstairs and read *Tennis Magazine* or something. Or play tennis, even better.

"And with most of the polls still open," a commentator was saying, "it's still too early to—"

"Oh, for God's sake," her mother said. "Someone change the channel."

Meg got up and flipped to the other networks, which concurred with the first channel. One minute her mother would be ahead; the next Mr. Griffin would be in the lead.

"Voter turnout so far has been higher than projected," a commentator remarked, "and we have a live report from outside a polling center in Trenton, New Jersey. Susan?"

"Thank you," a woman with a microphone said as the camera switched to the report. "This is Susan Gaines, and I'm standing outside the—"

"They hate me in Trenton," her mother said, getting up to change the channel. She turned the dial, and they heard an announcer saying, "—too close to call." Her mother shuddered and flipped the channel again.

"Now, we'll have a report from our correspondent in Chicago," the announcer was saying. "Take it, Bill."

"Boring, boring, boring." Her mother gritted her teeth. "They hate me in Chicago. Neal, you always know. What's on UHF?"

"The Bionic Woman," he said cheerfully.

Someone knocked on the door. "Meghan, you have a telephone call."

Meg jumped up, relieved to be escaping. "I'll take it upstairs." She went to her parents' room and closed the door before lifting the receiver. "Hello?"

"How's it going?" Beth asked.

Meg groaned.

"I don't know," Beth said. "She's doing pretty well so far."

"What channel are you watching?"

"Five."

"We're switching around mostly." Meg sighed. "Everyone's in really bad moods. Mom especially."

"Sounds like you are too."

"Yeah, kind of."

"Hey, wow," Beth said. "She just got a whole bunch in Virginia."

"Really?" Meg looked at her parents' television, tempted to turn it on. "I don't know if that's good or not."

"Of course it's good."

"No, see, some states she's *supposed* to win, so it's no big deal."

Beth laughed.

"What's so funny?"

"I don't know," Beth said. "I guess this is just a pretty weird conversation."

"I guess it is."

"If she wins, are you blowing off school tomorrow?"

"Either way I'm blowing off school."

"Yeah, right. If she wins, you'll have to come in and swagger around a lot."

"No way," Meg said. "I'm going to—"

"Hello?" someone asked, clicking on.

Meg sighed. "I'm kind of on the phone."

"Oh, sorry." The person clicked off.

"Sounds like you have to get off," Beth said.

"Yeah. I should probably get downstairs anyway. My parents are heavily into us doing togetherness."

"Sounds like fun."

"Absolutely," Meg said. "I'm glad you called though."

Downstairs, she found her family watching *The Bionic Woman*. The Candidate's Family being devil-may-care. Actually, they did look somewhat more relaxed.

"You know," her mother said as the Bionic Woman lifted a car. "If I could do that, I would have won. People would have been afraid not to vote for me."

"You haven't lost yet," Meg's father said, resting a calming hand on hers.

"You mean you think I'm going to?" She jerked her hand free. "Thanks a lot. I bet you didn't even vote for me."

"Sorry." He took her hand back. "I probably should have."

Meg and Steven laughed, and her mother actually cracked a smile. The mood in the room was sort of happy for a minute, but then Glen stuck his head in.

"Kate, you just took New York." he said.

Her mother jumped up, changing back to one of the networks.

"—Powers has a substantial majority in New York," the commentator was saying. "New Jersey is also going with the Senator."

"I thought they hated you in Trenton," Meg said, grinning.

"I did too," her mother said uneasily.

As more and more votes came in, most from Northern states, her mother started to pull ahead.

"You're winning, Mommy!" Neal bounced delightedly in his chair. "Look, you're winning!"

She shook her head. "We haven't heard Texas. Texas is going to be big. And California, we won't hear California for hours, and—"

"Griffin seems to have just edged Powers in Alabama," the commentator said, numbers going up.

From the quick nervous look her parents exchanged, Meg

knew Alabama was one of the states in which her mother should have lost *badly,* not been "just edged." Meg swallowed, feeling her stomach start to churn around. Good thing she hadn't eaten dinner. A few more states like Alabama, and her mother might— Meg drank some of her Tab, which was now flat, as well as warm.

There was a knock on the door, and Glen put his head in. "Okay if I come in?" He nodded at everyone, and stood next to her mother. "You took Missouri," he said quietly.

"I know, I was watching." She gulped coffee.

"No way should you have taken Missouri."

Meg had to swallow, hard. This was starting to get serious.

"And you took Georgia," Glen was saying. "My God, we never expected percentages like *that.*"

"I know," her mother said, a visible shudder jerking through her body. "Texas is going to be bad. He'll get me three to one in Texas."

"You don't need Texas."

"What do you mean, I don't need Texas? Of course I need Texas."

"You got Michigan," he said. "You got Pennsylvania. Believe me, you don't need Texas."

"Cut it out, all right?" Her mother's voice was irritated. "I don't want to speculate, I hate speculating. We haven't got Texas, we haven't got California, we haven't got—"

"You're *winning,* Kate."

No one spoke.

"It's early," her mother said finally, nervously. "It doesn't mean anything."

Meg looked at the television where the trend was in her mother's favor. *Strongly* in her mother's favor. She closed her eyes, wishing they could switch over to HBO or something. Except they would probably be showing *Mr. Smith Goes to Washington* or *The Candidate* or something.

"—and preliminary returns from Illinois are giving Powers an overwhelming majority of the votes," the commentator was saying, and Meg opened her eyes to see the numbers go up. "It's still too early to project a winner, but we're getting closer to—"

"Maybe," her mother sat down, trembling. "Maybe running wasn't such a great idea. Maybe," she was watching her hands shake, "maybe I don't want to be—"

Glen changed the channel, and they heard "Powers is holding strong in Wisconsin with a three to one—"

"Maybe," her mother got up, heading for the door, "maybe I'll just go upstairs for a while."

She was barely out of the room when Glen turned the channel again, and they heard an excited announcer saying "—early returns from Texas have Griffin and Powers running neck and neck—"

Silently, her mother came back in to stare at the television, then sat down, hands tight in her lap.

Glen moved to the door. "I'll come back in a little while."

Her mother was going to win. She was actually going to win. Meg watched more numbers go up, feeling dizzy.

"—so far, we seem to have an unprecedented—"

Meg concentrated on not listening. Her *mother* was going to be President. The thing that had never seemed real, that she had always dreaded somewhere in the back of her head, was now going to—or about to—or—

"In Arkansas, with sixty percent of the districts reporting, Powers is still hanging on to a slight edge."

"Well." Her mother crossed to the television and flipped the dial until she got to MTV. She studied the video. "Ah, yes. One of my favorites."

"She is so cool," Steven said to Meg, but loudly.

"Your father and I spend many an evening watching," their mother said. She frowned at Boy George. "This is a very strange young man."

The tentatively relaxed feeling was back, and they watched MTV, Meg *almost* able to convince herself that this was any old evening. There was a video that was on the obscene side, and her father changed to the sports channel, where a soccer game was in progress. So they watched soccer and Meg, by listening carefully, could hear the excitement in the voices from the living room. The phone was ringing and ringing, every now and then there were enthusiastic shouts or cheers, and her family was watching a soccer game. Unreal.

She looked around the room, seeing that none of them was really watching. Her father was holding Neal on his lap, being told some long involved story. Steven was sitting on the floor, patting Kirby. Her mother was the only one who seemed to be watching the soccer, leaning back in her chair, almost—not quite—slouching. Her shoulders were shaking, and Meg realized, horrified, that she was crying.

"Mom?" she asked uneasily.

Her mother looked over, and Meg saw that she was laughing so hard that tears were coming out of her eyes. "Is this possibly the funniest thing ever?" she asked, her voice shaking.

"Funny?"

"I mean, I—" Her mother laughed. "I've been horrible all day, and now we're watching little men in shorts and—" She broke up completely, covering her eyes with her hand.

Worried, Meg looked at her father.

"Katharine," he said, smiling.

"Don't call me that," she said, laughing almost too hard to speak. "I hate that name."

"Kate," he said, starting to laugh himself.

"She's flipped," Steven said to Meg. "She's really flipped."

Their mother laughed, getting up to change the channel, turning back to one of the networks.

"The trend is obvious now," the commentator was saying now, "and I think it's only a matter of an hour or so until—"

Their mother turned the television off.

"Well," she said, her voice weak from laughing. She looked at all of them, her expression softening. "I guess—I mean, it looks as if—"

There was a knock on the door and Meg sat up straight, knowing that this was it.

"Kate," Glen said. "You have a telephone call."

Griffin, calling to concede. Meg gulped, feeling her stomach tighten with incredible fear. President. Her mother was the President of the country. *Her* mother. Good God.

"Mr. Griffin," her mother said, sounding stiff and formal.

Glen nodded.

"Well then," she said. "I guess I'd better take it." Automatically, she reached up to straighten her hair, hands shaking slightly.

Meg's father stood up, his grin huge. "Think I might come for the walk," he said. Then, his grin widened. "Madame President."

CHAPTER THIRTEEN

Meg noticed one big change after the election—boys were breaking their backs to ask her out, quite a few of whom she barely knew. It was flattering, in a way. It was tempting, in a big way. But how could she say yes to a guy she knew was only asking her out because she was the President-elect's daughter? It was kind of demoralizing. Kind of very demoralizing. She had the feeling they were going to go out with her, see how much they could get, then run to the *National Enquirer* with the news.

Two days after the election, Linda came over when she knew Meg's mother wasn't home and sat Meg down for a Talk.

"You have to be careful," Linda told her. "Anything you do now is going to reflect on your mother—even more than during the campaign. We can't have you running around with a lot of boys or coming home drunk. And as far as sex is concerned—" She closed her eyes.

"Shouldn't my mother be doing this?" Meg asked stiffly.

"She trusts you."

"But *you're* expecting me to come home pregnant."

"You're sixteen years old, you're moving into a national spotlight, and I think we need to discuss it."

"I didn't know we were discussing," Meg said. "I thought you were telling."

"Meg, come on." Linda made an impatient gesture. "We have to work together on this."

"Then how come you tell me instead of discussing?"

Linda sucked in a hard breath.

"Well, you are," Meg said defensively.

"Look, I know you're pretty well politicized—"

That word again.

"—no conception of what it's going to be like. People are

125

going to be watching every move you make. So, your image—''

Meg grinned. Linda couldn't say ''politicized'' without saying ''image.''

''—very important.'' Linda frowned. ''Are you listening to me?''

Meg nodded.

''I'm much more worried about you than I am about your brothers. You're sixteen—it's going to be very difficult for you. You have to be prepared to—''

''Is my mother honest?'' Meg asked suddenly.

Linda blinked. ''What?''

Meg blushed at her reaction, but decided that now that she had asked, she really wanted to know. ''Is my mother honest?''

''Are you putting me on?'' Linda looked at her as if she were an extremely odd specimen.

''I was just—curious.''

''Shouldn't you and your mother be having this talk?''

Meg laughed. Unexpected humor from the Ice Queen.

''I just wondered,'' she said. ''What's your opinion?''

''That she is to a rather ridiculous degree.'' Linda shook her head. ''A difficult woman to work for, your mother.''

''You're not just''—Meg put on a serious expression— ''fabricating this for the sake of her image, are you?''

''Are you kidding?'' Linda obviously wasn't sure. ''I'll tell you, honesty isn't as easy to package as you might think. That kind of image, when it's genuine, requires—''

Meg sat back, grinning, knowing that Linda, with all her talk about Meg being politicized, would have given her a straight answer.

''—listening to me?''

Meg nodded.

''Well, I hope you're convinced.''

''Now,'' she looked down at her clipboard, ''insofar as you're concerned—''

''Hey,'' Meg thought of something. ''A man from the *Post* asked me what kind of birth control I used, and I said I was on the Pill. Was that okay?''

Linda looked at her with the same expression she'd had at the top of the mountain.

"I mean, I figured in the interests of honesty . . ." She let her voice trail off.

"I do not find your humor amusing." Linda said, half-smiling.

Meg grinned.

People kept asking her out. Knowing that Linda was right, though somewhat of an alarmist, Meg said no to almost all of them, giving in only to Rick Hamilton because she still had a wild crush on him and didn't care *what* his motive was for asking her.

She was on her way to chemistry one day when Carl Lewis, whom she knew from the Ski Club but almost never saw otherwise, stopped her, wanting to know if she'd go to the movies.

"I—I can't," Meg said, blushing. "I'm sorry, we have to—"

"Yeah, sure." He shoved his hands in his pockets, rocking back on his moccasins. "Heard you went snob on us."

"I didn't, I just—"

"Yeah, sure." He opened a piece of gum, putting it in his mouth and crumpling the piece of paper. "Well, see ya."

"Wait a minute."

He turned.

"How come you never asked me out before my mother got to be President?" She looked him straight in the eye.

"Dunno." He had the grace to blush. "Guess I never thought of it."

"Oh, please, you flatter me," Meg said.

"You sound like your mother."

"I do not! I sound like *me.*"

"Yeah, sure." He opened another piece of gum.

"If you want to go out with my mother, don't ask *me,* okay? And tell your friends! I don't go out with people who don't ask *me.*" Very angry, she started down the hall.

"You said yes to Rick."

"Yeah, so what? It's none of your business."

"Why you think *he* asked you out?"

"I—I don't know."

"Why you think?"

"I said, I don't know." She held onto her chemistry book more tightly, not looking at him.

"Well, think about it."

"It's none of your business." She hunched her shoulders, starting down the hall. "I'm late."

"Meg?"

"I'm late."

He caught up to her, putting his hand on her arm.

"I'm sorry," he said. "I didn't mean that. 'Sides, it's not why *I* asked you out."

"Yeah," she said. "Sure."

"Well, think what you want. Only I asked you out 'cause I always thought you were kinda—I don't know—quiet and stuff. Only, you got up and made that speech and were really beautiful and everything—you were kinda something else."

"I was being my mother."

"Naw, you were just wearing her blazer."

"Yeah, but—"

"Hey, think what you want, y'know?" He tossed his crumpled ball of gum paper and foil at a wastebasket further up the hall. "F'you don't want to go out with me, don't go out with me."

"What if you were only telling me that so I'd go?"

"Hey, think what you want." He went down the hall. "Maybe I'll try again sometime."

"Maybe I'll say yes."

"Hey, don't flatter me." He flipped her back a piece of gum. "See ya."

"Yeah," she nodded. "See you around."

She was late for chemistry, and when she walked in, everyone stopped working on their experiments, staring at her.

"Sorry I'm late," she said to her teacher.

"Uh, no problem," he said, blinking several times. "No problem."

"You're not going to make me go get a pass?"

"No," he said. "That won't be necessary."

She was going to go back to her lab bench where Beth and Sarah were already working on the experiment, but changed her mind and turned.

"Sir," she said quietly. *"Everyone* who's late has to go get a pass. It's a rule."

He straightened his glasses. "I told you. It's not necessary."

"Yeah, well, I think it is," she said.

Now everyone was *really* staring.

"Meghan," her teacher said, "I might remind you that tardiness to class is an automatic night's detention."

"So what? I broke a rule."

"Meghan—"

She looked at him, stubbornly folding her arms across her chest.

"Very well," he said. "Go get a pass."

"Thank you, sir." She left the room and went down to the office, where no one was very eager to give her a late pass. Finally, a reluctant aide wrote one out.

"Thank you," Meg said. "Where's detention tonight?"

"Um, room two-twelve," the woman said uneasily.

"Thank you."

"Hey, all right," the guy next to her, a senior who had been caught skipping, said. "Way to go."

She gave him a tough-kid grin, which he returned. "See you there."

Back in chemistry, she handed her teacher the pass. Then, because everyone was staring, she couldn't resist swaggering a little on her way to her lab bench.

"What a girl scout," Beth said, as she sat down.

"Yup, you know it," Meg said. "Law and order, damn it."

"Your parents are going to *kill* you." Sarah's voice was horrified.

"No way," Meg said. "Too much publicity." She turned up the flame under the Bunsen burner, the chemicals bubbling furiously in response. "Bet we could get *suspended* if we blew the lab up."

"That's not funny," Sarah said, turning the flame down. Meg and Beth laughed.

"Meghan, put on your safety glasses," her teacher said from the front of the room.

She grinned. "Yes, sir." She took her plastic goggles from the lab drawer, strapping them on.

"Know what we ought to do tonight?" Beth dropped some white powder in the test tube, and Sarah flinched as the contents bubbled up. "Let's knock over a liquor store."

"No." Meg dropped in some more powder. "Too boring. Let's rob a bank."

Her mother wasn't home much, but that wasn't anything new. She had to spend most of her time in Washington, figuring out her Cabinet members and other appointees, as well as working out the transition to office with the current President, Mr. Crandall. Her father flew down for a few days, and her parents went through the White House, deciding what furniture they were going to need and that sort of thing. The White House. Meg had never even been on one of those White House *tours*. Her father had left the firm now, so when he wasn't away with her mother, he was around more often, and her mother was home weekends without fail, sometimes coming in on Thursday, and a couple of times, even on Wednesday night.

Her father wasn't talking about it, but the press was giving him a pretty hard time, enjoying the idea of a First Gentleman. They kept asking him about his plans for White House redecoration, his ideas on fashion, what he was going to wear to the Inaugural Balls. Usually, he would pass it all off as a joke, saying things like he was going to do the East Wing in blacks and browns, but whenever he got home after a session with reporters, he would be tense, and they would all have to watch their step. Steven, with his usual tact, had asked him when he was going to start wearing lacy dresses, and their father had blown up, yelling at everyone in the house. One of those days when Meg thought about joining the Foreign Legion.

Hearing her parents come home one night in early December, back from a dinner in Boston, Meg came downstairs to find out if they'd had a good time.

"Darling," her mother's voice was quiet, but warning. "you really have to watch what you say in front of those people. *I* know when you're kidding, but—"

Meg paused in the doorway, seeing that they were in another fight. They'd had a lot of fights lately. Kind of scary.

"My dear Madame President." Her father spun around to face her mother, sounding calm but furious. "Let's get something straight. I will say whatever the bloody hell I feel like saying."

"I know, but—"

"As long as you know." He strode to the door, seeing Meg. "Hello," he said shortly, pushing past.

"Uh, hi," Meg answered, wishing she hadn't come down at all. She glanced at her father going up the stairs, then at her mother, who looked thin and tired in her bright-red, very Christmasy dress. Meg decided to pretend that she hadn't heard anything. "Did you have fun?"

"Lots." Her mother filled a glass with water, drank half of it, then dumped the rest in the sink. "They're not letting your father be a person." She refilled the glass, drinking another half. "He has every right to be angry," she added quietly, putting the empty glass in the dishwasher. She looked up. "Everything go okay tonight?"

"Yeah."

Her mother nodded, heading for the stairs. "Turn off the lights and everything, will you, Meg?" she asked.

Meg shrugged, going over to lock the back door even though there were agents outside, again feeling as if she really shouldn't have come down at all.

Her mother made a huge effort in the next couple of weeks to make the press be nicer to her father, and he got his own press secretary, which helped things considerably. Since he chose Preston, there was more publicity about that than anything else. Besides, having Preston around invariably took tension out of the air, and reporters loved him. He sat Meg down in the kitchen right after he got the job, looking at her with his stern-but-I'm-just-putting-you-on frown.

"I'm just going to say one thing to you, Meggo," he said. "Only one word."

"Plastics," Meg said, grinning.

He laughed. "Close. Style, okay? Style."

"In what sense?"

"No grandchildren for the next four years. No drug busts. Don't join the Nazi party."

"Is that all?"

"Keep your sexual activities discreet."

"What if I don't have any?"

"Even better, Meggo. Only I think it stunts your growth." He winked at her. "Watch yourself."

"Yes, sir."

"Style, kid. That's all you have to remember."

Steven and Neal got the same advice, although Meg figured he didn't stress the sexual activities as much with them. There was starting to be even more publicity—if that were possible—and most of it focused on the family, articles with titles like "The Storybook Family." Meg was kind of hoping for one called "The Stylish Family," but so far that hadn't happened.

"Quiet and bookish?" She had been appalled by that descriptions of her in a national magazine. "How come Steven gets 'a quick grin,' and I have to be 'quiet and bookish?' "

"You were," her father pointed out. "Remember when that man came to do the story? You kept turning red and muttering things about having to do homework. What was he supposed to think?"

"Daddy, do I have a shy smile?" Neal asked, worried.

"You have a beautiful smile." Their father lifted him up on his lap. "You were embarrassed that day too."

"Boy," Meg said. " 'Quiet and bookish.' "

"What are you complaining about?" her father asked. "It also says"—he picked up the magazine—"you 'inherited your mother's beauty with an adolescent charm all your own.' "

"Oh, well," Meg had to grin. "I liked that part."

Time was beginning to drag now, and she was looking forward to the Inauguration, even if it was just to get out of this uneasy period of waiting. Her mother took off a couple of weeks at Christmas, and they spent part of it at home, part of it in New York shopping for what her father called "proper presidential family clothes," and part of it skiing. In spite of the fun of running in and out of Bonwit Teller, Bergdorf Goodman, and Saks, Meg liked the skiing part the best.

Coming home one day right after school had started again, Meg heard music and laughing from the living room. She went in to see what was going on, not even pausing to take off her coat.

Peeking into the room, she saw all the furniture pushed back out of the way and the rug rolled up, as the dancing song from *The King and I* played on the stereo. Her parents, both laughing, were dancing around the room in a classic waltz. Her mother was laughing particularly hard and kept missing steps, which would confuse her father.

"Come on, Katie, cut it out," he was saying, eyes on the floor and where he put his feet. "This is serious."

"Oh, right." She changed her footing so she could lead him in the waltz, and they struggled for control, laughing.

They had gone mad, Meg decided. This time, the pressure had *finally* gotten to them and they had lost their minds. Or maybe they'd gotten that disease. There was some kind of disease that made you dance nonstop until you dropped dead. Actually, there were probably worse ways to go.

"Come on, can't you feel it?" her mother asked, letting him lead again. "One, two, three; one, two, three."

"No, it's one, two, three, *four;* one, two, three, *four,*" he said, dancing intently to *that* rhythm.

"But it isn't." She tried to slow him down. "It's one, two, three. Listen."

"I don't hear it."

"You guys do this a lot when we're not home?" Meg asked.

Her parents stopped, startled.

"All the time," her father said, and bent her mother over in a totally inappropriate and precarious dip.

"Every afternoon," her mother said, letting him sweep her back up.

Meg considered that, shrugged, and turned to go to the kitchen.

"Actually"—her mother crossed to the stereo to put the needle back to the beginning of the song—"your father has pointed out, with some rather reasonable concern, I think, that we will be dancing on national television in a couple of weeks, and we thought we might try some practicing while free from the prying eyes of small, pesty children."

Meg shifted her knapsack to her other shoulder.

"I'm not sure how to take that," she said.

They both grinned at her.

"Well." She shifted the knapsack again. "Guess I'll be on my merry way."

"We'll be done in a little while." Her father put his hand on her mother's waist. "Come on, Madame President."

"Now, remember," her mother was saying as Meg went to the kitchen, "it's one, two, three; one, two, three . . ."

CHAPTER FOURTEEN

It was a couple of nights before they were going to Washington for the preinaugural festivities, and Meg couldn't sleep. Tomorrow was her last day of school, there were suitcases all over the room, and she couldn't sleep.

Tab. She would get some Tab.

Moving Vanessa off her stomach, she got up. It was cold, and she had packed her bathrobe, so she put on a warm-up jacket and went downstairs. After rummaging around the kitchen, she came up with a ginger ale and some chocolate chip cookies Steven had made, which were large, misshapen, and delicious. Taking three, she wandered to the sitting room to see what late-night movie might be on and fumbled for the light switch.

"Before I scare you, I'm here," a voice said and Meg jumped, spilling some of her soda.

"How come the light's off?" She tried to sound as if she hadn't been startled at all.

"I don't know." Her mother's voice was sad. "I was thinking."

"Oh." Meg squinted, barely able to see her in the light from the hall, seeing only the tall outline of a figure sitting on the couch. Was she crying maybe? She had never seen her mother cry, except for that time when she was little. Cry from laughing maybe, but that was all. "Should I leave?"

"No, sit down."

"Should I turn on the light?"

"I guess so."

Meg flipped the switch, her mother blinking in the brightness. There was a half empty glass of dark amber liquid on the coffee table, a crumpled napkin beside it.

Maybe her mother *had* been crying. Sitting down, Meg looked at the napkin. Why else would it be crumpled? Un less her mother had a cold. If she had a cold, it made sense. Was she sniffling maybe? Except crying made you sniffle too. Meg frowned.

"You don't have to look like that." Her mother sounded very defensive. "I just felt like having a drink. My God."

"I wasn't—" Meg stopped. What was she going to say, she had been looking at the napkin to see if she'd been crying? Maybe it would be better to have her mother think she was pushing temperance. "Um, are you upset?"

"I guess, a little," her mother conceded, eyes faraway.

"Well, is it like something we did?"

"What?" Her mother glanced away from whatever she was seeing. "No. No, it isn't."

"Oh." Meg shifted. "Well, are you worried about your speech and everything?"

"No. I mean, I suppose so, but no." Her mother also shifted, one hand sliding up to massage stiff muscles in her neck. Then, she brought the hand down, folding it around the napkin.

That meant that she had been crying. Meg frowned, wondering what she looked like when she cried. The other time, she had been kind of small and hunched over.

"Actually," her mother was looking at the napkin too, "today was my father's birthday, and I guess I've been depressed."

It was? Meg hadn't known that. Her father should have said something. She thought for a second. Only maybe he had. At breakfast, he had been saying something about being nice to her mother today and Meg had nodded, tuning him out, thinking about having to start saying good-bye to people at school. Maybe that's why Steven and Neal had been so good all day—she couldn't remember hearing any fights.

"He would have been—sixty-nine?" she asked awkwardly.

"Seventy."

Neither spoke for a minute.

"Oh, I'm okay," her mother was brisk now. "I mean,

it's been almost six years, I'm fine." Part of her mouth smiled, the eyes staying dark. "I'm lying, of course."

"He, uh, he would have been really proud."

"I know." Her mother picked up her drink, holding it in both hands. She looked up. "It makes me feel alone."

"Well," Meg twisted in her chair, "you have us."

"Thank God." Her mother sipped the drink, and Meg remembered that her grandfather had been a scotch drinker—expensive scotch. "It made me think of my mother too," she said quietly.

Meg thought of the picture upstairs of the thin, beautiful woman holding hands with a little girl with dark braids and a smile like Neal's. "What was she like?"

"It's hard to say how much I remember and how much my father and everyone else told me. After all," her mother tilted her glass, rolling the scotch around, "I was even younger than Neal."

Meg nodded, wondering with a sudden cold shudder what it would be like to have your mother die, to be missing that huge part of your life. She looked up, relieved to see her mother's chest moving with light regularity, her face healthy and alive, not frozen in a photograph.

"What was it like?" she asked hesitantly.

"What?"

"Not—not having a mother."

"I wouldn't think you'd have to ask." Her mother's laugh was bitter.

"But you—"

"It's been the same thing, hasn't it?" Her mother took a very large sip of the scotch. "I haven't been here when you've needed me, I haven't been here when you've wanted me, I haven't been here for any of you." She put the glass down with a slightly clumsy movement, and it occurred to Meg that maybe it wasn't the first one she'd had. "Now, we're going to Washington, and it's going to be—you're all going to end up wishing—" She shook her head, picking up the glass.

"But, we don't—"

"Don't say things because you feel you have to, okay?

137

You've got every right to feel lousy about me, I've certainly never—'' She took a sip that was more like a gulp. ''Don't ever be alone. Alone is lousy.''

''But you're not alone.''

''I could be.'' Her mother finished the drink. ''You all might—'' She stopped, studied the empty glass, then put it down with a dull clink. ''I guess we've got self-pity talking here. Or, as Humphrey Bogart would say, maybe it's the bour-bon. They're a lot alike.''

''I thought you were coming right up.'' Meg's father was unexpectedly in the doorway. He noticed Meg in the easy chair. ''Terrific, a whole *family* of insomniacs. How about we all go up and get some sleep?''

Meg stood up, very relieved to see him. She saw her mother hesitate, not standing up. Maybe she was afraid she would look drunk and didn't want Meg to see. Meg decided to make it easy and go.

''Well,'' she stretched, trying to look tired. ''Night, I guess.''

''Good night, Meg,'' her father said, and she could tell he understood.

''Night,'' she nodded, then looked at her mother. ''Night, Mom. Have, uh, have good dreams and stuff.'' She left, not hearing anything behind her.

She went up to her room and, closing the door, sat on the bed. She lifted Vanessa onto her lap, staring at the shadowy suitcases.

Now, she *really* couldn't sleep.

In the morning, her mother didn't mention their discussion, so Meg didn't bring it up, concentrating on the craziness of these last couple of days at home, what with last-minute packing and good-byes. And arrangements. There were lots of arrangements. Like the caretakers who were going to move into the house, transferring school records to their new schools in Washington, things like that.

Probably the saddest thing was saying good-bye to Trudy, who was going to Florida to live with her son and his family. She would come visit them at the White House though, where her mother promised she would be waited on hand and foot. Trudy thought that sounded great.

On the last afternoon, Beth and Sarah came over, sitting on the bed to watch Meg throw a few last-minute things into the suitcase she was carrying with her on the plane.

"Wow," Beth said. "Can we like, have your autograph and everything? So people'll believe we know you?"

"Maybe," Meg said in an "if-you're-lucky" voice.

"Actually, get a couple from your mother too. I can probably sell them."

"Beth!" Sarah elbowed her. "That's no funny."

Meg closed her suitcase and struggled with the zipper, feeling a lump of homesickness starting before she even got downstairs. The zipper, actually, was quite happy to zip, but she kept struggling, not wanting to look up, afraid that she was going to cry or do something otherwise disastrous.

"You need help?" Beth asked, getting up.

"No. No, I'm—" Meg let the zipper close turning to look at them with a flimsy smile. "It's all set."

"Look," Beth said. "it's going to be great. *You're* going to be great."

"Yeah, sure."

"Beth's right," Sarah said. "You get to live in the White House, and I bet your school has thousands of cute guys, and—well, everything!"

Meg sat down at her desk, not sharing Sarah's enthusiasm.

"It *is* going to be okay," Beth said.

"Yeah, sure." Meg swallowed, really wondering if she were going to cry, really not wanting to. She fastened her hands tightly together, hoping that would help.

"Are you that scared?" Sarah asked.

Meg shook her head. "No. Just kind of." She smiled weakly. "Kind of a lot." Her smile weakened even more. "Kind of petrified."

"Well," Sarah sounded awkward. "You *look* nice."

Meg shook her head, going over to her dresser to check the drawers for the fiftieth time and make sure she hadn't forgotten anything.

"Miss Powers," Beth made her hand into a microphone, "looking nothing if not ravishing, recommends traveling in simple tweeds—"

"I'd call this flannel," Meg said, looking at her skirt.

Beth ignored her. "Tweeds, and a single strand of pearls. The President's daughter also likes a shoe with a low heel and favors a thin black vanity case for afternoon outings."

"I prefer a money belt," Meg said to Sarah, who laughed, uncertainly.

"Her makeup is subdued," Beth went on, "in muted blues for winter, accenting her best features."

"What are my best features?" Meg asked.

"Her best features being, of course, the young woman's knees."

"Oh, no," Sarah disagreed. "I think it's her eyes. Meg, you have great eyes."

"Well, maybe," Meg said. "But, have you seen my knees? I have kind of incredible knees."

Sarah frowned. "I never noticed."

"The President's daughter is also a very accomplished girl," Beth said. "She makes Christmas decorations out of egg cartons—"

"Hey, remember that?" Meg laughed, picturing the foil-covered monstrosities they had made when they were in junior high.

"She does very nice paint-by-numbers and shyly confesses that she's been known to read four or five romantic novels at a sitting," Beth said. "While much of her conversation is disjointed, if not, in fact, gibberish, she has been known to—"

Sarah shook her head. "Beth, you're terrible. Why don't you say something nice about her?"

"I was about to," Beth assured her. "Like I was saying, she has been known to make witty comments with biannual regularity."

"I thought it was more like biennial," Meg said.

"She also likes to show off her vocabulary," Beth told her unseen audience.

"Meg, come on!" Steven shouted up the stairs. "Every-one's waiting!"

Meg looked at her friends, swallowed, and opened her suitcase, rechecking the contents.

"You guys are going to come down during spring break, right?" she asked.

"Yeah," Beth agreed. "I'm going to bring my camera. Bet I can make a lot of money on the pictures."

Meg smiled; then they all looked at each other.

"I, uh," Meg had to swallow again. "I'm not so great at good-byes."

"This is only a see-you-later," Sarah said.

"I'm not good at them either." She gave each of her friends a stiff hug, then stepped back, managing a weak laugh. "I can't cry or anything if I'm going to walk out by all those stupid photographers."

"It would spoil the look," Beth agreed.

"But I kind of—" Meg had to blink fast. "I kind of—"

"Meg, come on!" Steven sounded irritated.

"Okay, I'm coming!" Picking up her suitcase, she took one last look around her room, feeling tremendously home-sick.

"Look," Beth put a friendly arm around her shoulders as they walked down the stairs. "Think how nice you look in your tweeds."

"They do hang well," Meg said. "Would you believe I've had them since college?"

"You guys are weird," Sarah said. "You really are."

"Oh, and remember," Beth said as they got to the bottom of the stairs. "It's been a few months, so you're about due for a witty comment. Don't waste it."

Meg nodded. "I'll try." Then she grinned. "Make sure you give Rick my love."

"Oh, you jerk," Beth said sadly. "You wasted it!"

CHAPTER FIFTEEN

The first few days in Washington were a blur of honorary breakfasts and dinners, special concerts and theatrical performances. And Secret Service agents. She and Steven and Neal were each going to have two guards; guards who would go to school, the movies, everywhere with them. Steven, who was really bugged about the whole idea, kept asking where the guards were going to be when he played baseball. Meg couldn't help wondering too. Like, when she played tennis, would she have to play doubles so they could play with her? She hated doubles. Her father had about five guards, and it seemed like her mother had hundreds.

Steven had also asked if Kirby and the cats would have to have guards. He was really pretty funny sometimes. Most of the agents were men, although a few were women. They would have these agents for six months, then they would get new ones because the Secret Service worried about people getting emotionally attached and relaxing on the job. Steven and Neal were going to have theirs changed every three months, because the younger people were, the more likely it was that attachments would form. Meg kind of wondered if the inference there was that she and her parents were too old to like. Anyway, for the next four years, they would all have official, constant protection. How depressing.

The day of the Inauguration, Meg woke up very early. They were staying in her mother's Georgetown apartment, and she went out to the kitchen, her brothers appearing almost simultaneously.

Neal sat up at the counter in his pajamas. "Where's Mommy?"

"Taking the first shower." Meg got down some cereal bowls. "I think she wants to go over her speech again."

Steven took out the orange juice and a carton of milk. "Want some juice, brat?" he asked Neal.

Neal hit him. "I'm not a brat!"

"You want some juice?" Steven held the carton over his head.

"Steven, don't be a jerk, okay?" Meg tried to get it away from him and they scuffled for a minute until she finally got the carton. "Mom and Dad'll be uptight enough without you starting trouble."

"Meggie thinks she can play mother," Steven grumbled to Neal.

She got out a loaf of bread. "Want some toast, brats?"

"Meg!" Neal hit her too.

"Think Mom and Dad'll want cereal, or something better?" She put four pieces of bread in the toaster.

"Why don't you make poached eggs?" Steven asked, and snickered.

"I know how to make them," she said defensively.

"And *boy,*" he dumped sugar on his cereal, "are they good."

Their father came into the kitchen in his plaid bathrobe. "You guys all set on breakfast?"

They nodded.

"Your mother and I are going to have omelets. Anyone else want one?"

Steven gagged. "Hey, Dad, what time do we have to be at the White House?"

"Who says you're coming?" their father asked, melting butter in a frying pan. He grinned at Steven's expression. "Eleven. President and Mrs. Crandall want to meet our *whole* charming family."

"Toto too?" Meg asked, scraping the burnt parts off the first batch of toast.

"I bet Meggie'll be quiet and bookish," Steven said, putting more sugar on his cereal.

"I bet you'll chew with your mouth open," Meg said.

"Bet I won't."

"Bet you will."

"Well." Their mother came into the kitchen, her hair

wrapped up in a large blue towel. "If it isn't the Storybook Family."

By ten-thirty, they were all dressed and sitting in the limousine that would take them to the White House.

"Well." Her mother looked them over, then smiled. "Very good." She straightened the front of Steven's hair, fixed Neal's even though he didn't need it, then lifted an eyebrow at Meg. "You look very old," she said.

"Is that bad?" Meg glanced at herself, worried.

"It's just frightening," her father said, looking from her to her mother, and shaking his head.

Meg slouched against the seat, embarrassed. The clothes *did* feel too old. The boots were great though—high black boots that kind of wrinkled at the ankles, they were really something. Spiffy, her father said. Her skirt, a soft grey wool, reached down to her midcalf—hiding her knees, too bad—and Meg was quite certain that it would look better on her mother. She was also wearing an even softer grey cowl neck, and a long wool coat they had gotten at the Chestnut Hill Bloomingdale's. She had gotten her hair cut so that now it just grazed her shoulders, and it was very full, making her look even more like her mother, except without quite the panache.

Instead of just being adorable, Neal was oddly masculine in little grey flannel pants and a blue blazer from Brooks Brothers. Sort of a miniature adult. Steven's jacket was a brown herringbone tweed, and she knew he was going to die when he grew out of it. He'd stubbornly insisted on wearing his Top-Siders, saying he didn't want to be seen in any queer patent leather, and following his example, Neal rebelled too. There was something appealing about the well-worn leather they'd both tried to shine.

She smiled at her brothers, who were sitting in the jump seats, and they gave her shy smiles back.

So, Steven was nervous. For all his big talk, he was nervous. He probably *was* scared that he would chew with his mouth open or something. She tilted her head, making a contorted face at him, and he laughed, the tight hands in his lap unfolding a little. She reached forward with her left boot and kicked him in the ankle, and he relaxed more, kicking back.

That taken care of, she looked at her father. She didn't think of him as being handsome, but he was. He looked solid, he looked healthy. His suit was charcoal grey flannel, bringing out the beginning grey in his hair. Very distinguished. This wasn't a man who burned omelets and swore; this was a man who was served a silver tray with poached fish, melon in season, light flaky croissants—she liked the man who burned omelets. She would miss him if he didn't come to the White House.

There was a myth or something about a person who could hold a bird in his hand and no matter how hard the hand was crushed, the bird would be safe—there was something so strong and safe about the person that he could always protect the bird, no matter what. Her father was like that, she decided.

Maybe her mother was like the bird. No matter what happened, her mother would pop out without a feather ruffled. She might be little and scared—birds' hearts always beat like crazy when you held them—but then, it would open its mouth, start to sing or whatever, and it would suddenly seem very big. Yeah. Yeah, maybe that was her mother.

Meg grinned. Like wow, how profound. She looked up, seeing that they had turned onto Pennsylvania Avenue and were now stopping to go through one of the White House gates. They drove inside, pulling up in front of the house at the North Portico, cars with Secret Service agents both in front of and behind them, reporters and photographers gathered around outside. They were ushered into the entrance hall where President Crandall and the First Lady were waiting, both cheerful and relaxed.

"Wow," Steven whispered, staring at the marble pillars across the great hall, a red carpet running down another hall behind the pillars. There were huge glass chandeliers, and open doors behind the red carpet revealed what could only be the Green Room, the Blue Room, and the Red Room.

"Why don't we go upstairs?" the President suggested,

and they crossed to the left of the hall to a tremendous red-carpeted staircase.

Dignified paintings of previous Presidents hung on the walls, and Meg thought about how much the one of her mother was going to stick out someday. They were taken upstairs and through the Center Hall, which was yellow and long, with lots of chairs and several small couches on wooden legs. Famous paintings, French mostly, hung on the walls, walls which also had built-in white bookcases. There were flowers all over the place—probably just because this was a big day, Meg figured. Having them all the time would be pretty expensive.

The President and the First Lady took them through one of the big mahogany doors and into the Yellow Oval Room. The Yellow Oval Room was where people like Popes and Queens were received. Again, there were lots of upholstered chairs with dark wooden legs and small antique tables covered with fragile china urns, candlesticks, and even more flowers. The draperies were golden—maybe silk—and Meg could see the Washington Monument through one of the windows. There was a marble fireplace, with more paintings above and beside it. Meg thought these looked more American, not that she was the world's leading authority on art.

Everyone was very friendly, and they were served coffee and cocoa in dainty cups, along with platefuls of small pastries and cookies. Steven wiped his mouth with his napkin about ten thousand times to make sure he didn't have a mustache, and Neal imitated him, giggling and wiping his mouth too.

President Crandall and his wife asked all the usual questions about school, how they felt about their mother being President, if they wanted to live in the White House. Meg thought all three of them answered rather quietly and bookishly. Neal dropped a pastry on the rug and looked terrified, but the President just laughed, leaning forward to scoop it up, saying that it happened all the time. It was nice that he hadn't run again. If her mother had beaten him, this probably wouldn't be as friendly.

At noon, aides came in to say that it was time to go to the Capitol for the ceremony. Downstairs, the Marine Band played "Hail to the Chief," and everyone shook hands a lot. Her mother and President Crandall got into the first limousine, the one with flags on the hood and all. The second two were for Secret Service agents; her father and Mrs. Crandall got into the next. The former vice-president, Mr. Kruger, and the other wives got into the fifth.

Meg and Steven and Neal sort of stood around, Meg baffled by motorcade protocol.

"This way, kids," an agent said. "We have to get moving, kids."

They got into the seventh car. Everyone else's children were married—President Crandall's were in the car ahead of them with their spouses, the vice-presidents' children in cars behind them.

"Wow." Steven reached for the button to open his window and look out at all the other limousines. "I bet this is really expensive."

"Hey." One of the agents in the front seat turned around. "You have to keep the windows up, kids."

Guiltily, Steven jerked back his hand.

"It's just a precaution," the man behind the wheel assured them. "We have a lot of rules around here."

They sure did.

At the Capitol, the Secret Service brought them up to the platform, facing out over the grassy mall that led to the Washington Monument. The theory was that the President could look west and out over the country that way. Pretty whimsical. They were supposed to sit in the front row, the entire Congress and other invited guests in chairs spreading out behind them. Everyone smiled as they went by, and cameras were going off like crazy.

"Where's Mommy and Daddy?" Neal wanted to know as they sat on one side of the podium.

"Back there." Meg gestured with her head. "They wait inside until everything's ready to go."

"Do we like have to keep smiling in case the camera's pointed at us?" Steven was letting all his teeth show.

"You think it's pointing at us?" Meg looked around, alarmed.

"They always film the families."

"Then, I don't know." Meg shrugged nervously. "Look happy or something."

There were hundreds upon hundreds of people below the platform, waiting to see the Presidents, hundreds and thousands of blurred faces.

"Meggie, I'm scared," Neal gulped.

"Why?" She took her eyes off the winter-clouded sky, afraid to look anywhere else, afraid of all the people.

"They're all looking at us."

"No," she lied. "They can't even see up here."

"But what if they can?" He looked at the blur of people, then around the platform, with small scared eyes.

"They can't. I swear they can't."

"I don't feel good," he said uneasily.

"Oh, God," Steven groaned. "I'll die if he gets sick."

"He's not going to get sick." Meg closed her eyes. Please, Neal, don't get sick.

"I feel like it, Meggie." Neal's face was very pale. "I don't like this. I want Mommy and Daddy here."

"Steven, trade places with him," Meg said. What if Neal got sick on national television? What if *she* got sick on national television?

Now, Steven looked scared.

"I'm not sitting over there," he said.

"All right, all right, trade places with me then."

"What if they wonder why we're doing it?" His face was now as pale as Neal's."

"They won't. Come on, just trade places."

He stood up nervously, and she sat down between them. Neal's hand shot over and she took it, praying that he wouldn't get sick, that none of them would get sick.

"Meg, I feel kind of funny too," Steven said, his voice small.

Who didn't? "Come on, you're fine." She made her voice hearty in comparison. "This is going to be fun."

"Aren't you scared at all?" Neal asked.

"Why would I be? Mom and Dad'll be out here in a minute." She changed the subject. "What do you think they'll have to eat at the luncheon?"

"Squab," Steven said glumly. "And I'll get sick."

"You know," Meg couldn't help grinning, "I bet everyone in the country with a color television thinks we have green faces."

"You mean, *you're* scared?" Steven said.

"Well, sure," she said, forgetting that she'd just said that she wasn't. "I'd be kind of a jerk if I wasn't. Besides, no one's looking at us anyway."

Neither of them looked convinced, and just as she was beginning to feel pretty sick herself, there was a flurry of activity on the platform, reporters and photographers scrambling to get into position.

"What is it? What is it?" Neal sounded scared to death, trying to see over all the people.

The Marine Band went into "Hail to the Chief."

"I think it's Mom and Dad," Meg said.

CHAPTER SIXTEEN

The Crandalls and her parents came out to the platform, and the crowd cheered and applauded for several minutes, the President and the President-elect waving, finally sitting down in the seats on either side of the podium.

Her mother, cheeks bright with excitement, smiled down the row at them, and her father leaned over, touching each one of their left shoulders for a second. Meg felt her nausea ebbing at the security of having their parents there and saw her brothers relaxing too.

After more applause and cheering, the excitement turned into silence, and it was time for her mother to be sworn in. Her parents looked at them, and Meg felt a strange long privacy in the seconds of eye contact, the people and noise blotted out, as if—for that brief moment—no one except their family existed. The intensity was kind of scary, maybe because it was so powerful, and no one else in the world had been a part of it. Her parents were up now, and she saw their fingertips touch before they got to the podium, where the Chief Justice of the Supreme Court was waiting with an open Bible.

And it was very quiet.

"Raise your right hand and repeat after me," the Chief Justice said, the sound echoing through the speakers.

Her mother put her left hand on the Bible, lifting her right hand, and Meg could see it shaking slightly.

"I, Katharine Vaughn Powers, do solemnly swear," he said.

"I, Katharine Vaughn Powers, do solemnly swear," her mother's voice clear and strong, going out over the people.

"That I will faithfully execute the office of the President of the United States."

"That I will faithfully execute the office of the President of the United States."

"And will to the best of my ability, preserve, protect, and defend the Constitution of the United States."

"And will to the best of my ability, preserve, protect, and defend the Constitution of the United States."

"So help you God," he finished.

"So help me God." Her mother's head tilted up for an instant, and Meg looked up too, hoping that if there were anyone up there, he or she was listening.

"Thank you, Mr. Chief Justice," her mother said.

"Thank you, Madame President," he said.

The Marine Band started "Hail to the Chief." Everyone was standing and applauding, the former President and other government officials moving to shake her mother's hand. Before any of them could, Meg saw her parents tightly grip right hands; then her mother turned, giving the three of them a quick, conspiring wink.

President. Her mother was the President of the country. Feeling sick again, Meg wanted to sit down, but everyone would see her.

"Meggie, clap!" Steven hissed, elbowing her.

Meg clapped, everyone clapped, and her mother—the President—stood there waving. And the entire country was watching. She gave her speech, and people went wild, interrupting her with applause about every third sentence. Speaking from only a few note cards, without prepared typescript—nothing new there—speaking with sincere conviction and strength, it was obvious that this was now the President of the United States. A calm, confident, and very hopeful President of the United States. Also, a very funny President of the United States.

After the ceremony ended in a confusion of handshaking and applause, they went to a Congressional luncheon, then down Pennsylvania Avenue in the motorcade to watch the inaugural parade, which was long and got very dull. Finally, they were in the White House, standing in the entrance hall where they had been only a few hours earlier. Only now they lived there.

"Well." Her mother smiled at the four of them, at Glen who was now her chief of staff, at Linda and Preston and all of the other aides.

"The only thing you have to do before dinner is sign those Cabinet appointments," Glen said. Then he smiled, which Meg thought made him look about ten years younger. "Madame President."

"Quite right." Her mother smiled back, then looked at the family. "What do you all want to do?"

"Can we look around?" Steven asked.

"Why not?" Their mother gave him a one-armed hug, then glanced at the various aides. "I'll want to see all of you in the Oval Office at five-fifteen for a few minutes. Linda, why don't you go to the Press Room, and tell them I'll be in to make a brief statement and answer a few questions at five. I think that's all."

"Madame President?" someone asked. "Do you want us to—"

"No, that's really all," she said. "I want to be alone with my family for a while." She nodded a nod of dismissal and her aides dispersed, most of them heading for the West Wing and their new offices. Her mother watched them go, then grinned. "This is kind of fun," she said.

Meg's father laughed, putting his arm around her waist. "You're a wonderful President."

"Come on, let's look around," Steven said impatiently.

"Quite right," their mother agreed. She struck out across the marble floor, between two pillars to the red carpet behind. They walked down to the East Room, past some guards who smiled. Neal stopped in the doorway, mouth open.

"It's beautiful," he said, voice hushed.

"Wow." Steven went in first, stepping carefully on the well-polished oak floor, staring up at the gold chandeliers and tall, gold-draped windows, paintings of George and Martha Washington dominating the huge room. He paused by the grand piano. "Come on, Meggie, play 'Greensleeves.' "

"I know other songs," she said.

"Then, how come you never play 'em?"

Meg glanced back at one of the guards, then hesitantly touched middle C on the piano, the sound echoing across the room. "Are we allowed to play this?" she asked.

"We live here," her father pointed out.

"Boy," She sat down on the gold-and-white upholstered piano bench. "I bet even 'Greensleeves' sounds professional in here."

"Hey, check it out!" Steven called from a door opening into another room. "What's this one?"

Meg went over to join him. "The Green Room, stupid, can't you tell?"

"Just 'cause it's green, they call it the Green Room? I think *that's* pretty stupid." He sat in a green chair, trying to look solemn.

Neal giggled and followed him, lying down on a stiff green and white couch and pretending to be asleep.

"Cute," Meg said.

"I think it is," her mother said, going over and pretending to tuck Neal in. She crossed to another door and opened it. "Steven, what do you think this room is?"

He got up, looked through the door, and snorted.

"The Blue Room, I bet," he said, and she nodded. "How queer." He wandered over to the windows of the large oval room. "Is that like the backyard?"

Their father nodded. "I guess you could call it that. The porch out there is the South Portico."

"And we came in through the North Portico?" Meg asked.

"You've got it, kid."

"What's portico mean exactly?"

"Porch."

"A porch with a roof supported by columns," her mother elaborated.

"Oh," her father put his arm around her waist. "The woman thinks she's smart because she's President."

"Oh, Christ," Steven said from another door. "This's the Red Room, right?"

"Watch it with the Christs," their father said, and Steven saluted.

Next was the State Dining Room, gold and austere, with a painting of Lincoln frowning down from above the mantelpiece.

"What, is this like if the Queen or someone comes?" Meg asked.

"If the Queen comes," her mother agreed. She crossed to one more door and opened it. "This is the Family Dining Room."

Meg stared dubiously at the formal mahogany table, a silver antique tray covering most of it. "We *eat* here?"

"Usually we'll be upstairs," her mother said. "Although it isn't much better."

Meg folded her arms, not wanting to start trouble. "Um, is the whole house like this?"

Her mother looked at her. "Pretty much."

"I figured," Meg said.

Her mother opened her mouth to say something, then stopped. "Would you like to look downstairs now?"

Meg shrugged and followed her, leaving her father and brothers behind.

"Mom?" she asked. "Are you guys mad about tonight?"

Her mother turned from examining a Monet painting. "It's not too late for you to change your mind and come."

Meg sighed. She probably shouldn't have brought it up— her not going to the Inaugural Balls had been an issue for weeks now. "I'm just really not into it," she said. "But I don't want you guys to be mad at me."

" 'Disappointed' is a better word," her mother said. "I think you'd have a good time."

"*I* think I'd die of embarrassment."

"Well, as your father and I have said, we're not going to *make* you come."

"But you're disappointed."

Her mother laughed. "Yes, we're disappointed. I may not go myself."

Meg smiled uncertainly. "That's a joke, right?"

Her mother just laughed, and Meg followed her to the

China Room, which had a lot of dishes displayed behind glass-covered shelves.

They met up with her father and brothers in the Diplomatic Reception Room, large and oval, dominated by painted wallpaper that showed early American scenes with a lot of what looked like Pilgrims. They checked out the rest of the floor—the Map Room, the Curator's office, a room for the Secret Service, the doctor's office, the housekeeper's office, a large kitchen with a special room for pastry making—all kinds of stuff. There was a movie theater further down and even a bowling alley. None of them had ever particularly bowled, but it was kind of neat to have it right downstairs, in case they wanted to or something.

"This place is really wild," Steven said as they walked upstairs to the second floor family quarters, although there were elevators they could have taken.

"This place is really *big,*" Neal said.

The floor was connected by three large halls—the East, the Center, and the West. The East Sitting Hall was gold and looked pretty comfortable. The Lincoln Bedroom and Sitting Room opened off one side of the hall, the bedroom stark in white and brown, the sitting room small and almost cozy. On the other side of the hall was the Queen's Bedroom, pale rose with a tall canopy bed.

"Bet you guys want me to sleep in here, right?" Meg asked.

"Yeah," Steven said. "Far away from us."

They went into the Treaty Room, which was red and black, very impressive with signed documents on the walls and one of the most beautiful chandeliers they'd seen so far. The White House was big on chandeliers.

Her mother sat down at the head of the heavy walnut table in a swiveling armchair. "This used to be the Cabinet Room."

"It's nice." Meg sat down at the other end, touching the polished black top. "Bet I could really get homework done in here."

"Yeah, me too." Steven sat along one of the sides, trying

to open the drawers built into the table. "Will you sign junk in here, Mom?"

Their mother looked around the room, a slow grin starting. "I don't think I'll be able to resist."

They went through the Center Hall, past the Yellow Oval Room where they'd had coffee that morning, continuing to the West Sitting Hall, where most presidential families spent a lot of time.

"Hey, that's our stuff!" Neal pointed at the couch and two matching armchairs.

"So you'll remember this is our house," their father said, ruffling his hair.

"Wow, I'm glad." Neal sat in one of the chairs, looking very pleased.

"You can see the Oval Office from here." Their mother pointed through a semicircular window to the West Wing.

Steven threw himself onto the couch, taking off his jacket. "Is this like, where we're supposed to hang out?"

"Basically," their father said.

Meg wandered around the hall, finding a kitchen with two cooks, who smiled and nodded, a dining room, and some bedrooms, two of which were very large and dignified, one of which was normal and one of which was very pink.

"Madame President?" A butler appeared. "May we get you or your family anything?"

"No, thank you. I think we're all set, Bill," her mother said. "Oh." She turned. "These are my children. My sons Steven and Neal, and my daughter Meghan."

"Hi," Meg said, her brothers also sounding quiet and bookish.

"Hey, yo," Steven said suddenly. "Where's Kirby?"

"Yeah, where's Vanessa?" Meg asked. She hadn't seen her cat since they left the apartment that morning. Staff people had been instructed to bring the animals to the White House.

"They have been put in kennels downstairs," the butler said. "For the time—"

"Kennels?" Steven said. "They don't live in *kennels!*"

"Traditionally," their mother said, "animals—particularly dogs—have—"

"If Vanessa has to live in a kennel, *I'm* living in a kennel," Meg said.

"*But*," her mother went on, "we just arranged to have them kept downstairs until we got here."

"Oh," Meg said. Steven looked as embarrassed as Meg felt.

"I'll have them sent upstairs," Bill said, moving to a telephone.

"Okay," her mother said. "We've got more bedrooms upstairs, a billiard room, the solarium—"

"What's that?" Neal asked.

"Oh, you'll love it," she said. "Lots of windows, plants, a stereo, television—the whole thing. You all will probably take it over. At any rate, your father and I figured that you would probably want a bedroom down here, Neal; that you'd take the other or go up to the third floor, Steven; and you'd be upstairs, Meg."

"I'd rather be down here," Steven said.

"I have to be upstairs by myself?" Meg said. "I don't want to be by myself."

"Oh." Her father looked surprised. "Your mother and I just assumed you'd want privacy."

Meg shook her head hastily. "I don't. I'd rather live with you guys." Especially here. At *home*, she'd want privacy.

"But you haven't even seen it up there yet."

"You want me to be away from everyone?" Meg asked, knowing that they probably meant well but still hurt.

"No," her father laughed, putting a calming arm around her. "We want you where we can always see your smiling face."

"Now you're making fun of me."

"A little," he admitted.

"Meg," her mother said, "I'd just as soon you were down here with us anyway—I like the idea that the family can be together. We need to be together. So"—she opened a bedroom door—"Neal, how would you like to be in here?"

He beamed. "Next to you and Daddy?"

She smiled back, giving him a small hug. "That was easy. Now you two can fight over the other two rooms," she said to Meg and Steven.

Steven and Meg looked at each other.

"I don't do pink," he said.

"Neither do I," she said.

"We'll have it redecorated,"' her mother said, an answer ready for everything. No wonder she was President. "I'm sure they can do it in blue or green, or whatever you want. We can get them started on it tomorrow." She glanced at her watch. "I think it's time to go work for a while."

"Can we come too?" Neal asked.

"I think maybe I have to be by myself. Dinner at six-thirty?" She smiled at all of them, then started down the hall to a presidential elevator, her walk much slower in this house than it was at home. A very dignified walk.

"There goes the President," Meg said.

Her father shuddered. "The mind boggles."

CHAPTER SEVENTEEN

Her family didn't really have many relatives—her father's sister and husband and their two sons, who were in their late twenties, then two great-aunts, both of them Vaughns, very old and very proper and kind of disturbed at the idea of a Vaughn female in the White House—so, a lot of her parents' friends had dinner at the White House before the Inaugural Balls. Meg felt like a bit of a jerk because she wasn't going, but she had this image of herself sitting alone in some corner, the wallflower of all-time, and people like the Speaker of the House—who was a really good friend of her mother's—asking her to dance because they felt sorry for her.

Dinner was a major production, with roast beef and Yorkshire pudding, which just happened to be the President's favorite meal. Only people were too excited to eat and kept jumping up to make toasts and everything. Every time someone shouted "Toast!" Meg wanted to play *Rocky Horror Picture Show* and throw bread at them. She managed to refrain. At one point, Steven leaned over and said that the painting of Lincoln—they were in the State Dining Room—was frowning because he was disgusted by Meg's table manners, and they laughed so hard that their father had to frown at them. Decorum. *Toujours,* decorum.

When her parents left for the Balls, they looked about as good as Meg had ever seen them. Her father, very formal in white tie, was wearing gloves and carrying a silk hat that he was too embarrassed to put on. Her mother had had her dress designed—by an American, naturally—and it was a smooth simple black with immeasurably flattering lines. She didn't look over forty. She didn't look over *thirty*. The neckline was a thin, sort of oval, V-neck that would probably become one of the most popular fashions in the country. The Presidential Look, magazines would call it. Her father was right, the mind had to boggle.

Her mother had put her hair up, and soft tendrils curled around the high cheekbones. She wore elbow-length gloves and a short, elegant jacket that had been designed for the dress. Her father had an evening cape. They were both flushed with excitement and, standing together, made a pretty incredible picture. They also made Meg glad that she wasn't going—she really would have felt in the way.

Alone in the house, Meg and her brothers wandered for a while, met more butlers and maids, unpacked a little. They ended up in the solarium—which *was* a great room, all couches and windows—watching the Balls on television and watching their parents. Kirby stayed with them, the cats came in and out, and a butler named Felix brought up some food.

"This is pretty excellent." Steven took a cookie and leaned back on his couch. "I didn't know they waited on us and everything."

"They're probably kind of glad we're here." Meg took a cookie too. "There haven't been any kids living here for a while." Meg looked over to see what Neal was doing, saw that Kirby had climbed up next to him when no one was looking and now, the two of them were asleep next to each other.

"The kid practices being cute," Steven said.

"Kirby's probably not supposed to be up there."

"This junk's not antique."

"Well, I guess it's okay," Meg said uneasily.

The television was focusing on her parents dancing together, and they looked very happy. Earlier, one of the bands had played a tango, and her parents had danced it, her mother's expression very amused, her father's a little terrified. Dancing wasn't his best skill. Probably most people were watching her mother anyway. The woman looked good. Very good.

Meg watched as she whispered something to her father, he whispered back, and they both laughed, still dancing. It was nice to see them look so much in love. The song ended, he brushed his lips across her hair, and Meg could tell that they had forgotten about the cameras and all the people watching.

After a while, Steven fell asleep too, and Meg got them both downstairs and into bed. The cats' litter box was in the presidential bathroom, which would probably horrify the country, and she carried Humphrey and Vanessa down from the solarium, putting them in the bathroom to remind them. Adlai and Sidney were asleep on her parents' bed, and she figured they remembered.

"Miss Powers?" Felix, the butler, appeared. "Would you like to have us take the dog out?"

"Do I need guards if I do?"

He nodded.

Guards. She wasn't really in the mood for guards. "Is it a pain if you guys do it? I mean, like, just this once?"

"Not at all."

"Um, sir?"

He turned, smiling.

"Is it all right if I make a phone call? I mean, are there rules?"

"No," he said. "No rules. Would you like me to get the number for you?"

"Are you supposed to?"

"It's no trouble."

"That's okay, sir," she said. "I mean, thank you, but I'm fine."

"If you need anything . . ."

"Thank you." She decided to use the phone in her room. Her very pink room.

Beth answered on the third ring.

"Hi," Meg said.

"Oh, God," Beth said. "Thought I'd heard the last of you."

"Guess not."

"You didn't break down and go?"

"No."

"What a jerk."

"Yeah," Meg said. "What's going on?"

"Same old whirlwind of activities. You know. What's it like there?"

"I don't know." Meg looked around at the stiff and unfamiliar bedroom. "Scary."

"It'll get better."

"Yeah. I guess." Meg brought her knees up, putting her free arm around them. "I don't like it much."

"You haven't even been there overnight."

"Yeah." Meg sighed. "I know."

"What, you called me long distance to grouch?"

"Yeah."

"Well, don't."

"Yeah, but—"

"Don't be a jerk," Beth said. "My God, Meg, they're going to be afraid of *you.*"

"But I'm just normal."

"Well," Beth said, "let's not get carried away."

Meg laughed. "And you call *me* a jerk."

They talked for a while longer, mostly about stuff going on in Massachusetts but a little about Washington. It was Beth's opinion that Meg and her brothers had been, as Meg suspected, rather pale green during the Inauguration before her parents had come out. Chartreuse even.

"Oh, I forgot," Beth said as they were hanging up. "Is it okay if I taped this conversation? Bucknell wants me to keep in touch with you—so the class can like share your experiences and everything."

"You know what Bucknell can do?" Meg asked.

"I *am* taping this."

"You'll be hearing from my lawyer," Meg said.

When they hung up, Meg felt very lonely again. For a place that was full of people—guards and aides and everything—the White House was about as quiet as any place she had ever been. She wandered up to the third floor to watch a little more of the Inaugural Balls on television. The third floor had huge record and videocassette collections—it seemed like practically every one ever made. As far as she knew, companies donated copies of things to the White

162

House. The video collection was a pretty recent addition. Not a bad fringe benefit.

She went back down to the second floor and played around for a while: sitting in the Yellow Oval Room, the Treaty Room, then remembering that Lincoln's ghost was supposed to be around at night and running—quietly—back down to the west end of the floor there were people right in the kitchen if she got too nervous. She went into her very pink room, looked at her somewhat unpacked books, and pulled out *The Final Days*. Kind of a fun book to read in the White House. She carried it out to the West Sitting Hall, deciding to read until her parents got home.

It was pretty comfortable there, sitting on the couch from home with her feet resting on Kirby's back, and she must have fallen asleep because suddenly she smelled delicate perfume and saw her mother sitting next to her.

"What time is it?" She tried to wake up, wondering who had covered her with a blanket.

"Almost three," her mother said, smoothing her hair back.

"Oh." Meg yawned, feeling half-asleep. "You guys have a good time?"

"We had a marvelous time."

"Your mother was the belle of the ball," her father said, taking off his gloves.

Felix came out of the kitchen. "Is there anything we can do for you, Madame President, Mr. Powers?"

"No, thank you," her father said. "We're fine."

Felix nodded, returning to his post.

"Steven and Neal asleep?" her mother asked.

"Yeah, they were pretty tired." Meg yawned again.

"Maybe you ought to get some sleep yourself," her father said.

"Yeah, I guess." She glanced around, remembering all the company. "Where is everyone?"

"Downstairs celebrating," her mother said. "If tonight is any indication, I'm afraid my administration is going to be known for drunken revelry."

Meg grinned. "Does that mean you guys?"

"Nope." Her father stumbled and fell on the couch.

Her mother laughed. "Will you stop?"

"Melly, I ain't so very drunk," he mumbled.

Her mother laughed again, running her hand through his hair, and Meg put on an intelligent smile, almost sure that he was referring to a scene in *Gone with the Wind*. She hated it when she didn't get her parents' references. Last of the big-time Babbitts.

"Take your hands off me, woman!" Her father's voice was slurred.

"You're so cute." Her mother kissed the top of his head, then looked at Meg. "I love this man very much."

"Should I, uh"—Meg edged toward her room—"maybe leave on that note?"

Her father got up, no longer drunk. "Sleep well, kid."

"Night, First Gentleman." She shook hands with him, then with her mother. "Night, Madame President."

Her mother smiled. "Good night. Do you need any—"

"No, thanks. Think I can deal with it. I'm glad you guys had a good time."

"The revelry hasn't even *started*," her father said, drunk again.

Meg grinned back at them and went to her room, noticing that someone had turned down her bed and laid out a night-gown. Generally she slept in old, very large T-shirts. She heard a scratch on the door and let Vanessa in, then started to get undressed. This room was extremely pink. The sooner she turned the lights off, the better.

She was up and dressed by nine the next morning, deciding to wear a skirt—just in case, but hoping she'd be able to get back to regular clothes soon. The plan was for her family to have a private breakfast in the Presidential Dining Room while everyone else slept late.

The dining room was deep blue, its wallpaper covered with scenes from the Revolutionary War. The table was already set beneath the huge chandelier with an arrangement of fresh flowers, mostly yellow, as a centerpiece. As she hesitated on the threshold, yet another butler came to greet her. How many *were* there?

"Good morning, Miss Powers." He bowed slightly. "What would you like for breakfast?"

Meg resisted an urge to curtsy back.

"You mean, I can choose?" she asked.

He nodded.

"Wow, not bad." She thought for a minute. "What do you have?"

"Just about everything."

"Orange juice?"

He nodded, smiling.

"And—cereal?"

"What kind would you like?"

"Hmmm." She shot a glance at the door. "Do you have Captain Crunch?"

He nodded. "We weren't sure what you and your brothers liked."

"Oh, wow, great," Meg said, impressed. "All we get at home is boring junk. Mom and Dad always say—" She stopped, deciding not to mention that her parents thought cereal with added sugar would rot their teeth out. "Yeah, that sounds good. I'd like some Captain Crunch, please."

"Anything else? Toast? English muffins? Doughnuts?"

Meg grinned. "Sure. Oh, and could you bring the box, please?"

"The box?"

"I like to read the cereal box. It's kind of a habit."

"I'll bring the box." The butler left the room, smiling.

Meg glanced around, finding the bold Revolutionary scenes on the walls somewhat intimidating. She'd read somewhere that a previous Administration had taken the paper down and painted the walls a nice cheery yellow. Why would anyone have wanted to put the war scenes back up? It was going to be like eating in Cyclorama.

She crossed to the table, studying the five place settings. She touched one of the glasses, very thin and delicate. Boy, the staff was going to hate Steven. He was always breaking things. She sat down, deciding on the chair that corresponded to her position at home. This wasn't a table you leaned your elbows on. You couldn't throw mashed potatoes here either. In spite of age and maturity and all those things, she and Steven generally threw mashed potatoes. It had gotten so Trudy refused to make them anymore.

She heard uneasy footsteps, and Steven peeked into the room.

"Hi," she said.

"Hi." He came in, subdued in neat flannel slacks, a dark blue Lacoste sweater and a white Oxford shirt.

"Where's your tie?"

"What?" He stopped, looking down at himself. "Do I have to wear a bloody tie just to have *breakfast?*"

"Hey, watch your mouth!" She hissed, checking the door.

"Yeah, well, I'm not wearing a stupid tie!" He hissed back. "Mom won't make me!"

The butler came in with a silver tray. "Good morning, Master Powers," he said, pouring juice from a crystal pitcher into Meg's glass.

"Uh, hi," Steven said.

"What would you like for breakfast?" The butler set a pitcher of milk on the table, along with a basket of hot muffins. He tipped the box of Captain Crunch, filling Meg's bowl.

"What she has looks pretty good," Steven said. "We never get to have decent cereal."

The butler smiled and brought the box over.

"Would you like anything else?" he asked, after pouring Steven some juice as well and making sure that they both had muffins.

"No, thank you," Meg said.

"No, thank you," Steven said.

When the butler was gone, he put down his spoon.

"Some room," he observed.

"That's for sure. Don't the walls make you nervous?"

"Yeah." He looked up at the chandelier. "If that thing falls, we're in trouble."

"Good morning." Their mother came into the room, smiling.

Being President agreed with her, Meg decided. After no more than a couple of hours' sleep, she still looked cheerful and refreshed.

"You look nice, Mom," she said.

"You think?" Her mother checked her outfit, adjusting one cuff of the sweater dress, pushing her gold bracelet down. She lifted an eyebrow at Steven's bowl. "Captain Crunch?"

"Want some?" he asked.

"Why not." She sat down and reached for the box.

"Madame President?" The butler hurried in. "What may I bring you?"

"Good morning," she said, smiling at him. "Just some coffee, please."

"The President of the United States should have protein," Meg remarked.

"So should the President's daughter," her mother said.

Neal and their father came in with Kirby, who went under the table the same way he did at home, presumably expecting people to sneak him food.

Neal stopped when he saw Steven, giving his father an accusing look. "He's not wearing a tie—how come I have to?"

Steven took another muffin. "Can't make me wear a bloody tie."

"Then, *I'm* not wearing a bloody tie!" Neal yanked his off.

"You two looking for trouble?" their father asked.

"Ground them," Meg advised, reading the nutritional information on the box.

"Ah, another joyful morning with the Storybook Family," her mother said, taking half a muffin and spreading butter on it.

"You're going to try to be President without protein?" Meg's father asked.

Her mother laughed, skimming the morning edition of the *Times* some aide had read and underlined for her.

"Katie, make me happy," he said. "Have an egg. Have a poached egg."

She laughed, merrily spooning up some cereal.

"Wow, Captain Crunch!" Neal grabbed the box. "Do we get to have this all the time now?"

"Yes," Steven and Meg said.

"No," their father said.

Neal looked at his mother. "Mom?"

"No comment." She picked up the morning *Post*.

The butler came in with coffee. "Mr. Powers, what may I get you?"

"Could I have a poached egg, please?" He gave the entire family a pointed look. "And some coffee."

"Right away, sir." The butler turned to Neal. "Master Powers?"

Neal giggled.

"Would you like an egg? Or some french toast, or—?"

Neal shook his head, giggling.

"How about, 'No, thank you?' " their father suggested.

"No, thank you," Neal said.

"Robot," Steven snorted, grabbing another muffin.

"Sexist, unscrupulous puppet," Meg said, taking one too.

"Bad-mannered children," their father said.

The butler waited until they were finished, smile hidden. "Would anyone else like anything? Madame President?"

"Um, yes. Thank you." Her mother lowered the newspaper, eyes terribly amused. "You wouldn't happen to have any Frosted Flakes back there, would you?"

CHAPTER EIGHTEEN

Meg and Steven kept trying to count all the White House employees, but there were so many people like laundresses, switchboard operators, and night doormen—to say nothing of the butlers, cooks, maids, and gardeners—that they gave up after a while, deciding to just call it the Cast of Thousands. Weird place, the White House.

Her mother was having constant receptions—for members of Congress, for new staff members and their spouses, for the media people assigned to cover the White House. When Meg and her brothers didn't have to make appearances, they kept exploring the house and grounds. When they walked around outside, agents accompanying them, tourists beyond the cast-iron fences would point and wave. Between ten and twelve in the morning, they were supposed to stay out of the way because tours were given through the downstairs reception rooms, Steven thought it would be funny to wander down some morning and play the piano in the East Room, but their parents made a point of discouraging this idea.

There were all kinds of special gardens outside: the Rose Garden, the Children's Garden, the Jacqueline Kennedy Garden. The Children's Garden was near the tennis court—where Meg planned to spend every free moment of her time once the snow melted. Most of the trees and shrubs were marked with little signs, and Steven got a kick out of taking Kirby over to the Warren G. Harding Magnolia Grandiflora or the Richard M. Nixon Fern-leaf Beech.

On Saturday, her parents were going to a reception for a bunch of people from the embassies, and her mother suggested that the three of them spend the afternoon exploring the city a little, getting the feel of it. Having nothing better to do, Meg and her brothers agreed.

After brunch, while Steven was in the kitchen getting more to eat, Meg went to find out what was taking Neal so long. She found him in his room, on the bed with his shoulders slouched, looking close to tears.

"What's wrong?" she asked. "Come on, we're ready to go."

He shook his head.

"Come on, it's going to be fun. We can go to the museum with all the rockets and everything. Remember that one? With all the planes?" His expression didn't change, and she sat next to him. "What is it? Don't you feel good?"

He looked up at her with very worried eyes. "Are Mommy and Daddy safe?"

"Well—yeah," she said. "They just went to a thing at the Mayflower. It's no big deal."

"Jimmy told me," he gulped, quoting his best friend back in Massachusetts, "he said we had to have guards because people wanted to hurt us. Like—like with guns." He drew a small fist across his eyes, closer to crying, "Like Presidents get hurt, and he said Mommy might—"

She put her arm around him. "No one's going to get hurt. It's just a rule that we have to have agents."

"But Jimmy said—"

"Who do you believe, me or Jimmy?" She hugged him closer. "The agents are just part of it, that's all. Like, does it bother you that people bring dinner in for us? Does that scare you?"

"No," he said slowly.

"Well, the guards are like the same thing. They're there to take care of us when we're outside the White House, and the butlers and everyone take care of us when we're inside. It's just part of it. Look," she tightened her arm. "Talk to Mom and Dad about it, okay? They can explain it better."

"I guess," he said.

"Well, make sure you do." She fixed the knot in his tie. "Come on, let's go find Steven and—"

"I'm not wearing this." He yanked the tie off. "I don't like it."

"But we have to. We're not supposed to—" She stopped,

considering the fact that he would never have to wear a tie to go around Boston on a Saturday afternoon. Why should he have to here? "You're right." She threw it onto the dresser, one more incongruous touch in this room where stiff Victorian furniture and little boy possessions were fighting for control. "You don't have to."

"Will I get in trouble?"

"No."

"But *you* look nice."

She looked at the dress she had worn to the brunch.

"Do me a favor," she said. "Wait here, okay? Don't move." She started for the door, hearing him get off the bed. "Hey!" She turned around. "I said not to move."

He giggled and got back on.

"That's better." She opened the door, waiting for his second attempt, turning when she heard it. "I thought I said not to move."

He giggled harder and climbed back up.

"I'll be right back." She hurried down to her room, changing into an old sweater, a button-down shirt, and jeans. Shoes. What was she going to wear for shoes? She looked out the window at the grey winter slush, grinned, and pulled on her L. L. Bean hiking boots. She went back down the hall, feeling normal for the first time since they'd come to Washington.

Neal was still sitting on the bed. "Wow," he pointed to her jeans. "Can I too?"

"Sure," she said, gesturing expansively.

"Are we allowed?"

"Sure," she said in a less certain voice, with a more expansive gesture.

He put on jeans and sneakers, traded his grey V-neck for one of Steven's old crewnecks, then turned and smiled at her. "Can we go to the place with the rockets first?"

"Sure. Hey, Steven," she called as they went out to the West Sitting Hall. "Come on, let's go."

He came out of the kitchen, holding two chocolate doughnuts. He saw their outfits and grinned.

"Hot damn," he said, pulling his tie off.

On their way downstairs, they met Preston.

"Hmmm." He frowned at them.

"Hi," Steven said in one of his most arrogant and defiant voices.

"The cats didn't drag in anything very stylish today, did they?" Preston said, flashily dignified in a dark blue pin-striped suit, his shirt and handkerchief lighter blue, tie navy.

Neal and Steven looked at Meg.

"No, guess they didn't," Meg said.

"Hmmm." He leaned forward, straightening Neal's scarf.

"Meggie said it was okay," Neal said defensively.

"Oh, did she now."

"Sure did," Meg said, in *her* arrogant and defiant voice.

"Tying them might help the look," he said, indicating her boots.

"I like them this way."

"Well, whatever. You might want to pick up some colored laces though." He smiled. "You know how many reporters are waiting down there?"

They looked guilty.

"Oh, don't worry about it." He put Meg's jacket collar up, adjusted Steven's hat more rakishly. "You're kids—of course you dress this way."

"Okay now," he said as they walked down the stairs. "Have a good time and don't talk to too many strangers. And go to the National Gallery if you have time. You'll learn something."

"I'm not going to any stupid art museums," Steven said. "Mom always makes us go to art museums. We're going to the FBI."

"The FBI?" Meg asked. "We're not going to the FBI."

"Yeah, we are. I'm not going to any stupid—"

"I thought we were going to see the planes," Neal said, worried.

"Good idea." Preston patted him on the head, then adjusted his hat. "Take the kid to see the planes."

They ended up going to see the planes. That is, after the

photographers downstairs took their pictures and the reporters asked a few questions—like where they were going, and if they were dressed casually to avoid getting spoiled by the glitter and glamour of the White House. Meg repressed an urge to say that they were dressed that way because the cats hadn't dragged in anything very stylish. She had this image of Vanessa dragging home a bunch of designer outfits she'd found foraging through the closets of stylish Washingtonians.

They got into a car which had two of their agents in the front seat and a car with their other four agents behind them, and drove away from the White House through one of the front gates. Tourists who were gathered outside stared at the cars, and a few took pictures.

"We should like charge 'em for those," Steven said.

Meg hit him. "Don't be a jerk."

"Don't hit me."

"Don't be a jerk then."

"The Air and Space Museum, kids?" Barry, one of the agents, asked and they nodded.

The Air and Space Museum was part of the Smithsonian Institution. There were art museums—like the National Gallery, the Natural History Museum, one of American history, and a couple of others Meg couldn't remember. There was a long grassy mall—maybe a mile, maybe more—between the Capitol and the Washington Monument and the Smithsonian buildings were along it. A lot of people jogged along the mall.

The Air and Space Museum was really modern, white with black windows, kind of like the Kennedy Library in Boston. Their agents parked in front of it, and they went inside. Everyone they passed stared and nudged companions. Meg could kind of take planes or leave them, mostly leave them, but Steven and Neal loved the exhibits, standing open-mouthed in front of World War II fighter planes which Meg found rather dull. They looked at some moon rocks, a couple of Apollo spacecraft, and models of Sky-Lab. Meg thought that spaceships were a waste when there were starving people in Appalachia and that sort of thing, but she made a practice of keeping her political opinions to herself. It was easier that way.

They walked across the mall to the Natural History Museum, lots of people taking pictures of them. Meg kind of wished she could have a copy of one since six well-dressed and nervous-looking men walking along with three kids in ski jackets and jeans was probably an hysterically funny sight.

The Natural History Museum was more to Meg's tastes, although taxidermy always made her think of the movie *Psycho*. Steven and Neal made a bit of a ruckus, calling each other wombats and ring-tailed lemurs and that sort of thing, Steven yelling, "Yo, it's Meg!" in front of the Dogs of the World exhibit. None of them was too enthralled by rocks, but they went to the mineral and gem section to look at the Hope Diamond, Steven making a lot of loud remarks about how they were going to steal it and that the agents were their gang. Meg thought he was pretty funny, but most of the people around them stared.

In the Museum of American History, they looked at some old trains and automobiles, but then went to the part devoted to the history of the political process—definitely Meg's scene. She wasn't into the idea of running for office—much too hard on families—but sometimes she had this fantasy that she would grow up to be Elizabeth Drew or someone and write long political essays that everyone would read and admire. At least read.

There was a special exhibit focusing on their mother, mostly a pictorial history of her career, from Radcliffe on, with campaign memorabilia like bumper stickers and pictures of her doing things like accepting the Democratic nomination. There was even a picture of the family at Stowe, the one the *Times Magazine* had used a few years ago, looking tanned and All American, Neal three years old and the focus of attention on tiny little skis. She and Steven both had snow in their hair and she vaguely remembered their having had a fight right before the picture was taken.

The only thing funnier than that section of the museum was the section devoted to First Ladies. This part had, behind glass, reproductions of rooms in the White House during various points of history—like the Red Room as it was in 1870—and in the rooms were life-size mannequins of all the First Ladies in their Inaugural gowns. In the room that had Mrs. Kennedy right on up through Mrs. Crandall, there was a little empty space at the end and a white card: "COMING SOON: RUSSELL JAMES POWERS." They laughed for about ten minutes, attracting many stares, Meg picturing a tall model of their father in white tie and tails.

Since nothing could top "COMING SOON: RUSSELL JAMES POWERS," they left the museum, fighting about where they were going to go next. The FBI building didn't give tours on Saturdays, so Steven said they should go to the Watergate Apartment Complex, an idea Meg and Neal rejected. They ended up at Baskin-Robbins, and had to get back into the car with their cones because so many people were looking at them. "Oreo, mint chocolate chop, pralines 'n' cream!" Meg wanted to shout at them. Kind of weird to have so many people recognize them—the agents were a dead giveaway.

It was starting to get dark, and they drove out to the Lincoln Memorial. It was large and square, supported by marble columns, and as stately and dignified as a piece of architecture could be. The kind of place where Meg automatically whispered. They walked up several flights of stone steps, where between the two middle columns sat the statue of a serious but benevolent Lincoln. Meg felt sort of as if she were approaching the gates of heaven, the statue lit up in the darkness, looking as if it were sitting in judgment. She could have stayed there all night, but Neal decided that he was scared, Steven decided that he was hungry, and their agents pointed out that they should be getting home for dinner.

So they left, taking a scenic route home, past the Jefferson Monument and the Washington Monument, slowing to stare up the Mall at the Capitol Dome, all three lighted up and magestically golden against the winter sky.

"Wow," Steven whispered.

"Wow," Neal said, also whispering, and Meg felt the

same mingled pride and fear, thinking about how important it was to be the President.

They were driving past the South Lawn of the White House, which was also bright with golden spotlights, the fountains spraying into the night. They drove through one of the gates, the East Room chandeliers visible through the first floor windows. They got out at the North Entrance, said thank-you to their agents, and went upstairs, none of them talking much.

"That was really something," Meg said finally.

"*All* of this is really something," Steven said, and Meg and Neal nodded, the three of them stepped very carefully and quietly on the red-carpeted marble stairs.

CHAPTER NINETEEN

By Sunday night, all of the company was gone, and they spent the evening together privately in the West Sitting Hall, sprawling on the couch and chairs from home. Meg had been trying to read *The Making of The President: 1960,* but gave up, taking a cream puff from the coffee table—First Family refreshments—and killing a little time by trying to eat it without making a mess.

Finished with that, she looked around the room. He mother was sitting with Neal on her lap, the two of them smiling and talking quietly. Neal was lucky to be young. Looking at her mother's relaxed expression, Meg thought about the man nearby, probably in the Center Hall, who was holding the black box—the briefcase that had to be with the President twenty-four hours a day in case she had to make an immediate decision about nuclear war. Meg didn't quite understand the logistics of it all, but the controls and authorization were inside that briefcase. Walking to breakfast that morning, she had seen the man, silent and expressionless, sitting near her parents' bedroom. Pretty scary stuff. If Meg were in charge, her inclination would be to invite the Soviet premier over for some vodka and talk things out, but that was probably kind of simplistic. It made sense though.

She looked at Steven who was sitting on the floor with Kirby, stuffing his face with pastries. Did he think about stuff like war? Probably not. But it was hard to tell—he was always so reserved. Was "reserved" the word? "Restrained" was probably better. *"Con*strained." "Controlled." Very, very controlled. As always, his mother's child.

Sometimes—sometimes, she just felt like grabbing him when he walked by, giving him a big hug, and saying, "You know what? I love you." He'd probably hit her. Or pretend to throw up. There wasn't a single member of her family, except Neal maybe, who wouldn't think she was really weird if she walked up and hugged them. She was a little on the constrained side herself.

She leaned forward to get a pastry, and Steven grinned up at her, showing her a mouthful of mashed cupcake. Nice. Definite charm school graduate. She sat back, eating the raspberry tart she'd chosen. He also went back to eating, but when he glanced up a minute later, she opened her mouth for an equally disgusting demonstration of masticated raspberry tart. They both laughed, and she had to grab her Tab and gulp down half of it so there wouldn't have to be a demonstration of the Heimlich maneuver. Her father looked over his glasses at them, and they gave him angelic smiles. Proper presidential children. Yeah, right.

Her father had been sitting at the other end of the couch reading First Gentleman briefing notes all night. Hard to believe that there was such a thing. He was going to have to give speeches and do good works and all of that. Meg figured that he would probably concentrate on the environment. As far as she could tell, the idea that *he* could accomplish things too made him feel better about being First Gentleman. At least, he seemed pretty secure lately.

Neal went to bed early, her mother disappearing with him; then Steven went in around ten, and her mother left again so she could say good night to him. It was weird to have her mother home and able to say good night to them. In spite of the fact that she was President, they were seeing more of her than they ever had. Kind of ironic.

Alone with her father, Meg put her book down. "Dad?"

He took off his reading glasses, blinking to focus. "What?"

"I'm kind of"—she kept her hand in the book so she wouldn't lose her place, then just closed it altogether—"scared about school tomorrow."

"Well," he smiled. "That's normal."

"What if they hate me?" She brought her knees up, wrapping her arms around them. "They'll all have their own friends, so no one'll talk to me, and because of the agents, they won't talk to me even more.''

"Of course they'll talk to you." He moved over next to her. "Just be nice and friendly. Say hello to people. And don't worry about Jeff and Barry—they'll stay out of your way.''

"No one else is going to have two men following them.''

"No," he agreed. "But most of them will be government kids. It won't seem strange to them. Just be yourself.''

"What if they hate myself?''

"They won't.''

"How do you know?''

"I just do. You'll end up being the most popular person there.''

"You're only saying that because you're my father.''

He lifted his eyebrows. "You accuse the First Gentleman of lying?''

She nodded.

"Not only," he said, "are you going to be the most popular, but every boy in that school is going to ask you out—I guarantee it.''

"Because I'm the President's daughter.''

"Because you are *extremely* attractive.''

Meg snorted. "Are there going to be reporters?" she asked, more serious.

"Well, some," he admitted. "But just getting out of the car—they can't follow you inside. I had Preston make sure that no one's going to be able to bother you once you get in there.''

Meg tightened her arms around her knees.

"Look," he said, "it's not too late for me to come with you. You can just go in a little later. Steven broke down and is letting me come with him after we take Neal.''

Meg shook her head. "I can do it myself.''

"I know you *can*, but—''

"It's okay," she said. "I'd rather go by myself.''

He nodded.

"I really would.''

"Well, just remember that you can change your mind, okay?"

"I won't."

"Well, the offer's there." He turned over her book, reading the title. "Don't you ever read anything for fun anymore?"

"Well—" Meg grinned sheepishly. "It's sort of interesting. I mean, like, we're expected to know stuff, right?"

"You don't," he smiled, "enjoy it or anything?"

"No way," she said.

She saw her mother coming back and stood up, figuring her parents might want to be alone for a while. "Well, back later maybe." She passed her mother on the way to her pink room. "Hi."

Her mother nodded. "Hi. Was it something I said?"

"What?" Meg tilted her head, not getting it. "Oh. No, it wasn't."

"Going to bed?"

"Not yet."

Her mother nodded and Meg continued to her room. Once inside, she opened the closet, trying to figure out what she was going to wear. She'd asked Beth during their conversation that afternoon, and Beth had suggested that she wear her tweeds. Lots of help. She should probably wear a skirt though. But if she were too dressy, they would all think she was some rich jerk. Only, if she dressed down, she would look like a rich jerk who didn't give a damn. Besides, she had to consider reporters. Pictures of her first day at school could show up anywhere—*Newsweek, Time,* lots of places. Maybe she could arrange to be tutored at home.

"Having trouble deciding what to wear?"

"Hunh?" She turned, saw her mother in the doorway, and flushed, putting the clothes on her bed aside as if she were just doing inventory. "No. No, I'm all set."

"Oh." Her mother stayed in the doorway. "What are you wearing?"

"I don't know." Meg began putting things back in the closet.

"A skirt might be a good idea."

"Don't worry" Meg said, irritated. "I'm not going to embarrass you or anything."

"I didn't say that."

"You were going to."

Her mother's gaze sharpened, but she didn't say anything, moving all the way into the room, hands going into skirt pockets. "Are you nervous about tomorrow?"

"No."

"Not at all?"

"No."

"Oh." Her mother leaned against the Early American desk. "Well, I would be."

Meg was going to say, "Well, I'm not you," but rather than start trouble said, "I don't know, maybe I am. It's not important."

"I think it is."

Meg shrugged and reached down to the end of the bed to pat Vanessa.

"You know," her mother said, "I feel as if we haven't talked to each other in months."

Meg shrugged.

"Are you angry at me because of that night before we came down here?"

"I'm not angry at you." Meg looked at her. "I'm just—I don't know."

Her mother came over to the bed, sitting somewhat hesitantly at the bottom. "You and Beth had a pretty long talk today."

"Yeah, kind of."

"She and Sarah can come down here during their vacation."

"Yeah."

"Are you sure you aren't angry at me?"

"I said I wasn't."

"Maybe it's my imagination then. You seem a little brusque."

"Good word," Meg said.

"Thank you." Her mother sighed. "You know, you make me hate myself."

"For bringing me into the world?"

Her mother grinned. "Because you're such a nice kid and you have this defensive chip on your shoulder all the time."

"I do not!"

"What would you call that reaction?"

Meg frowned.

"Exactly." Her mother reached over to squeeze her shoulder. I keep trying to take it off, and you put it back on, and I take if off, and you put it back on—" She paused, seeing Meg's grin. "Having a laugh at my expense, are you?"

Meg shook her head, but let her grin get bigger.

"I rather thought so." Her mother smiled too. "Could you do me a favor?"

"What?" Meg asked, not committing herself, just in case.

"Tell me how you feel about something."

"About what?"

"Anything," her mother said. "Just tell me how you *really* feel about something."

"I'm against the draft."

"How about something a little more personal."

"I don't like olives."

"Even more personal than that."

"Yeah?" Meg glanced at her. "Can I say what I really think?"

"I want you to."

"Okay." Meg folded her arms across her chest. "I don't like reporters, Secret Service agents, or starting school tomorrow."

"No argument there."

"I wish we lived in Massachusetts, I wish you were an English teacher, I wish—"

"My God"—her mother fumbled around the floor—"where's the chip?"

"I was only going to wish for world peace."

Her mother laughed, hugging her even though Meg's

182

arms were folded. "Do you really wish I were an English teacher?"

"I don't know."

"Just anything but President?"

"It could be worse."

"What do you mean?"

"You could be Pope."

Her mother laughed again, kissing her on the top of the head before releasing her.

"Do you really hate my being President?" she asked.

"I don't know."

"Well, do you—"

"Mom, don't push me, okay?" Meg asked. "We haven't even been here a week."

Her mother nodded. "I know, I'm sorry."

"You don't have to say you're sorry. I'm just not sure how I feel."

Her mother nodded.

"You know what I wish?"

Her mother shook her head.

"I wish Mel Gibson would ride up and carry me off."

Her mother grinned. "That sounds exciting."

"Carry me off to the frozen tundra and—"

"I get the picture," her mother said.

"And we'd go skiing together."

"Oh, well, that sounds like a nice time," her mother agreed.

"I thought so."

Her mother smiled, leaning over to kiss her forehead. "It's late. You ought to get some sleep."

"I always stay up this late."

"I'm sorry, I forgot." Her mother stood up. "You know, Meg, I think all of this is going to be okay. We're all going to be together a lot more, spend some time with each other, find out a lot about our family. I think you're going to end up feeling better about it, I really do."

"I guess so."

"I really think you are. That all of us are." Her mother

paused at the door. "Come out and say good night before you go to bed, okay?"

"Maybe," Meg said in her if-you're-lucky voice.

Her mother drew her breath in-between her teeth. "Did I ever tell you that you can be an extremely irksome child?"

Meg nodded cheerfully. "SAT word."

Her mother tried, but wasn't able to keep her smile back. "Perpetually impudent. Unabashedly churlish."

"Oh," Meg said, "some applause for the woman who swallowed a thesaurus."

"Incessantly obstreperous."

"Oh, very good," Meg said, impressed.

"Thank you." Her mother opened the door. "Come out and say good night before you go to bed."

Meg nodded.

CHAPTER TWENTY

After agonizing again the next morning, Meg decided to wear a pleated wool skirt and an Oxford shirt with a sweater over it. Surely that would be casual enough, yet dignified enough to please everyone. She solved the shoe problems with knee socks and Top-Siders. How very sixteen-year-oldish. She would reflect well upon the Administration.

She rode in the back seat of the car, her agents in the front.

"Nervous?" Jeff asked, slowing for a red light, not very casual in his blue suit and tie.

"Nope," she lied. Then, she leaned forward. "You think someone who walks into school holding two pens and a brand new notebook looks like a jerk?"

"The person looks prepared," Barry said, even less casual in his grey suit.

"The person looks quiet and bookish." Meg sat back. "I don't want to go."

"I think you're stuck," Jeff said, turning right and pulling up in front of the school, reporters and photographers moving out to meet the car. A couple of other agents had gotten there earlier to check the crowd for crazed gunmen or whatever. A comforting thought.

"Do I have to get out of the car?" she asked, her throat getting tight as she looked at the crowd.

"I think it might be a good idea," Barry said, both agents scanning the waiting group.

"Should I swagger or slink?"

"Stroll," Jeff said. He got out to open the door for her.

Stepping onto the curb, she saw cameras go off and flinched, even though she had been planning not to.

A man in a tie and jacket moved forward, his hand out. "I'm Thomas Lyons, the headmaster."

"Hi." Meg shook his hand, then he nodded at Barry and Jeff, whom he must have met when the school security had been checked.

"Miss Powers, how do you feel about starting school?" a reporter from one of the networks asked.

"Nervous," Meg said without thinking, and everyone laughed.

Her agents ushered her inside, to her relief, and Barry went off with the assistant headmaster to the guidance room, which had been converted to a communications center with the White House. He and Jeff would take turns sitting there or outside her classroom. Fun job. The White House had to keep track of where everyone was in case of an emergency. They even all had code names—she was Sandpiper. She couldn't help wondering what they called her behind her back. Steven was Snapper and Neal was Snowflake. Her mother was Shamrock, her father Sunflower. What a team. The Secret Service liked to keep things innocuous and neat, everything beginning with the same letter. Barry was probably already contacting the White House: "Sandpiper safe and sound. Mission successful." They talked like a bunch of astronauts.

As she walked down the hall with Jeff and Mr. Lyons, teachers came up and introduced themselves, passing students just stared.

"Everyone's very excited about having you here," Mr. Lyons said.

Meg blushed. "I hope they're not going to be disappointed."

"I'm sure they aren't."

After going through the red tape of checking her schedule, as well as meeting the entire office staff, Mr. Lyons took her down to the last half of her first-period class, junior English with a Mrs. Simpson.

"Your grades from your old school are very good," he said.

"Thank you."

"We hope you'll do as well here."

"I hope so too, sir."

"Well, I'm sure you will." He paused in front of a door and opened it.

"Do it up, kid," Jeff said, sitting down in the chair outside.

Meg smiled weakly, then followed the headmaster into the room. All work stopped, and what seemed like hundreds of faces looked up.

Don't look, she ordered herself. Focus on something in the back. They were hostile, she could tell they were all hostile.

"This is Meghan Powers," Mr. Lyons said. "As you all know, she is going to be a student at our school from now on."

Meg nodded stiffly, afraid to look at anyone. The room was very quiet, and she could hear her heart up in her ears.

"Do you like to be called Meghan?" Mrs. Simpson, a short woman with pleasant gray hair, asked.

"Just Meg." Her voice squeaked a little. Way to go, Sandpiper.

"Well, we're really looking forward to having you in here, Meg." Mrs. Simpson handed her a thick anthology and a worn paperback copy of *1984.* "These are the texts we're using. Why don't you choose a seat?" She gestured toward two empty desks in the front row.

No way. She couldn't sit in front. She'd be sure that people were looking at her. Not that she was paranoid or anything.

"Meg?" Mrs. Simpson asked pleasantly.

"Right." Seeing a place in the back, she made her way to it, face painfully hot as everyone watched her. She stumbled as she pulled out her chair, but she managed to sit down, flushing even more as all the heads turned in her direction.

"I think we're all set here," Mrs. Simpson said to Mr. Lyons, who nodded at her, at the class, and left the room. "Now, why don't we go back to our discussion? We were talking about the concept of double-think, I believe."

Meg took stiff, obedient notes, knowing that she couldn't concentrate, anymore than anyone else seemed to be concentrating. People kept looking at her, and she had to keep looking away, embarrassed. There were a lot of guys in this class, some of whom—on quick glance—looked as if they might be handsome. Glancing around, she met eyes with one of the best-looking boys she had ever seen, a boy sitting diagonally across from her. She looked back—the way you always did, whether you wanted to or not—and saw him grinning at her. Redder than she had been so far, she focused on the board, copying down Mrs. Simpson's block-lettered "WAR IS PEACE, FREEDOM IS SLAVERY." A hand flashed over to her desk and away, leaving a small crumpled piece of paper. She unfolded it and saw "You blush more than anyone I've ever seen" in quick handwriting. She blushed again, and heard him laugh, a quiet masculine laugh.

I'm in love, she decided. He was *really* sexy. Forget Rick Hamilton. She looked at him, admiring the blond hair and charm-school smile. He dressed right too. Most of the other boys were wearing shirts and sweaters, but he had on faded, not too faded, jeans and a blue-and-white rugby shirt. They sold that kind at home—long-sleeved, with material like soft sailcloth, and she had a sudden desire to touch his arm, wanting to feel the material. Boy, was he handsome. He probably had a girlfriend.

She watched him from behind, studying the wide shoulders and the muscles that showed through his shirt. Very handsome. Very, very handsome. A 9.3. No higher because she had never given a 10, and she wanted to leave the possibility open. He was a strong 9 though.

She squinted at the board, scribbling down "IGNORANCE IS STRENGTH" on the clean, neatly dated page in her notebook. Before long, there would be drawings of cats, concentric circles, and small figures running or skiing, but right now, it was very neat. That made her nervous, and she scrawled a fast cat curled up on a rug. It was out of proportion and very ugly, but relieved the perfection of the page.

Sometimes. She drew a flag proclaiming "War is Peace." Sometimes she had these really graphic thoughts. Not often—she tried not to encourage them, but sometimes —like if she saw someone really, really handsome—like she had a feeling that she was about to have some good ones. It was kind of funny that people could have graphic thoughts without really having a frame of reference. It was like this movie she had seen once where this character was going on and on about sex and passion and that sort of thing, and another character said, "How do *you* know?" "Well," the first character admitted shyly, "I read a lot."

Once, when she was thirteen, she was in her parents' room—putting on makeup because no one else was home—and she found a copy of *The Sensuous Woman,* which she hid in her room and studied at great length. It was more confusing than informative, and one night when her mother was home and they were alone in the sitting room, she asked her if she were a sensuous woman. Her mother, who was drinking wine before dinner, choked, and then laughed for about ten minutes.

"What do *you* think?" she'd asked finally.

Meg wasn't sure how to answer.

Then, her mother had gotten serious, and they discussed Sex in much more detail than the time her mother explained that there was going to be a little sister or brother because she and Meg's father loved each other so much. Meg had never gotten the connection. She was given one of those *A Doctor Talks to . . .* books, which was equally obscure, and she forgot about sex until the night she got her period and her father had to deal with it because her mother was in Washington. He was very calm, seemed proud, but kept turning red. He'd hurried out to the store, returning with several brands of pads and tampons so she could choose. In retrospect, it was kind of funny to imagine what the clerk in the store must have thought of this man who was buying out the feminine protection department. Meg hadn't been able to decide which was best and called her mother for suggestions. Tampons weren't as easy as the directions led her to believe, and she'd had to practice for a few months before catching on. Until then, she had been convinced that she was deformed, which her mother assured her she wasn't, finally offering to take her to a gynecologist so she could get an expert opinion. The idea of *that* was so embarrassing that Meg immediately learned how to use them, never mentioning the problem again. It took a long time to go through all the boxes her father had gotten.

She heard Mrs. Simpson asking a question and looked up, realizing that she had been in this school for about twenty minutes and was already having trouble paying attention. Junior year was the most important, at least according to guidance counselors, and she had to make sure she kept up her average. She also wanted to reflect well on the Administration. Of course, being the President's daughter, she would undoubtedly get in anywhere she applied to college, but it would be nice to get in, or not, on her own merits. Nice, but probably a moot point. Since Harvard was a Vaughn tradition and they would be sixth generation, either she or one of her brothers was going to have to go there. Maybe she would make Steven go. She would rather be at some little school in the mountains where no one would know who she was. She glanced around the room, seeing almost everyone sneaking looks at her. She would rather go *anywhere* where no one knew who she was.

"Hard to pay attention the first day," Mrs. Simpson said, smiling at her.

Realizing that the bell had just rung, Meg blushed. "Kind of," she said in a low voice.

"Well, we're very happy to have you in here."

Wait until you get to know me. "Thank you," Meg said, still blushing. She gathered up her books, feeling scared again. Her next class was U.S. history, Room 217. Thank God Jeff was out in the hall—at least, she'd never have to worry about walking alone.

"Hi," a chubby blond girl said. "I'm Gail. Do we call you Meg?"

Meg shrugged affirmatively, shyly.

"What's it like, living in the White House?" another girl asked, most of the class still in the room.

"Uh, I don't know." Meg shifted her books, flustered. "Big. Very big."

"Do you get to go wherever you want?"

"I thought you had guards."

"Do you get waited on?"

This was like reporters. Worse even. She gripped her books, too intimidated to answer right away.

"Toldja the kid'd be a snob," she heard a boy mutter, heading for the door.

"It's, um"—her voice still wasn't coming out right, "it's kind of weird, I guess." That's it, Meggo. Nice and articulate.

"Hadn't you all better get along to class?" Mrs. Simpson suggested from the front of the room.

People started for the door and Meg let a small relieved breath escape, arms relaxing around her books.

"Hi." The boy with the rugby shirt came over, a confident hand stuck out. "Adam Miller."

"Hi." She tried to shake his hand just right, not holding on too long, not letting go too quickly. What a production. She let go. "I'm Meg Powers." Except that he already knew that.

"Oh, yeah?" he asked. "How do you feel about being called Meghan?"

She was definitely in love.

"Must be something, living in the White House." He held the door for her.

"I guess. I—it doesn't seem very real yet." She smiled nervously at Jeff, and he stood up, ready to follow her to her next class. "Hi. Um, Adam, this is Jeff Traynor. Jeff, this is Adam Miller."

"Hi." Adam glanced at her, "Friend of yours?"

She nodded. "My husband. He's very possessive."

Adam looked surprised, maybe not expecting her to have a sense of humor, then laughed.

"Where are you going now?" he asked, his voice very interested.

"History. It's in two-seventeen."

"So'm I. Let me see your schedule."

She handed him the little card, and he ran down the list, nodding.

"You're going to have the same kids from English in almost all of your classes." He gave her back the card.

"What, were you a brain at your old school?" He grinned. "Or do your parents have pull?"

"Um, well—" Meg wasn't quite sure how to answer that.

"These're the stairs up here." He turned left, Jeff close behind them. "He always follow you around?"

"Kind of, yeah."

"What happens if you go out or something?"

"I don't know." Did that mean he maybe wanted to ask her out sometime? She would probably die. Too bad she couldn't take his picture and mail it to Beth and Sarah.

"This is it up here." He pointed down the crowded hall. "Patterson—he's the teacher—he's been looking forward to you coming for days."

"Oh, yeah?"

"Oh, yeah." He smiled, holding the door.

She smiled back. Nice teeth, very nice teeth. Nice mouth too. He probably never had chapped lips in his life—she should stop looking at his mouth already. She should look at his eyes, you were supposed to look at people's eyes. Very nice mouth though.

"Hope you're ready to tell about 'your experiences,' " Adam went on. "He's really into it."

"My experiences?" Meg forgot about his mouth.

"Yeah. He can't wait."

She made an effort to keep her sigh inaudible.

CHAPTER TWENTY-ONE

Mr. Patterson *did* want her to share her experiences—it was almost like being home again. As usual, she stuttered a lot and couldn't think of anything to say. Why did they always do that? On the first day even.

Barry and Jeff switched at lunchtime, Barry taking a position on one side of the cafeteria. What a job.

Adam brought her over to his table and spent five minutes introducing her to everyone: Gail, blond and chubby; Matt, black-haired, wearing a Georgetown sweatshirt; Phyllis who had suspicious eyes and kept her arm locked through the arm of a tall, very good-looking black guy, Nathan; Zachary, almost as good-looking; Alison, who was wearing a tie, reminiscent of Annie Hall; and Josh, a boy with brown hair and somewhat darker brown glasses, who ate with quick motions, either tense because she was there—probably *not*—or just generally tense. But his sweater was pretty nice—argyle and all.

Keep them straight, she ordered herself, wishing she had her mother's ability to memorize names.

"Whatsa matter, Josh?" the boy in the Georgetown sweatshirt—Mike? Matt?—asked. "Where's the jokes?"

"What jokes?" Josh concentrated on his sandwich, nervously shy.

"Usually we can never get him to shut up," Adam said, taking a napkin out of the holder, brushing her arm with his.

What a nice arm. She wanted to grab him—throw him down, and kiss him. *That* would attract attention. She glanced at Josh to take her mind off these graphic thoughts, and he flushed and dropped his sandwich, both of them looking away. With her luck, he would be the one who ended up liking her.

"Hey," Alison noticed her brown paper bag, "who packed your lunch?"

"Your mother?" Adam asked and they all laughed.

"No, um, I did," Meg said.

"You mean, a chef did," Phyllis corrected her.

"No, I did. See, I always figure—" She stopped, wishing she could just crumple herself up, along with the bag, and get rid of the whole conversation.

"What?" Matt asked when she didn't go on.

"It doesn't matter, it's pretty stupid." Looking around, she saw that they wanted her to finish. "See, the thing is—I guess I'm repressed or neurotic or something, I don't know—but I can't stand tomato seeds. And just about everyone puts tomatoes on sandwiches, so I always make my own, so I can take the seeds out."

"How do you do that?" Gail asked dubiously.

"Just cut off the top and—" Meg pantomimed squeezing a tomato, then blushed, realizing that they all probably thought she was a maniac.

"Like this kid here." Zachary pointed at Josh with a half-eaten apple. "He won't eat hot dogs or bologna or anything."

"Are you kosher?" Meg asked him.

"N-no, only at Passover." He didn't meet her eyes. "I saw a film about how they make all that stuff, and I kind of haven't been able to eat it since."

"The film was probably fifty years old," Matt snorted.

"Beef lips?" Josh looked up in sudden animation. "You like to eat beef lips? And hearts? And—"

"Enough already," Nathan said. "I got a sandwich to finish here." He frowned at his bologna sandwich, then bit off about a third of it.

He *was* cute, Meg decided. No wonder that kid Phyllis was hanging on to him. Oh, God, if looks could kill, she had just gotten one. Meg Powers, femme fatale. What a joke.

"What's that?" Matt demanded.

Meg looked at the Baggie of delicate cookies in her hand. "What do you mean?"

"Did someone bake them, or do they buy them, or what?"

"Uh, they were leftover."

"Leftover?" Gail asked.

"There was a reception yesterday, and there was some stuff leftover." Meg put the Baggie down, too embarrassed to eat now.

"Did the chefs bake them?" Matt asked.

"I guess so." She held out the Baggie. "You want some?"

"Yeah. Can I?"

"Sure."

"Anyone else want some?" she asked uncertainly.

Just about everyone did, so she put the Baggie in the middle of the table. Even Phyllis took one. Meg took a bite out of one of the two that were left. They weren't even all that great—she'd take a good Oreo any day.

It was a relief when school ended, and she could go home. Today she had felt like a deer in a zoo, having everyone come up to the fence, then say nervously, "Does it bite?" Some guy had held the door for her as she left French class, and two girls had given her incredible scowls. Being the President's daughter was a royal pain. Why couldn't her parents own a vegetable stand or something?

When they got back to the White House, she couldn't decide what to do. She talked to Willy, the doorman, for a few minutes, then went down to the East Room to play the piano for a while. She played "Greensleeves," which really was the only song she knew, then the first half of "Hill Street Blues," the first nine bars of "Deck the Halls," and the introduction to "No Business Like Show Business." Her repertoire exhausted, except for the last part of "Mapleleaf Rag," which she quickly played, she got up from the piano and went to sit in the Green Room. She lounged in a Sheraton mahogany armchair, resting her feet on an undoubtedly priceless New York sofa table. After a few minutes of that, she got bored and decided to go to the East Wing and see if her father was busy.

She took time to lie down on a yellow Hepplewhite sofa in the Diplomatic Reception Room, then continued to the East Wing. Preston was just coming out of his office, singing "I Got Rhythm," pausing to twirl her around twice, still singing, before continuing down the hall.

"Have you seen my father?" she asked.

"He's being bourgeois with *Gentleman's Quarterly.*"

"He's reading?"

Preston grinned. "He's being interviewed. How was school?"

"Everyone stared at me."

"Did you stare back?"

She nodded.

"Good. Remember what I always say, you should never—"

"Preston?" A woman on his staff came out of an office. "I have ABC on the line."

"Tell them I'm on my way." He smiled back. "Philosophy later, kid."

She smiled back. "I'll hold my breath."

"Do that. I'll tell the father you were down here."

"Thanks." She watched him go, then tried to figure out what she was going to do next. She *could* go down to the Oval Office, but her mother would be busy, and she would be in the way.

The Oval Office was very impressive. Her mother had taken them in there the second day, and it was the kind of room that made Meg stand up straight. It had been redecorated, her mother giving the room a soft blue emphasis, and there were quiet hints of gold to coordinate with the Presidential seal. There were two darker blue couches and a low walnut table in front of the fireplace, a fireplace her mother planned to keep burning for the rest of the winter. How very rustic. There was a huge, mostly blue, impressionistic painting by Childe Hassam in the White House collection, and her mother had had it hung over the fireplace, replacing the stern male statesman that had been there.

The desk was dark gleaming oak, and on it her mother had a telephone, a thick appointment book, a leather pen set,

a primitive clay paperweight—it was supposed to be a cat—
that Meg had made when she was nine, and an ashtray that
Steven had made. Not that her mother smoked. Instead, she
used it for paper clips and things.

"What about me?" Neal had asked, and she had shown
him the framed drawing that was going up on the wall.

"What about me?" Meg's father asked, and her mother
grinned at him. Her parents might be under a lot of pressure
lately, but they sure seemed to be getting a kick out of each
other. Thank God.

There were pictures of everyone—including Kirby and
the cats—on the table behind the desk and the tall, black
chair. It was Meg's opinion that the school pictures of her
brothers and the one of her were absolutely horrendous. Her
mother liked them.

"How come there's one of everyone but you?" Steven
asked her, studying the pictures and laughing uproariously
at the one of Meg with braces.

"I know what I look like," her mother said. "I want to
feel as if you all are keeping me company all day."

Going upstairs to the family quarters, Meg decided that
her mother wanted figurative company, not literal. She
found Steven and Neal in the solarium, drinking Coke, eating brownies, and watching a *Brady Bunch* rerun. That was
so refreshingly normal that she flopped down on the couch
next to them.

"How was school for you guys?" she asked.

Steven belched.

"Me too," Meg agreed. "How about you, Neal?"

Neal giggled and tried to burp, making a noise that was
more like a squeak.

"Absolutely," Meg said. She looked at the television.
"Which one is this?"

"Jan gets glasses."

Steven held out the back of his right hand for her to exam-
ine.

"What am I looking at?"

He sighed deeply and indicated the bruised knuckle.

"Oh, God, Steven, what did you do?"

"Some guy said I looked like a fag in my tie." He grinned. "Guess *he* won't be bugging me anymore."

"Steven, you can't go around hitting everyone who makes you mad."

"Why not? Gets 'em off me."

"Yeah, but—" Meg stopped, not having any way to contradict that. "What did your agents do?"

"Broke it up and yelled at us."

"Did you get in trouble?"

"Nah, no teachers around." He put most of a brownie in his mouth. "Kid'sa nice guy," he said with his mouth full. "Said he plays baseball. They have like a school team."

Meg looked at Neal. "What about you? Did you hit anyone?"

Neal giggled and shook his head.

"Girl tried to kiss him," Steven said.

"Really?" Meg looked at her little brother. "What did you do?"

"Let her," Steven said. "What else?"

"Really?"

"On the lips," Neal giggled.

"Said she was pretty." Steven gave Kirby half a brownie, Kirby thumping his tail and going under the coffee table to eat it.

Neal nodded, giggling.

"My God." Meg shook her head. "Rocky and Romeo."

"What did you do today, Meggie?" Neal asked.

"Nothing much."

"The boys all thought you were ugly, hunh?" Steven said.

"Looks that way."

"But you're not," Neal said.

"Is that an expert opinion?" Meg smiled at him, then gestured toward the television. "What's on after this?"

Steven checked the *TV Guide*. "*Gilligan's Island*."

"Which one is it?"

"The one where they eat radioactive vegetables."

"Great," Meg said. "I love that one."

* * *

School wasn't working out to be quite as bad as she had anticipated. In a couple of classes, like French and chemistry, she was ahead; in most of the others, she was just about even. She had some catch-up reading to do in English, and her new trigonometry book was sort of confusing, but she figured she would just put extra time into those two subjects for a while.

Most of the people in her classes were either still intimidated or else asking constant questions. And girls were being very possessive with their boyfriends. It didn't look as if she was going to be making female friends any time soon.

Adam, on the other hand, was still very attentive. Sometimes she had the uneasy feeling that he had staked her out and that it was more of a prestige thing than anything else, but since she had a pretty irreversible crush on him, she pushed away any suspicions easily convincing herself that they would be a perfect couple. Now all she had to do was convince him.

Then one Tuesday he asked her out. It was a Tuesday and he wanted to know if she could go to a movie or something on Friday.

"Um, yeah," she answered, trying not to sound as excited as she felt. "That would be nice."

"How's it work?" He glanced back at Barry, a few feet behind them in the hall.

"I'm not sure." She glanced back too. "I think they have to follow me in another car."

"Do they come in the movies and everything?"

"I think they have to."

"What if we go somewhere after?"

"Um, I guess they have to sit at another table."

Adam didn't say anything.

"Well, we don't have to go if you don't want to," she said, trying not to sound as hurt as she felt.

"That's not what I meant." He shifted his weight. "I don't know. It's just kind of weird."

"It's not my fault."

"Yeah, yeah, I know." He kicked at the floor with one Top-Sider, hands sulkily moving into his pockets.

Adam, don't turn out to be a jerk. She didn't want to find out that he was a jerk.

"It's just—" He touched her shoulder, moving his hand down her arm and she felt a warm tremor of excitement in her back, trying to repress threatening graphic thoughts, trying not to move closer to him. "I wanted to be alone with you."

He wasn't a jerk, she knew he wasn't a jerk. He *did* like her.

"Well, how do I pick you up?" he asked. "Will they let me in?"

"If I tell them you're coming."

"Okay. Seven-thirty sound good?"

Six in the morning would sound good.

"Yeah," she said. "It sounds fine."

CHAPTER TWENTY-TWO

Her parents didn't react the way she had expected. Her father pulled the possessive-father act, as if not sure that anyone was good enough to take out *his* daughter. Her mother looked worried, saying that she wasn't very happy about the idea either. Meg found this extremely annoying. She had been talking about him for days—where had they been?

"So what am I supposed to do?" she asked her mother that night after Steven and Neal had gone to bed. "Tell him I'm sorry, but my parents won't let me go?"

"I didn't say you couldn't go." Her mother lowered the papers she was studying. "I said that your father and I didn't like the idea of your going out with some boy we haven't met."

"So, it's my fault you aren't going to be home?"

"Last I heard, you were coming to the play *with* us," her mother said calmly.

"But Adam asked me out. God," Meg shook her head. "Don't you understand anything?"

"Probably more than you think."

"I didn't say I was definitely going to the play, I said maybe. Then, when he asked me, I forgot. Is that why you're mad?"

Her mother put the papers down. "There's a very simple solution to all of this. As I said before, invite him to dinner on Thursday, and that way, your father and I will get a chance to meet him before you go out."

"I can't do that." Meg sat in a Kennedyesque rocking chair, very discouraged. She had expected her parents to be pleased and send her off with their blessing. It had never occurred to her that they might not let her go.

"Why can't you do that?"

"That might scare him off—to have to come here and sit through dinner and everything."

"What's wrong with us?" her mother asked, smiling.

"Oh, forget it." Meg picked up the *National Geographic*. "You don't understand anything."

"Meg, I'm sure he's a perfectly nice boy, but there are a lot of strange people out there, you're in a highly visible position, and can't you understand why your father and I might be a little concerned?"

"I'm going to have two stupid guards with me," Meg pointed out. "How much safer can I get?"

"Granted, but—" Her mother sighed. "What can you tell me about him? The only thing we've heard is that he's handsome."

"I don't know. He plays football."

"That's it? That's all you know? Where does he live, what do his parents do? Is he a good driver?"

"I think his father works for the FCC," Meg said uncertainly.

"And that's all you know?"

"We don't talk about that kind of stuff." Meg said, aware that she wasn't making a very good case for herself.

"What *do* you talk about?"

"Sex, drugs, liquor. You know how it is."

"If you're trying to reassure me, Meg, it's not working," her mother said.

"What do you want to hear?" Meg asked. "My God, we're only going to a movie. I'm even going to have two stupid chaperones. How much trouble can I get into?"

"Probably not very much." Her mother sighed again. "I still don't like the idea."

"But I can go?"

"I suppose so. I suppose," her mother fingered her coffee mug with one hand, "that I should trust your judgment."

"Yeah," Meg agreed. "Don't worry, he really is nice."

"And handsome?" her mother asked wryly.

"Very handsome."

* * *

Her father wasn't too happy that her mother had given in, saying that if the boy was really all right, he wouldn't mind putting it off until they could meet him, but Meg won him over with the agents-as-chaperones argument. Needless to say, she didn't tell Adam that her parents were uptight about the whole thing.

Friday, in the locker-room after gym class, Alison MacGregor, the girl who reminded her of Annie Hall, came over to talk to her, both her expression and her voice hesitant.

"Hi," she said, very chic in baggy pants, an oversized Oxford shirt, and a man's vest.

"Hi," Meg said, her smile shy, hoping that this girl, who seemed like one of the nicer people she had met at this school, was going to treat her normally.

"I hate gym," Alison said. "Don't you?"

"Yeah, really," Meg said. "How many times can you play volleyball?"

"Last fall we did square dancing."

"Sorry I missed it."

"That's what *you* think." Alison shifted her weight. She started to say something, then stopped. "You look a lot like your mother," she said finally.

"Yeah, kind of."

"Kind of a lot." Alison shifted again.

"Um," Meg was starting to get uneasy too, "is there something wrong?"

"No, it's just—"

The bell rang, and both of them automatically looked at the clock.

"We'd better get to French," Alison said.

"It's just what?"

"Nothing."

Meg sighed. Adjusting her knapsack on her shoulder, and started for the door.

"Wait a minute." Alison caught up to her.

Meg paused.

"I was new last year," Alison said.

"Oh yeah?"

"It takes people a while to loosen up."

"How long?"

Alison laughed. "Is it really that bad?"

"It's not that great."

"It'd probably be easier if you looked like your father instead."

"What—you mean, masculine?"

Alison laughed again. "No. Just so it would be easier for people to forget, you know?"

"I guess." Meg pushed the door open and saw her agent's somewhat relieved expression. "Hi."

Jeff nodded. "Hi."

Seeing Adam moving down the hall, Meg moved her hair back over her shoulders, hoping that she looked all right. She should have checked the mirror in the locker-room.

"Do you like him that much?" Alison asked.

Meg blushed. "He seems like a nice guy," she said, not committing herself, managing not to stare as he came down the hall. How could any human being be that incredibly good-looking? She glanced at Alison. "Don't you think so?"

"Yeah. Sure." Her voice wasn't very convincing.

"Hi," Adam said, his grin both charming and sensual.

"Hi," Meg said. She smiled back shyly, hoping that she wasn't as flushed as she felt, flushing more as he slid his arm around her waist. "Adam, come on." She pushed at his hand. "Don't."

He grinned. "Why not?"

"I guess I'll see you guys later," Alison said, edging away.

"Well, wait—" Meg started, but Alison had already joined some other people from their gym class and was heading down the hall. She turned back to Adam, noticing that she was much closer, his other hand on her shoulder. "Come on, don't," she said, knowing that her arms wanted very much to go around his neck, to have him kiss her no matter *what* anyone else thought.

"Why not?" he asked, leaning closer.

"Everyone's looking."

"Yeah," he glanced around, grinning, "So?"

"Just don't, okay?" She pulled free, very embarrassed.

He shrugged, put his arm back around her waist, and walked her down the hall toward class.

She saw her parents and brothers off to the play that night, her mother warned her to be careful, still not looking happy about any of this; her father warned her not to give her agents any trouble and to be home by midnight. Steven had been giving his agents trouble lately, like trying to escape from them, and her parents weren't too pleased about it. To say nothing of the agents.

She took a shower, then paced around her bedroom, trying to decide what to wear. Adam was the type who would show up in a jacket, maybe even a tie, so she ended up wearing a skirt and the grey cashmere sweater she had gotten for Christmas. She put on some perfume—too much?—grabbed her Bloomingdale's coat from the closet and went downstairs to wait for him. He was supposed to be coming to the North Entrance, so she decided to wait in the Red Room, sitting on the American Empire sofa that had legs in the shape of what Meg thought were very unattractive gold dolphins. She checked the clock above the mantelpiece several times, drumming on the red damask arm of the sofa with her right hand, getting more and more nervous about this date as it got closer.

Promptly at seven-thirty, a butler appeared.

"Mr. Miller has arrived, Miss Powers," he said.

"Oh." She stopped drumming. "Thank you."

"Should I show him in?"

"No, thank you. I'll come out." She stood up, checked her reflection in the window, and went out to the entrance hall.

He was standing by the main door, wearing, indeed, a jacket, with a tie underneath his sweater.

"Hi," he said. "I mean, hello." His eyes went down her outfit. "You look nice."

"Thank you," Meg said. "So do you."

"Your family isn't home?" he asked and said.

"They went to a play at the Kennedy Center."

They stood awkwardly for a minute, not looking at each other.

"Guess we should probably be going," he said.

"Yeah." Meg nodded, relieved that he hadn't asked her to take him on a tour or something. She'd feel like a jerk doing that, even though she could tell from his expression that he wanted one. "My parents are going to be home around eleven or so. Maybe after you can come up and meet them. They were sorry they had to miss you."

"Sounds good," he said, nodding.

They didn't say anything else until they were in his car, pulling out of the long driveway, her agents in a car behind them. He glanced over, now not shy about letting his eyes move.

"You look good," he said.

She blushed, focusing out through the windshield.

"You sure this movie is okay with you?"

"Oh, yeah," she lied. When they had made the plans, he suggested going to one of the ax murder movies Hollywood was always churning out. He'd obviously wanted to go, so she agreed without blinking, even though she would be much happier at the revival of *The Philadelphia Story*. He probably wouldn't be so thrilled by that idea. At dinner, her father had asked what movie they planned to see, and when she told him, he frowned, exchanging glances with her mother who asked if it had been her idea or Adam's, Meg feigned confusion and changed the subject by asking her to please pass the salt.

She should have suggested *The Philadelphia Story* though. Granted, the White House had that private theater, and they could get just about any movie, so she could see it anytime she wanted, but the thought of going to a really gratuitously violent movie wasn't very appealing. She should have said that she wanted to go to *The Philadelphia Story*.

"Why you sitting way over there?"

"Am I?" she asked.

"Yeah. Come on, move over." He patted the seat next to him.

Meg looked at him, at the seat, then behind her at the car with her agents, and didn't move.

"What," he gestured with his head toward the rear of the car, "you uptight about them?"

"Kind of." She looked through the windshield at the crowded city streets, ignoring the battle the emotional and intellectual parts of her head were having. The emotional part was insisting that he was really nice, really handsome, really everything, while the intellectual side was saying very quietly that he was kind of a jerk, and she ought to face up to it.

"You okay?" he asked.

"What? Oh, sure."

"You look good tonight." He reached over and touched her face with his right hand. "I wasn't kidding."

"Thank you." she said, feeling her intellectual arguments weaken. Yes, Adam, flattery will get you everywhere.

The theater was very large, and they had no trouble finding seats. They could go where they wanted as long as her agents could sit a few rows behind them. Adam chose seats far over on one side, letting her go in first.

"You want popcorn or anything?" he asked, taking off his jacket.

"If you do."

"Am I allowed to leave you to go get some?"

"They're right back there."

He nodded wryly, heading out of the row and up the aisle, returning with a medium popcorn. He settled back into his seat, putting his arm around her as soon as the lights went down, and she spent the first few minutes of this movie, thinking about how much she liked the opposite sex and how great their arms felt. She felt warm, she felt safe, she felt very female, she felt like throwing him down and kissing him. Yeah, the emotional argument was winning.

"You still here?" he asked, pulling her closer.

"What? Oh, yeah."

"You like it?"

She nodded, looking up at the screen, seeing that the movie was in the middle of its third embarrassing sex scene which, if the plot stuck to its current course, would end with the beautiful girl lying on the floor in a pool of blood. She closed her eyes.

His hand was creeping down from her shoulder and she moved, avoiding it. She really didn't want him to turn into a jerk. His hand tried only once more, then got the hint, staying on her shoulder.

The fourth murder was particularly offensive, and even Adam seemed uncomfortable.

"I didn't know it was going to be this bad," he whispered.

"It's not that bad," she said bravely.

"It's awful." He glanced over his shoulder, then at her, moving closer. "You really do look good tonight."

"Well, so do you." She also glanced over her shoulder, sensing that he was about to kiss her, wondering if her agents would be able to see. The place was uncrowded enough so that no one else would notice, and they were way over on the side anyway. Did she really want him to kiss her so much that she was willing to do it here? The answer was very easy, and she blushed in the darkness. Better to have him kiss her here in the dark theater than in the car with her agents right behind them. They were behind her here too, but it was different—they were a few seats over and could pay attention to the movie.

"Come here," he whispered.

"What?"

He turned her face to him and kissed her, one hand on her cheek. She couldn't keep back a quick, shuddering sigh of relief, having been wanting him to do that ever since she'd met him, then pulled her head away, embarrassed as well as startled by the intensity of her reaction.

"You okay?"

She nodded, blushing, and as he kissed her again, she let a tentative hand move up into his hair, kind of—embarrassingly enough—new at all of this. She opened her eyes, seeing that his were closed, turning her head just enough to see if her agents were watching, which they weren't, thank God. His breathing was faster, and she hoped that it was something *she* had done and not just puberty. His arms were warm around her, and she noticed how good he smelled; he was wearing some kind of really sexy aftershave. And—his hand was up underneath her sweater. She flinched, surprised that it felt so good, surprised that he had managed it so deftly. But this was the first time they'd ever—and they were sitting in a movie and—she really couldn't let him—

"Adam, don't," she whispered.

"Hunh?"

"Come on, don't." She pushed his hand down, looking around to make sure no one was watching or listening.

"Why not?"

"Because I don't want you to."

"Why not?" he insisted.

"Because it's—I mean, because we're—" She tried to think of a way to explain it. "I just don't."

"I don't believe it." He sat back in his seat, scowling up at the screen, and Meg sat back too, folding defensive arms across her chest.

"We didn't see you as a tease," he said quietly.

"I'm not!"

"You led me on."

"I did not!"

"Yeah, well, guess we didn't see you as being frigid either." He watched the fifth murder.

"I'm not—" She stopped, shoulders crumpling. "You said 'we.' "

"So what?"

"Oh, God." She turned her head away, not trusting her expression, fumbling for her coat.

"What are you doing?"

She got up and put on her coat, walking—almost running—up the aisle, and her agents jumped up to follow her.

"Meg?" One of them caught up to her in the lobby. "What's wrong?"

"I don't feel very good." She didn't look at him, fighting

back a strong urge to burst into tears. "I think I'd better go home."

Adam hurried out after them. "Meg, what are you doing?"

"I have to go home. I don't feel very good."

"You're gonna leave? Just like that?"

She didn't answer, just pushed the door open and stepped outside.

"You're not gonna let me drive you?"

"I have a ride." She kept walking.

"Meg, come on." He touched her arm, and she shook his hand off. "Look, let me drive you, okay? I'm sorry."

"I have a ride."

"Okay, okay, look." He glanced at the agents following them. "Just get in my car for a second. I have to talk to you, okay?"

She hesitated.

"Just for a second, okay?"

She thought about that, then got into his car, staying close to the passenger's door.

"Look, uh—" He put his keys in the ignition, then turned to face her. "I'm sorry. What did I do?"

"Did you ask me out because of *who* I am?"

"No, I—" He shifted uneasily. "I mean, it's not that you're not—"

She nodded stiffly and opened the door.

"Meg, wait." He put his hand on her arm. "I didn't meant it that way—it was before you even came. Everyone figured you might go with me, and then we could—"

"Find out how far I went?"

"No, I—" He stopped. "Well, sort of."

"Terrific." She shook his hand off. "Make sure you tell them."

"Meg, come on." He moved his hand to her shoulder and she shrugged it away. "I really am sorry. I like you. I didn't know I was going to—I thought you'd be a snob. But I like you. When we started fooling around, I didn't even think about those guys. I kissed you because I wanted to. Really."

She nodded, pushing the door all the way open.

"Well, can we try again sometime? I'd like to."

"Well, I wouldn't." She got out, very stiff. "Tell your friends that too."

"Look, at least let me—"

She slammed the door, ran over to her agents' car and got into the back.

"Is everything—?" one of her evening agents started.

"Just take me home, okay?" She folded her arms. "I mean, please."

The other agent nodded and started the engine.

CHAPTER TWENTY-THREE

At the White House, she went directly upstairs to her room, took off her coat and put it on the bed. She'd checked with the doorman and her family wasn't home yet. Of course, why would they be home? It was only ten. She took off her sweater and skirt, slamming them onto her closet floor, and changed into a battered, too big chamois shirt, a pair of very old navy blue sweatpants, and her hiking boots. At the kitchen door, she met Felix at the door.

"Did you have a nice time?" he asked, smiling.

"Yeah." With great effort, she smiled back. "Do you think I could have a Tab, please?"

She took the glass, smiling her thanks, and carried it up to the solarium, where she could be alone for a while. She sat on one of the couches, knowing that she was going to cry but afraid to start.

To distract herself, she turned on the television, then slouched down to stare at the last half of a very inane movie. She was going to call Beth, but remembered that it was Friday night and any *normal* person her age had friends and was out with them. She sipped her Tab, occasional tears sliding out and down her cheeks, tears she didn't bother wiping away.

At around eleven-fifteen, by which point she had given up on television and was just plain crying, she heard footsteps in the hall and quickly dragged her sleeve across her face to get rid of any traces of tears.

"Hi," her mother said.

Meg didn't look at her. "When'd you come home?"

"Just a few minutes ago. Felix told me you came in, but I wasn't sure where you were."

Meg didn't answer, drinking Tab.

"Do you want to tell me about it?"

"About what?" Meg looked up at her mother, who was, naturally, ravishing in a slim red velvet dress. So beautiful, in fact, that Meg felt a strong, unexpected flash of hatred, hating her for always looking and being so perfect.

Her mother must have felt something because she paused on her way across the room. "May I keep you company?"

"Why? So you can gloat?"

"I don't think you mean that."

Meg scowled and folded her arms across her chest as her mother moved Kirby off the couch and sat down, neither of them speaking; Meg scowling, her mother brushing at an invisible piece of lint on her sleeve.

"Well?" Meg said finally. "Aren't you going to say I told you so?"

"No. What happened?"

"He only asked me out because of you, okay? You were right, are you happy?" Meg clenched her right fist, feeling tears trying to get out.

"I'm sorry." Her mother put her arm around her.

"Don't!" Meg moved away. "Please don't touch me."

Her mother slowly withdrew her arm. "I want to help you. What can I do?"

Meg shook her head, bringing her right hand up to cover her eyes, the flow of tears starting again.

"I really am sorry." Her mother reached over to rub her back. "I wish I could—"

"I just want to be by myself," Meg said, feeling the tears come harder, not wanting anyone to see them. "Please?"

"Oh, Meg." Her mother kept rubbing her back. "I don't want to leave you alone."

"You have been for sixteen years. Why stop now?"

There was a silence so silent that Meg was sure she could hear both their hearts beating, especially hers.

Why had she said that? She never should have said that. "Mom," her heart was loud in her ears, "I'm sorry, I didn't mean to say that, I don't know why I said that."

Her mother sat back, looking suddenly smaller, her face expressionless.

"I'm sorry, I didn't mean it."

"I expect you must have," her mother said, so quietly that Meg almost couldn't hear her. She stood up, her eyes as distant as a *Time* magazine photograph. "Excuse me."

As she started toward the door, Meg knew she didn't want her to leave first, knew she'd be afraid to go downstairs if she did. She jumped up, getting to the door first and running downstairs to her room, running inside and slamming the door, leaning against it, too out of breath to cry.

Why had she said that? She shouldn't have said that. She should have just said she hated her or something. Lots of people said they hated their parents when they were angry, and her mother would know that she hadn't really meant it. And she hadn't. Well, she had, but not really. It just came out. How come, when you were hurt, you had to turn around and hurt someone else? A hell of a thing to know about yourself.

Slowly, she pushed away from the door, realizing that she was crying again. She hadn't even shouted it in anger—she had said it calmly, maliciously. Vindictively. Somehow that made it worse. Anyone could get mad and yell things. Nothing like going for someone's weak spot though.

She sat down on the bed, taking off her hiking boots and sweatpants, then getting under the covers and reaching up to turn the light off. She lay on her back in the darkness, staring at the chandelier, tears sliding down her cheeks, into the pillow. She lay there, feeling a lot of tired hatred, almost all of it directed toward herself.

The next morning, she was afraid to go to breakfast. Only she would have to face her sooner or later. So, she got up, took a shower, put on jeans and a thick ragg sweater, and went out to the Presidential Dining Room with its stupid wallpaper. She paused at the door, seeing her parents at the table, eating silently. They glanced up, neither looking very happy to see her.

Her father. She had forgotten about her father. He was probably ten times angrier than her mother was. She backed up toward the hall, afraid to sit down, figuring she would just skip breakfast.

"Meggie, come on!" Neal pushed her from behind, trying to get in, so she took a deep breath and went over to sit in her usual place.

"Morning." Neal hugged their father. "Hi, Mommy." He went up to the other end of the table, fastening his arms around their mother's waist.

"Hi, Neal." She hugged him back, her face hidden by her hair as she kissed the top of his head.

Meg tentatively checked her father's eyes, found them very cold, and focused on her place setting.

"What would you like for breakfast?" a butler asked.

"Just cereal, please," she said, not looking up.

"What kind?"

"Uh," she tried to think of a brand, "Rice Krispies."

Once she had her cereal, she tried to eat, but her stomach felt like lead. Neal kept up a high-pitched, running conversation about the play they had seen the night before, which he had apparently loved.

"And then," he bounced in his chair, "when the man came out and danced, and his friend, his friend came out, and *he* started dancing—"

"Hi." Steven came in, wearing sweatpants and a sweatshirt, which meant that he had a new athletic conditioning plan to get ready for baseball. He took a boxer's stance and gave their father several light quick punches on the arm. "Hi, Pop," he said breezily. Then, he saluted the other end of the table. "Hey, Prez." He sat down, slapping Neal on the head. "How ya doin', brat?" He grinned across the table at Meg. "Betcha looked pretty ugly last night. D'ja have to pay him to take you?"

Something snapped somewhere inside, and Meg jumped up, throwing her cereal and milk at him, then put the bowl down, running out of the room. She saw the surprise on the butler's face, hearing her father's furious, "Meg, get back here!" She didn't stop running down the hall, not sure where to go. She ducked into the Lincoln Bedroom, lay down on the antique bed, wishing that Lincoln's ghost would come along and carry her off.

She knew they wouldn't follow her, and no one did, so

she stayed there for what seemed like a very long time, hands folded behind her head, staring up at the chandelier, which she decided she hated. She hated all of the chandeliers in the house; in fact, she hated every chandelier in the world. They didn't have chandeliers at home, they had lamps. She liked lamps. She lay there, hating chandeliers, sitting up when she heard a gasp.

"Glory, and you startled me, Miss Powers," the maid in the doorway said, holding a dustcloth. "I'm sorry, I didn't expect—I'll just come back later."

"No, I'm finished." Meg got off the bed and smoothed out the wrinkles. "Sorry." She moved out into the East Sitting Hall, not sure where to go now. Well, the longer she put it off, the angrier her father was going to be. She would just go back to her room, where she could lock herself in, and if she ran into him on the way, she could at least find out how angry he was.

He was on one of the couches in the Center Hall, holding the morning *Post,* obviously waiting for her, and she wondered what time it was. Seeing her, he stood up, folded the paper under his arm, and indicated the Presidential Bedroom with one jerk of his head.

"I—I don't feel good," she said. "I have to sleep."

He just looked at her with the cold anger and she swallowed, going into the room. He followed her, closing the door behind him.

He couldn't actually *kill* her. It would be all over the papers.

She sat in a rocking chair from home, and he sat across from her on a small sofa. He put the paper down, folded his hand, and she wondered if he was going to crack his knuckles. Sometimes he did, although it drove her mother crazy. He looked at her, cracking them halfway.

Yeah, he was mad all right.

"I didn't mean it," she said, making an effort not to sound nervous, holding on to the worn wooden arms of the chair.

"Why did you say it then?"

"I was mad."

216

"A little below the belt, don't you think?" His voice was very calm, almost conversational. People in her family didn't raise their voices much.

"Does she, uh, hate me?" she asked, not looking up.

"What do you think?"

Meg shrugged, running her hand along the right arm of the chair.

"Do you hate her?" he asked.

"You know I don't."

"I'm not always convinced."

"As usual," she nodded, watching the bones and muscles of her right hand move as she tightened and loosened her grip on the chair arm, "taking my side."

"Hey!" He grabbed her arms, holding them just above the elbows so she would have to look at him. "Let's get something clear. I don't want any more fresh remarks out of you. Not to your mother, not to me, not to your brothers. Is that clear?"

"You're hurting my arms."

"You know I'm not," he said, but loosened his grip. "Is that quite clear?"

She jerked free, folding her arms.

"Well, it had better be," he said.

"What happens now?" she asked.

"Well, first of all, you're grounded—more because of what you did to your brother than anything else. For two weeks, and if you don't shape up by then, I'll add on more time."

"Just moving here grounded me," she said, standing up.

"Where are you going?"

"I thought we were finished."

"We aren't."

She sat down.

"Look, Meg," he said. "I know you were upset last night. Neither your mother nor I is even exactly sure what happened, but we both know how upset you were. Do you want to tell me about it?"

She shook her head.

"Are you sure?"

She nodded.

"You might feel better."

She shook her head.

"Well, all right, but I think it would make you feel better." He sighed. "I know how difficult it's been for you—it's been difficult for all of us. What it means is that we all have to try harder, especially with each other, okay?"

"I'm sorry," she said stiffly.

"Neal and I aren't the ones who deserve apologies."

She nodded, standing up. "How angry *is* she?"

"She's more hurt than anything else." He let out his breath. "You and I both hit below the belt, Meg. It's something we need to work on."

"Yeah, I guess." She opened the door. "I'll be in my room."

The hall was empty, although she could hear a vacuum cleaner going somewhere on the east end of the floor. She went to her room, closing the door behind her. Vanessa, who had fallen asleep on her chamois shirt, woke up and stretched out a front paw, flexing her claws.

"I wish it were this time yesterday," Meg said, Vanessa purring in response. She took out a book by Rona Jaffe out of her bookcase and flopped down on her bed to read some fun fiction for a change. Vanessa moved up to sleep next to her.

Sometimes, she wished she had a sister. Having a sister would probably have made it easier. Being a son of the first female President meant having a successful courageous mother. Being the only daughter meant having something to live up to. Her mother was beautiful, a phenomenal tennis player, *President*—Meg could never do anything *as* well. It was like she was defeated before she even tried.

She flipped over on her stomach, deciding that all she wanted to do was read for a while. Take a vacation from real life. For weeks, if possible.

At twelve-thirty, there was a knock on the door.

"Do you want lunch?" Neal asked.

She hesitated, deciding in favor of cowardice.

"No, thanks, I'm not hungry."

218

"It's onion soup and stuff."

"Thanks, but I'm not hungry."

"Are you sure?"

Fratricide. She got up, opened the door and looked down at him.

"Neal, I'm just not hungry," she said. "Thanks anyway." She closed the door.

When the next knock came, she was reading an Irwin Shaw.

"May I come in?" her father asked.

"Uh, yeah." She turned over so she would be facing him.

He opened the door, dressed to go out in a dinner jacket and black tie.

"Are you going somewhere?"

"The Palmers' party."

"Oh, right," she remembered.

"They'll have dinner ready for the three of you in about fifteen minutes. We'll be home fairly late, so keep an eye on your brothers."

Meg nodded.

"It might be a good idea for you to go in and say goodbye to your mother."

"Now?"

"I think it would be a good idea."

She got up, following him down to the Presidential Bedroom. The door was open, but Meg knocked.

"Come in," her mother said.

"Uh, hi." Meg went in uneasily, hands going into her pockets.

Her mother nodded, not turning from the mirror.

"You, uh, you look nice."

Her mother nodded again, putting on her earrings.

"I'm sorry."

"Oh?" Now her mother turned, looking less than convinced.

"I really am. I was upset, so I wanted to make someone else upset. I'm sorry, and I didn't mean it."

"Okay." Her mother picked up her brush, but lowered it. "I'm sorry I haven't always been there."

"I told you I didn't mean that."

Her mother lifted the brush to her hair, and Meg eased back toward the door, very uncomfortable.

"Uh, have a nice time." she said.

"Thank you. Please keep an eye on your brothers."

Meg nodded, they looked at each other for a short uneasy second, and Meg left the room.

CHAPTER TWENTY-FOUR

The next day, for the most part, she stayed in her room, sometimes doing homework, mostly just reading. She had apologized to Steven, who seemed to think that getting hit with cereal was funny, but her mother was still distant. It wasn't blatant or calculated, but it was uncomfortable, and Meg felt better in her room, since on Sundays, her mother was generally around all day.

She spent a lot of time worrying about school, dreading having to face people. Adam was sure to have gone around telling everyone, and she didn't know what was worse—having people laugh behind her back or laugh in front of her. Both were sure to happen.

Getting dressed on Monday morning, she thought about Scarlett O'Hara. Scarlett had been caught with Ashley once in what looked like an affair but wasn't, and she had to go to a party that night to face all of Atlanta's society, society that was whispering about her. So, she went looking her best, her attitude a damn-the-torpedos sort of courage. So, Meg decided to look *her* best, an outfit that included her black boots, her Inaugural Day skirt, and a black velvet blazer. She spent a long time blow-drying her hair so that it would be thick, full, and dramatic, sweeping back from her face. What did she care if Adam had spread rumors all over the place? She cared a lot, but no one else was going to know it.

She was at her locker, getting her books before homeroom, when Josh Feldman walked by, eyes nervous behind his glasses but smiling at her.

"H-hi," he said, reddening at the stutter. "How was your weekend?"

Meg stiffened and concentrated on her books, not answering. What was he trying to do—get her off the rebound? What a jerk.

Josh hesitated, saw that she wasn't going to answer, and reddened more, backing away through the morning crush of students.

Except for that beginning lapse, she was careful not to be rude to anyone, but she didn't go out of her way to be friendly either. Adam never spoke to her, his male friends seeming just as embarrassed. She avoided the opposite sex in general, which got her quite a few smiles from girls in her classes. She was in trigonometry, waiting for class to begin, when someone sat next to her.

"Hi," Alison said cheerfully, wearing tapered pants and a large but slimly cut wool blazer with a belt on over it.

"Hi." Meg smiled briefly, then returned to her notes.

"What's with you and Adam?" She gestured up a few rows to where Adam was sitting and laughing with some of his friends. "I thought you guys went out on Friday."

"We did."

"Well, how'd it go?"

"It didn't."

"What happened?"

"I'm sorry. I'd really rather not talk about it," Meg said, her hands tightening on her notebook.

"Yeah." Alison opened her own notebook. "You never feel like talking about it."

Meg shrugged. Who needed friends, right? Everything she'd ever read said presidential children had trouble making friends.

"How come you make it so hard for people?" Alison asked.

"*I* make it hard for people?"

"Up until now, like the only person you ever talked to was Adam. Now you aren't talking to anyone. No wonder they think you're a snob!"

"Who thinks I'm a snob?" Meg asked, carefully expressionless.

"It doesn't even bother you, does it?"

"Maybe."

"Yeah, that's what I figured." Alison leaned on one

222

hand, frowning at chapter six in their book, even though they were on chapter twenty.

"It bothers me," Meg said.

"Oh yeah? You don't look it."

"It bothers me a lot," she said quietly.

Alison closed her book. "Can I tell you something?"

Meg shrugged and nodded at the same time, hands tightly together under her desk.

"Adam is just a big, conceited—well, you name it." Alison scowled at the back of his head as he laughed and said something to a group of boys. "If we weren't all scared of you, someone would have told you. I almost did after gym on Friday."

"Scared of *me*," Meg said. "Why?"

"You're kind of intimidating."

"No, I'm not."

Alison grinned.

"Well, I'm not." Meg closed her notebook, feeling grumpy, fretful, and irritated at the same time. "You guys are the intimidating ones."

"*We* are. Look at you today." Alison gestured toward the outfit. "My God, you look like the cover of *Seventeen*."

"I do not." Meg blushed, wishing she'd worn sweatpants. "You dress better than I do."

"I wish."

"At home I used to wear just jeans and hiking boots," Meg said, running her pen down the spiral of her notebook.

"No shirts?"

"I don't like shirts much."

"I said, settle down, everyone," their teacher was saying, sounding very annoyed.

Alison shot a note over, and Meg picked it up, unfolding the paper.

"Are you really quiet and bookish?" it asked.

Meg thought about that, scribbled "Sometimes" and flicked the paper back. It returned almost immediately.

"Me too," it said.

* * *

So, at lunch, she sat at the same table where she had been all along. Adam sat somewhere else with friends of his from the football team, and she found herself at a table that was mostly female and mostly friendly. Nathan was there too, Phyllis keeping her possessive arm through his, and Josh sat at the far end of the table with Zachary.

Meg watched him eat, wondering if maybe he wasn't much of a friend of Adam's after all. Maybe he was just a bundle of nerves. She shouldn't have been such a jerk to him.

He looked up and saw her, his left hand promptly knocking over his milk. He flushed, blotting the liquid up with some napkins.

"But no one's scared of you," Alison muttered next to her.

"He's not scared of me."

"Right."

When the bell rang, Meg managed to get over next to him as he threw away his lunch bag.

"I'm sorry about this morning," she said. "You kind of caught me at a bad time."

"No, I'm sorry," he said, not looking at her. "I didn't mean to—"

"You didn't," she said. "I did. Don't take it personally."

"Oh, I—I didn't," he said, his gaze a little to her left. "I mean, it's okay."

"Well, I'm really sorry," she said, and they both nodded, going in different directions.

After school, she walked with Alison down the hall toward the junior lockers, Barry behind them.

"You play racketball or tennis or anything?" Alison asked.

"Uh, yeah," Meg said. "I play some tennis."

"Oh, right." Alison grinned, flipping up her blazer collar and tying a cashmere scarf around her neck. "Guess I read that somewhere. Anyway, you maybe want to play sometime this week?"

"Yeah—" Meg stopped, sighing. "I mean, no."

"Oh." Alison looked embarrassed. "Well, okay. It was just an—"

"I kind of got grounded, I was a jerk this weekend, and I got grounded for two weeks."

"Your parents do that?"

"Oh yeah," Meg said wryly.

"Wow." Alison finished tying her scarf. "I never would have thought—two weeks, hunh?"

"Unless I can talk him down."

"Do you think you can?"

"Probably not. But maybe," Meg hesitated. "Well, I guess it's too cold to play outside, but maybe you'd like to come over to my house anyway. I'm going to be like, trapped there for a while."

"You're allowed to have people over?"

"Sure, why not? If you come with me after school, you won't even have to go through a big production at the gate or anything."

"That sounds good," Alison said. "Yeah, sure, whenever."

"Maybe tomorrow or the next day or something?"

"Yeah, sure—oh, wait." Alison grinned. "Gail said for me to ask you if you were in the drama club at your old school."

"Yeah. Why?"

"Well, they need help backstage. I'm working on it, and so's Gail, and so are some other kids from our class, but they need a few more people. They're starting to paint the sets this week. You interested?"

"Sure," Meg said, very interested. "How come she didn't ask me herself?"

Alison just grinned and shook her head.

So, things at school were getting much better. She blushed furiously every time Adam walked by, but he seemed pretty uncomfortable too. Her main problem switched from school to her mother. It wasn't even that they weren't speaking or anything obvious, but it was like those months during the primaries when they had gotten in some pretty bad fights and spent time being careful with each other. Conversations were a major effort.

Of course, being President took a lot of time, and Meg wasn't even seeing her all that much. The first few months of a President's term were called the honeymoon, which meant that everyone was going to be pretty cooperative, so that the new President could get used to the job, and that meant that it was a great time to get a lot of policy ideas through Congress. Plus, there was a huge state dinner coming up in a few days, a summit meeting with world leaders in Geneva in about a month, her Cabinet members and aides were all over the place advising and briefing—there was a lot going on. Nights that she and Meg's father didn't go someplace or have company, her mother was either working through dinner, or coming up to eat, then hurrying back to the Oval Office or her study to put in a few more hours. Meg hated to look out the West Sitting Hall window at the lights on in the Oval Office at nine or ten at night and think of her mother hunched over the desk, practically killing herself to run the country. They were all supposed to be going up to Camp David soon, but it was indefinite. Her mother was busy, much more busy than she had ever been in Congress.

It wasn't just being busy though. The only time she ever seemed to come in to Meg's room was when she thought Meg was asleep. Twice Meg had been awake, but hadn't moved, afraid to start anything. But she couldn't stand the thought that they were going to keep being careful like this.

It was Sunday night, and she was watching *Return of the Jedi* on the VCR with Steven, when it occurred to her that if her mother was down in the Oval Office, her father was probably alone, and she could talk to him.

"Where you going?" Steven asked as she got up.

"Downstairs for a minute."

"You're going to miss like the most excellent part."

"I'll be back." She left the room and went to the second floor, where she found her father in the West Sitting Hall, deep in a book.

"Um, Dad?"

He lowered the book.

"Are you busy, or can I talk to you for a minute?"

He gestured toward the couch. "I bet I know what this is about," he said.

"It's like during the primaries when we had those fights. I don't know what to do about it."

"It's also for a lot of the same reasons," he said. "She pushes herself too hard and then doesn't have enough energy left for anything else. It's not that she's mad at you—or at any of us, for that matter—but when she gets this exhausted, she knows she has a tendency to start arguments, so she makes an effort to avoid controversial situations."

"Like me?"

"Like all of us. But to a large degree, it's been you lately, you're probably right there," he conceded.

"Well, what do I do about it?"

"Give her a while. She's just in the middle of a couple of very difficult weeks of work."

"I guess." Meg slouched into her turtleneck. "Why's she always so quick to think I hate her?"

"Why do you ask such complicated questions?"

"Well," she frowned, "is it my fault?"

"Sure, sometimes that's part of it. There're a lot of reasons though." He fingered the gold ring on his left hand.

"Like what?"

"A lot of it is that she hates *her* mother."

"But she never really had one."

"That's why she hates her." He let his hand fall. "Oh, hate's a strong word—it's not even that simple. But her feelings toward her mother have a lot to do with the way she sees yours."

"But—"

"I know you don't." He half-smiled. "I just can't always convince *her*."

"Well, what'm I supposed to do, tell her I love her or something?"

"It might be nice."

"But," she twisted uncomfortably. "I don't tell you."

"I don't need to hear it."

She slouched down, folding her arms across her chest.

227

He picked up his book but after reading for a minute, he looked up. "Meg?"

She stayed slouched. "What."

"Do you?"

"What."

"I don't know. Like me?"

She shrugged, blushed, then nodded.

"Do you," he ran his finger along the binding of the book, "like me a lot?"

She blushed more, but nodded.

"Do you," he put the book down. "Maybe even love me?"

"Yes, okay?" She blew out an irritated and embarrassed breath.

"Just wanted to make sure." He picked up his book and cheerfully resumed reading.

"Well?"

He looked at her over his glasses. "Well, what?"

"Aren't you going to say you like me?"

"Are you sure I do?"

She slouched until the bottom half of her face disappeared into her turtleneck. He laughed, reaching over to hug her.

"Yes, I like you." He kissed the top of her head three times. "And yes, I even love you."

"Does that mean I'm not grounded?"

"No."

"Hmmm." She pulled out of the hug, arms going back across her chest. "Maybe I don't love you after all."

"God, you're a brat." He ruffled up her hair. "Okay, you're paroled."

She grinned, leaning up to kiss him on the cheek.

"This is not a precedent."

She just grinned.

It was past midnight, and Meg was in bed, scrunched up on her side, patting Vanessa and trying to fall asleep. The door slid open, and she smelled perfume. She stayed huddled on her side, not sure if she should pretend to be asleep. The gentle perfume was closer, and she felt her blankets being adjusted, then the soft warmth of the quilt from the bottom of the bed being spread out over her. There was a tiny sound, maybe just a breath, maybe a light sigh, and she felt a different kind of warmth, that of her mother's hand on her forehead, then on her cheek, before pulling away, the perfume fading.

"Mom?"

"What?" Her voice was near the door.

"Um, I'm awake."

"So I gather."

She turned on her other side, Vanessa giving her a good paw slap in protest. "Um, get a lot of work done?" she asked.

"I don't know." Her mother dragged a tired hand through her hair. "Not really, I guess."

"You've like, been working hard lately."

"I know." Her mother sighed. "The harder I work, the more there seems to be to do."

"Are you tired?"

"I think it's a permanent condition."

"Oh." Meg idly tugged at a loose piece of wool in her quilt. "I thought we could maybe talk for a minute."

Her mother sat down.

"You're so tired you fall over?"

"It only feels that way," her mother said, and Meg could hear the laugh in her voice. "How are you liking the drama club?"

"It's pretty good. The kids seem nice."

"I'm looking forward to meeting your friend Alison."

"Beth and Sarah'll be down in a couple of months, and maybe by then I'll know enough people to invite some over."

"I would expect so."

"I hope." Meg stopped pulling at her quilt. "I, uh, wanted to ask you. Are you still speaking at that NOW convention?"

"Yes."

"Be, um, kind of a big deal if you sold them on the Pershing recall."

229

Her mother glanced over, Meg grinning shyly at her.

"Indeed it would," her mother said.

"Can I come watch you? I'd like to."

"Really?" Her mother sounded pleased. "It's not going to be very exciting, I'm afraid."

"I'd still like to."

"Well, sure. If you're sure you want to."

"Can you write me a note to get dismissed early?"

"Well, sure." Her mother frowned. "Can you miss class?"

"It's only gym."

"Okay, then. I think that would be great."

"Can you write the note yourself? I mean, like, in handwriting?"

"Sure," her mother said. "I'd like that."

CHAPTER TWENTY-FIVE

"Hi," Josh said, passing her locker the next morning. "H-how was your weekend?"

He really was kind of cute. "Not bad," she said. "How was yours?"

"Fine." He nodded several times.

"Are you always so uptight?"

"Who, me?" He coughed. "No, not always."

"When aren't you?"

"Um, well," he coughed again. "Sometimes I sleep."

She laughed, and he allowed himself a small grin.

"You have a very nice smile," he said.

She blushed, feeling herself turn into the shy one.

"You really do."

"Oh," she kept blushing, "I don't think—" She noticed Adam swaggering down the hall with some of his friends and turned away, pretending to be busy in her locker.

"You might as well give up, Feldman," Adam remarked. "She doesn't talk to guys."

"Look, Miller," Josh said. "Why don't you—"

"Watch out for your glasses," Adam said, shoving him and continuing down the hall with his friends.

Josh recovered his balance, very red, and took off his glasses, shining them. He looked different without them. Younger? Less nervous?

"He's really a jerk," she said.

"Yeah." He cleaned his glasses harder.

"You look different without them."

"Yeah."

"If you hate them so much, why don't you get contacts?"

"I don't know. Guess I should." He studied his frames. "Guess these're kind of a turnoff, hunh?"

"Some people look good in them." Meg noticed that he

was taller than she'd thought, that she had to look up to see his eyes.

"Yeah." He put them on. "Men with greying temples. Or women who wear them on their heads." He paused. "You really do have a nice smile."

"Thank you." She went back to feeling shy. "But I don't think—"

They both looked up as the warning bell rang.

"May I carry your books?" he asked. "Or were you brought up to carry boys' books?"

She grinned and took his books.

"Thanks, they're pretty heavy." He put his hands in his pockets. "And I'm very weak."

"You don't look it." He didn't either, she decided, studying his deceptively muscled build. He probably played squash or something.

"Brought up to be a diplomat too, hunh?" He took the entire stack of books from her. "Which is your homeroom?"

"Mr. Duvall."

He nodded, walking down the hall with her.

He was cute, she decided. She wasn't interested, no *way* was she interested, but he was cute. Very cute.

School felt much better. Or she felt better, one or the other. The novelty of being the President's daughter was wearing off. She could open her lunch bag without everyone wanting to see what she had. She could make a joke without getting too much attention. Best of all, she bumped into some guy in the hall—a senior, she thought—and he just said, "Christ, will ya look where you're going?" instead of falling all over himself apologizing. Sure, some people were still treating her like a being from Oz or someplace, but it was getting better. She was playing tennis with Alison on Thursday, a couple of people had wanted to see her trig homework before class, she got reprimanded in French for talking—it was almost like being at home. And Josh was turning out to be very nice. She wasn't interested, no way

232

was she interested—but he was nice. One of these days, she might even have a couple of graphic thoughts. Maybe.

"Are you still thinking of coming tomorrow?" her mother asked the night before the NOW speech.

"Maybe," Meg said in her if-you're-lucky voice. "Are you still thinking of writing me a note?"

"Maybe." Her mother had an even better if-you're-lucky voice and Meg laughed.

So the next morning, Meg carried in her little note on White House stationery. It was in two envelopes and everything—her mother was being pretty funny, signing the polite request for her to be dismissed early with a large dramatic "Katharine Vaughn Powers."

"What's that?" Josh noticed the envelope when he paused by her locker before homeroom, an action that had become a habit.

"I have to get out early today." She put her books and the note on top of his books, stuffing her empty knapsack into her locker.

"So someone wrote you a note?"

"My mother," she said, feeling sort of proud.

"Yeah?" He touched the envelope with an exaggeratedly reverent hand. "Is this kind of like kissing the Pope's ring?"

"It's even better."

"Wow." He smiled, bowing low. "May I have the honor of escorting you to homeroom, Miss Powers?"

"Well, I don't know." She looked him over. "Jeffrey, darling?"

Her Secret Service agent grinned, a few lockers away. "What?"

"Do something with this young man, will you?" She brushed Josh away as if he were a small, annoying fly. "I cawn't seem to get rid of him."

"Talk about Boston accents," Josh said.

"I can only assume that you're jealous."

"In your dreams, kid."

"No," she shook her head, "I have to have my dreams screened before I can have them."

Jeff laughed, but Josh just looked at her, his expression—what? Intent? Interested? Attracted. Very, very attracted. So attracted that she blushed in confusion, adjusting the collar of her shirt, which didn't need it. The warning bell rang, and she started down the hall, Josh next to her, neither speaking.

"Uh, here you go," he said at the door of her homeroom, handing her her books.

"Oh, thank you," she said, keeping her eyes down.

"Meg?"

"What?" She let them up for a second, noticing that his shy smile was very appealing.

"I, uh—" He changed his mind about whatever he was going to say. "S-see you in English."

She nodded. "See you there."

Last period, she got out of gym and was driven back to the White House to go to the speech with her mother. She changed into a skirt and sweater, then they went out to the limousines that would carry them to the convention hotel.

"Hunh." Meg looked around the inside of the car. "I usually get stuck way back in the motorcade."

"I get tired of protocol." Her mother was going over a handful of file cards, very tense.

"What are you going to say?"

"I don't know," her mother admitted. "I'm never quite sure. I really want to do a good job though—I always feel as if I owe women's groups something extra."

"Haven't you done enough?"

"It just makes them expect more." She put the file cards in her coat pocket.

"I thought Glen or someone would be in here briefing you."

Her mother grinned. "I exercised protocol. They're a few cars back. I get tired of people telling me what to say."

"They must get tired of telling you."

"No doubt." Her mother smiled, then looked worried, taking her file cards back out.

At the hotel, one of Linda's aides took Meg into the huge reception hall to her seat in the front row, along with her agents. She looked over her shoulder at the packed room. She would be petrified to speak in front of that many people. How did her mother do it? The audience was very excited— they had even been excited to see *her*. Indicating, to Meg, anyway, that they were pretty hard up. But this was a pretty big deal, having the most important meeting of the year of the National Organization for Women and having the first female President of the United States speak at it.

Everyone turned to watch the door suddenly, and Meg saw her mother, surrounded by Secret Service agents, being ushered to the stage.

After being introduced to great applause, her mother stepped up to the podium, the applause turning into a standing ovation. For someone who had been so nervous in the car, she sure looked calm now, going into her speech and getting a big laugh on the first line, never even taking out the file cards. Meg noticed that Linda and Glen both had their eyes closed. Odds were they weren't sleeping.

The audience was very receptive, laughing and/or cheering at almost everything her mother said. Including the artfully phrased Pershing recall. At one point, her mother took off her blazer in what she called "abandoning male trappings" and got the biggest laugh of all. She winked at Meg, throwing the blazer out to her during the laughing, and Meg leaned forward to catch it, wondering what it was about her mother that made even *that* presidential.

She held the blazer in her lap, smelling the vitality and elegance of the perfume, not really even listening to her mother speak, just watching the audience's reactions: clapping, laughing, communal nodding. Meg got the feeling that they thought her mother had met God. Of course, knowing her mother, she probably had. Maybe she'd spent a weekend in Heaven campaigning.

Meg watched her mother finish the speech to great applause, wondering if she ever relaxed. Sometimes she thought her mother looked much happier holding Neal on her lap or sitting with Steven than she ever did doing political stuff. And lots of times with Meg's father. She had probably never seen her mother as happy as the day she caught the two of them dancing. Meg had to wonder why she went through all the rest of it.

Now the applause was a standing ovation, and her mother looked happy enough, but maybe it was like the difference between happiness and joy. Her mother didn't seem to get any joy out of this. She was winking again, and—only a little embarrassed—Meg winked back.

Sometimes she thought the President was a pretty soft touch.

When the applause finally died down, there was a reception in one of the hotel ballrooms. No one could say her mother wasn't a friendly President—nor could they accuse her of ducking out after speaking engagements. Meg made a halfhearted attempt to go over to her, but the crowd was so big that she decided it wasn't worth the trouble. She could always see her in the car. Her mother was looking for her; Meg waved, her mother smiling and waving back, most of the women around her smiling too. That taken care of, Meg wandered over to some of the tables to check out the food. Steven and Neal were going to be mad that they hadn't come—there were platters of frosted pastries, whipped cream puffing up all over the place. Maybe she could steal them some.

Feeling a little bored and a little bratty, she decided to make her agents nervous and eat a few. They had a poison fixation, always watching everything she put into her mouth. It was enough to make her want to stuff her face.

She ate a couple, then got a plate to take some home. A woman who was coming over to say hello saw the pastry-laden plate and looked very surprised. Meg blushed. "I was sort of stealing them for my brothers. Is that okay? If you want, I can put them back."

The woman laughed. "That's great. That's really great."

Meg reddened more and covered the plate with a napkin. A lot of people came up and talked to her, which was embarrassing as she stood there with a bunch of stolen pastries.

"Barry, can you hold these?" she whispered.

"Meg, you know I can't—"

"Please? Just so I can go to the ladies room?"

He glanced at his watch, then sighed and took the plate, gesturing for Jeff to escort her.

Meg followed him out to the lobby. Major drag. No wonder Steven was always trying to escape from his agents. It would be nice to be alone for once. Jeff knocked on the door, said, "Secret Service," and went in with her to make sure everything was okay. The two women standing by the mirror left quickly.

"Don't take too long," he said, looking at his watch.

Meg saluted grumpily, and he went out to the hall to wait for her. She sat down on the couch in the lounge section of the room. This was the first time she had been alone in public for weeks. It felt great. She glanced around, one idle foot tapping against the floor. Jeff, she knew, would keep everyone out, being paranoid as usual. She could stay in here all day if she wanted.

Tapping her other foot to make a little rhythm, she noticed that there was another door across the room. Did Jeff know that? Probably. Only, what if he forgot? She stood up with a sudden impish idea. It would be pretty funny to go out the wrong way, then come up behind him. She had never tried anything like that before, and it might be kind of fun for once.

She opened the door, seeing a long hall with a door to the far left. There was no one in sight, so she stepped out, closing the ladies room door behind her, and walking down to the other door. She opened it, finding herself in another hall, all red and gold, with some boxes stacked along the walls. Maybe this was a back passageway. She headed left, figuring that that way she would make a full circle and end up in the lobby.

It was really weird to be alone in public. It was really *great*. She kind of hoped she ran into someone who yelled at her, thinking she was just some kid off the street. A janitor or a cook or someone.

She found another hall, only it led to the right, which wouldn't take her back to the lobby. She didn't think. She hesitated, then turned in that direction. She would just try for another minute, then give up and go back the way she was supposed to go. She made a couple more turns, realized that she was completely lost, and stopped. She went back to the door she had just come through and opened it, but the hall there didn't look right at all. Maybe she had come through one of the other three doors. Two were locked, and the other opened on to a flight of stairs.

Maybe a door had locked behind her. She shivered with a sudden nervous fear. Jeff was going to kill her. How was she going to get back?

She went into the one open hall, not sure if she had come from the left or the right. She went down to the right and found a bunch of locked doors, went down to the left and found another stairway. Since stairways were now her only choice, she went down, finding herself in a pipe-crowded basement. She could hear a steady dripping from somewhere, and an irrational fear skipped up her back, sliding down again as she heard a loud crash that was maybe a machine starting up, maybe something falling over, or maybe some*one*—she wasn't waiting around to find out. She ran up the stairs and back into whichever hall she had been in. She tried doors until she found an open one, located the other staircase, and ended up in an ominously empty storage room.

Maybe this deciding to surprise Jeff hadn't been such a great idea.

She came across an unlocked door and stepped into a grey, uncarpeted hallway. It looked like the set for every rape she had ever seen on television, and she came to the conclusion that this had definitely been a lousy idea.

She heard a draft behind her and spun around, scared. What if someone was after her, what if—talk about paranoid. She shouldn't be paranoid. But why else did she have Secret Service agents? Because people were afraid that someone might go after her.

This had been a terrible, awful idea.

She followed the draft, tentatively opened the door from underneath which it was coming, and saw a dimly-lit, car-crowded parking garage.

No *way* was she going down there. Everyone knew that people got kidnapped in parking garages. Damn it, this had been such a stupid idea.

Panicking, she hurried through open doors, through grey halls, up some stairs, and finally arrived at a red and gold hall. That meant that she was back up on the first floor. There was a God.

Trying to find her way back, by now totally confused, she opened a door and saw one of the extra agents assigned to protect her mother striding down the hall, walkie-talkie out.

"Uh, hi," she said guiltily.

"Where have you been?" he asked, sounding furious.

"Well, I, uh, I kind of took a wrong turn."

He was already on his transmitter, relaying the information that Sandpiper was secured.

"Come on," he said, finished. "The President is waiting for you."

"Am I, uh," Meg cleared her throat, "in trouble?"

He nodded, ushering her along.

CHAPTER TWENTY-SIX

The agent knew his way, and after only two doors, they were out in the very crowded lobby, other agents swarming around her, everyone else staring. The word "embarrassed" took on a whole new dimension. She let the agents hustle her out to the limousine, noticing how particularly angry Jeff and Barry were. Flashcubes were popping, and she could already picture the morning papers telling about the President's klutzy daughter who had gotten lost on her way out of the ladies room.

Meg looked down at the red carpet, feeling as if she were being taken to her execution. As they got to the sidewalk, her mother, in spite of very nervous agents, jumped out of the car, looking about as angry as Meg had ever seen her.

"Where have you been?" she demanded.

"Uh, well." Meg put her hands into blazer pockets that weren't even hers. "I sort of—"

"Why do you think you have agents? Didn't it occur to you that everyone might be—"

"I'm sorry." Meg flushed, feeling all the eyes and cameras.

"Terrific," her mother nodded, "You're sorry. Get in the car!"

"Kate," Linda muttered. "Not in front of—"

"I can't be angry?" Her mother whirled to confront the cameras and reporters, her posture challenging. "I'm furious at my daughter, I think I'm quite within my rights, and you may quote me! I'm certain that any one of you who is a parent can understand." She shook an agent's hand from her arm. "Will you please get off me?"

Meg watched her, suddenly grinning, suddenly not minding all the attention.

"I thought I said to get in the car!"

Meg climbed into the limousine, still grinning, and her mother followed a few seconds later. As the motorcade pulled away, her mother spun to face her.

"Meg, I thought we made it very clear—"

That word again. Her parents loved to be clear.

"—that you weren't to give your agents any trouble. Do you know what could have—"

"Yes."

"I don't think you do! I was afraid you had been—"

Meg grinned. "You're yelling at me."

"Damn right I'm yelling at you!" Her mother missed the connection, furious. "You're grounded, got that?"

"Again?" Meg asked, grin bigger.

"Yes, again! And get that smile off your face!" Her mother ordered. "It's not—"

"I love you." Meg reached over and hugged her, hanging on, feeling the hard thumping of her mother's heart.

"Don't pull that!" Her mother tried to move away.

"But I love you." Meg held on more tightly. "I really do." She leaned up to kiss her mother's cheek, still hugging. "I love you a lot." Tired from saying all of that, as well as embarrassed, she let go and moved over to the left side of the seat, afraid to look at her mother. "Even though you're President, I love you," she muttered.

She didn't hear anything on the seat next to her and finally looked over. Her mother was sitting very still, face averted, and Meg recognized Steven and herself in the slight slouch of her mother's shoulders.

"Mom?"

Her mother reached out a tentative left hand, and Meg took it, seeing a small braceleted wrist, a thin hand. She looked at the older, but familiar fingers. She had always thought of her mother's hand as being bigger, but they were the same size. Her mother was really holding on, as if she needed to or something.

"Do you look like this when you cry?" Meg asked quietly.

"No." Her mother turned, and Meg saw the brightness in her eyes. "I look like this when I'm trying not to." She moved over, taking Meg into her arms for a quick hard hug. "Could I ask you something?"

"Sure."

"Did you mean that?"

"Could I ask *you* something?" Meg tilted her head to see her mother's face.

Her mother laughed. "I might have guessed. Why not?"

"Are you insecure?"

"Yes." Her mother laughed again. "Yes, I am very insecure."

"Did it feel good to yell?"

"Yes."

"Are you going to do it all the time now?"

"I just might." Her mother leaned back, leaving her arm around Meg's shoulders. "Are you ever going to pull a stunt like that again?"

"No." Meg slouched. "I'm sorry."

"Mmmm." Her mother lifted her hand to give her a very gentle slap. "Are you going to watch your step, brat?"

"Maybe." Meg used a champion if-you're-very-very-lucky voice.

"Oh, God," her mother groaned with extra theatricality, dropping her face into her hands. "You are totally—recalcitrant." She sat up with a sudden grin. "Would you like a martini?"

"What?"

"They keep this thing stocked." Her mother leaned forward, opening compartments in the back of the front seat, taking out two glasses.

"Very dry?" Meg asked.

"Absolutely."

"With an olive?"

"Sure."

"Are you kidding?"

"Yes."

Filmed reports of the President yelling at her daughter made every newscast that night. Her mother's aides all had heart attacks—except for Preston, who thought it was great.

Steven thought it was hysterical, Neal was worried that Meg was in big trouble, her father groaned a lot. Meg and her mother grinned a lot.

"Boy, Meggie," Steven said, watching the clip on network news, "they're gonna make fun of *you* in school tomorrow."

"Probably." She flipped a piece of cheese from the hors d'oeuvres tray at him.

"They're going to make fun of me too," her mother said.

"Is Meggie grounded again?" Neal asked.

"Meggie is grounded until she's thirty," their father said, lifting his glass at Meg before taking a sip.

Meg grinned, lifting her Tab back at him.

"Meggie is grounded until she's fifty," their mother said.

"Oh, right," Meg said in a yeah-sure-anything-you-say voice.

Her mother didn't even flinch. "Malapert. Overweening."

"You forgot 'a joy to be around,' " Meg said.

Her mother smiled. "No, I didn't."

Steven was right, and people did harass her about getting yelled at on national television, but she was right, and it didn't bother her. She had apologized to Jeff and Barry, who laughed and said they would forgive her, just this once.

"You're pretty chipper," Josh remarked after school, at her locker. "I mean, for having been chastised."

"You mean, chaste, right?"

"Whatever you say." He lifted her knapsack onto his shoulder.

"I could probably manage that on my own."

"Probably," he said. "How about you hold the door?"

"Fair enough." She moved ahead of him and opened the main door of the school with a flourish.

"Thank you, young lady."

"Young woman," she corrected him instantly.

"Sorry," he said, the attraction she'd noticed before sud-

243

denly strong in his eyes. "You—you look good happy, Meg."

"What?" she asked, that particular remark unexpected.

"I'm just glad you're happy." He coughed, stopping near the dark car at the curb. "Guess you, uh, have to get going."

"Yeah." She took the knapsack, just as uncomfortable. "You need a ride anywhere?"

He shook his head. "I'm all set."

They both nodded.

"Uh," he cleared his throat. "Hypothetical question."

She nodded.

"If I were to ask you out—to a—a movie, say. How do you think you'd feel about that?" He looked everywhere but at her.

"This is just hypothetical, right?"

He nodded, eyes on the flagpole in front of the school.

"I think I'd feel good," she said. "Can you wait thirty-four years?"

"What?"

"I kind of got grounded until I'm fifty."

"Y-you did?"

"Yeah, kind of." She shifted her knapsack to her other shoulder. "Do you like Katharine Hepburn?"

"Sure."

"Do you like *The African Queen?*"

"Sure."

"They're showing it at the house tonight—it's one of my mother's favorites. Would you," she blinked a couple of times, tense herself, "uh, maybe like to come over and see it?"

His eyes got very wide. "T-to your house?"

"Yeah."

"Big white job, right? Pennsylvania Ave'?"

Meg nodded. "That's the one."

"It's okay for you to have people over?"

She nodded.

"Geeze." He took his glasses off, absently wiping them on his sweater. He put them back on, squinting as if he'd only made them worse; then grinned, his whole face brightening. "What time?"

"Eight?" she guessed. "They usually run them around eight-thirty or nine."

"Black tie?"

"Wear what you have on."

"Oh, yeah?" He glanced dubiously at his sweater and jeans.

"Hey," she remembered something. "What kind of car do you drive?"

"Would it make a difference?"

"Yeah. If I don't tell the guards, they won't let you in."

"Plymouth Duster, dark green, pretty ugly."

She laughed. "Okay. Great."

Adam Miller and a group of his friends came laughing out of the school. Meg saw him, and without thinking, leaned forward and kissed Josh, who had also noticed.

"You just used me," he said quietly.

"I know." She turned very red, regretting the impulse. "I'm sorry."

"Don't be," He rested his hands lightly on her shoulders. "Now it's my turn." He kissed her, and they moved closer together, forgetting about Adam, forgetting about his friends, forgetting about agents who might be watching. Remembering, they pulled apart, embarrassed. "Wow," he said. Awkwardly, he touched her face, then dropped his hand. "I'm sorry."

Adam and his friends had passed now, very quiet.

"I'm not," Meg said. "Eight?"

At the White House, she had her agents drop her off at the West Wing and went straight to the Oval Office.

"Is my mother busy?" she asked the receptionist in the outer office.

The receptionist smiled.

"Well," Meg amended that, "is she *really* busy?"

The receptionist smiled.

"Actually, Meg," she looked down at the schedule,

"you might be able to catch her for a minute between appointments. Do you want to wait?"

"Sure." Meg sat down.

After about twenty minutes, after some Congressional leaders left the office, she was buzzed in and found her mother frowning at her reflection in the window, straightening her hair.

"Hi," she said cheerfully.

Her mother turned. "Hi. There's nothing wrong, is there?"

"Nope." Meg sat down behind the desk, swinging her feet up, enjoying the feeling of power. Maybe there *was* something to public office.

"How was school?"

"Not bad." Meg picked up her mother's phone without pushing any buttons down, pretending to be a President answering it. "God damn it," she said in the receiver. "I told you that I wasn't to be disturbed. I'm entertaining." She listened for a second. "Well, get on the stick, or I know someone who's going to be increasing my unemployment figures. Yes, they are *my* figures. *Everything* is mine. *I* am in charge."

"Having a nice time?" her mother asked.

Meg sighed impatiently. "Miss, please. I'm really terribly busy. If you'll just—oh!" She let her eyes dawn with recognition. Lots of recognition. "The interview—of course. Good God, I'm sorry." She studied her mother, then leaned forward to scan imaginary papers on the desk, nodding. "Yes, you're in luck. We *do* have an opening for an exotic dancer. If you wouldn't mind—"

"You're invading my space, small pesty child," her mother said.

"Well," Meg said huffily, "we *are* a mite presumptuous, aren't we?"

Her mother laughed. "We are indeed." She jerked her head to the left, indicating for Meg to get out of the chair.

"Boy," Meg said, standing up. "Some Presidents sure are grumpy."

"I'm not grumpy." Her mother sat down, swinging her own feet onto the desk. She grinned. "I'm possessive."

"That's for sure," Meg said grumpily.

Her mother got up. "I hate to do this to you, brat, but I have to kick you out."

"Boy," Meg said, kicking at the carpet. "You don't even want to talk to me."

"Perhaps we can find a more opportune time," her mother said. The phone on her desk rang, and she picked it up. "Thank you, I'll be right in." She hung up, glancing in the silver stand of her pen/pencil set, checking her hair again.

"You look fine," Meg said. "I mean, considering how old you are."

"Thank you." Her mother frowned at the phone as it rang again. "Do you still hate being the President's daughter?"

"Maybe," Meg said in a bet-you-wish-you-knew voice.

Her mother nodded. "That's what I figured."

Meg grinned, moving to give her a hard, reassuring hug before leaving.

"Are you coming to dinner tonight?" she asked.

"Maybe."

"No, really, I mean it."

"Sure," her mother said, her smile bright with far more joy than just plain happiness. "I'll be there."

ELLEN EMERSON WHITE grew up in Naragansett, Rhode Island. She graduated from Tufts University in 1983 and now lives on Manhattan's Upper West Side.